The Funerals of Key West

Dear Jeff:
Welcome to my
Fantasy!

9/15

The Funerals of Key West

Edgardo Alvarado-Vázquez

The Funerals of Key West

Printed in the United States of America
ISBN 978-1-936818-42-6
Library of Congress Control Number: 2014948597

SeaStory Press
305 Whitehead St. #1
Key West. Florida 33040
www.seastorypress.com

If the shortest distance between two points is a line,
I will make it an arch, always.
Understanding this,
And embracing it;
it's my life journey.

DEDICATION

To my mother, who taught me to go on, no matter what is going on.
To Raúl and Adalberto.
To Stephen who is always there, to pick up the pieces.

To my sister Laurie who, without her knowledge, has argued with most of the characters in this book.
You know I owe you much more than that.

To my Key West family, which is so dysfunctional, it is delicious.
Thank you for the support, the fights, the drama (fictional and real), the lessons in life and the affairs of the heart.

To the Memory of Lois Busto Kline who inspired the setting and insisted that I write some of her experiences and about Key West.
Thank you, Lolo.

FORWARD

This book is a work of fiction. While in all fiction the literary perceptions and insights are based on experience, all characters and incidents are products of the author's imagination. All names and places are used fictitiously. No reference to any real person is intended or should be inferred. Some characters are wholly fictional and some are composites of historical figures.

The language of this book is experimental. I believe that language is a living organism that evolves and adapts to the circumstances that surrounds it. It is a reflection of the social, historic, economic and topographic forces that are shaping constantly the area and the people that it is using such means of communication. The grammatical, syntactical, orthographical and the spelling of some words have been subverted to reflect this evolution.

My apologies to the people of Key West, some events have been displaced historically to enhance the plot and narration devices. The first version of the story titled "Siña María" appeared in the Winter 2003 issue of *Blithe House Quarterly Magazine: a site for gay short story fiction*, on the Internet. The author wants to thank the staff of the magazine for their support and encouraging the reader to visit their website at www.blithe.com to read about an award winning e-zine dedicated to gay-lesbian-transgendered short stories.

All pictures, unless noted, are a product of the author's camera. Mike Hentz (smhentz@comcast.net, or alternatively mhentz@comcast.net, mhentz@keysnews.com) contributed the original cover picture; it was manipulated using PhotoshopTM, to display a particular angle. Rob O'neal (www.roboneal.com) contributed other photos for the book. Mike and Rob are award winning photographers and good friends, thanks guys.

A project-based grant from the Anne McKee Artist Fund helped with the publication costs of this book. Thank you: Ms. Anne McKee, Mrs. Roberta DiPiero, foundation's staff and the board of directors.

The Key West Citizen, *Key West The Newspaper* (aka *The Blue Paper)*, *Conch Color*, and the *Miami Herald* are all trademarked publications in the state of Florida.

Dearest Reader:

I'm, one more time, breaking Elmore Leonard's rule No.2 of writing, avoid prologues. In doing so, I would like to address how to get this book into your hands (or hand-held device). As I thought about this, I remembered one of those classics that everybody reads at least once in their lives; and how its 16th century writer pondered that question, and discussed it with a friend:

> *'Say, I pray thee,' quoth I, hearing what he had said, `after what manner lest thou think to replenish the vacuity of my fear, and reduce the chaos of my confusion to any clearness and light?'*
>
> *And he replied: `The first thing whereat thou stoppedst—of sonnets, epigrams, eclogues, etc., (which are wanting for the beginning, and ought to be written by grave and noble persons)—may be remedied, if thou thyself wilt but take a little pains to compass them, and thou mayst after name them as thou pleasest, and father them on Prester John of the Indians or the Emperor of Trapisonde, whom, I know, were held to be famous poets; and suppose they were not, but that some pedants and presumptuous fellows would backbite thee, and murmur against this truth, thou needest not weigh them two straws; for, although they could prove it to be an untruth, yet cannot they cut off thy hand for it.*

(Cervantes, Miguel De. *The First Part of the Delightful History of the Most Ingenious Knight Don Quixote of the Mancha.* Trans. Thomas Shelton. NY: Collier & Son Co. 1970. p.7)

I thought that was good advice then, so why not try it now? And remember, this is the fruit of my own fantasies. Welcome to my world, and grant me the wish of keeping my hand and my tongue intact when you leave it.

EAV

PREFACE
A CAUTIONARY TALE ABOUT KEY WEST

Key West is an implausible and startling place.
Its air will jump-start your soul transmigration.
Reality in the Keys holds a candle to idle fiction.
Writers, poets, painters and performers
race against feral cats, geckos, iguanas and chickens.

Where, in the 21st century, still today,
you can be drinking with someone at the bay,
and an unchartered treasure map you can obtain.
It will take you to a cache of emeralds in the soft clay,
valued in millions of dollars that day,
but deemed only trinkets the next by Judge Kay.

Revelers, troubadours, ex-fashion models,
devout Buddhist developers,
hackers of history, city prowlers,
religious peddlers,
speakers of tongues
and undiscovered singers
come down here to deconstruct their fortunes.

Thieves, demagogues, drug runners at the bight.
Politicians and other escapists hide in plain sight.
They try to lay low and let the world go by the light.

By car, only one way in and only one way out,
many other means, by air, by sea, by mind, sprout,
to bring things in and scout them out,
like a smoking square grouper,
a fiery wooden barracuda
or a dry papier maché lionfish in a waterspout.

But the lasting treasure of the Florida Keys,
its string of islands,
its 42 bridges,
is the people that populate these forever lands.

They have seen power, money, prestige,
despair, dissolution, poverty and disregard
populate the mangroves,
which are cleaned away by the next tide,
and completely purified by the next hurricane.

Its good people hear the call of the conch shell
and extend a welcoming embrace to all who arrive.
For poorer, for richer, for loser, for winner,
all find accommodations and locations.

Sometimes, they all learn to coexist with the other,
most of the time, in spite of each other.
And they lend the place its paranormal aura.

Because they were here before,
because they are here today,
because they will be here tomorrow.

So be careful,
be aware, be watchful.
The next time you are:
having a drink with a stranger,
breaking bread with a foreigner,
sharing a little, or a lot with another …

You could end up:
as a mug in the sheriff's office files,
part of the crime report of the paper,
a role in a play,
a muse of a poem,
a reflection in a song,
or a spirit in a novel.

1

The Cathedral at the *Plaza Mayor* in *La Habana*, still standing guard, is an architectural testimony to the resiliency and spirituality of the Cuban people.

JUAN ZÚÑIGA Y VALDEVIESO

The personal papers and chronicles of Bishop Javier Arrigoitía y Ramírez are part of this story as researched at the Biblioteca Nacional de Cuba during the 20th century. The action takes place circa 1898.

"Your Eminence, a letter has arrived for you," said the monk as he came onto the terrace. The bishop was taking his afternoon coffee and crackers.

"Who delivered it, Eustacio?" asked the bishop, disturbed.

"It was a lackey. He was wearing a hat and I couldn't identify him."

"It does not have a rubric or signature," said the bishop, rising from his rocker and looking down at the plaza in front of the cathedral; the messenger was gone. The monk left.

"This is serious; innocent people could be harmed. Damned plots and schemes. Nothing but envy disguised as accusations." The bishop caught himself thinking out loud and looked around to make sure that no one was within earshot of the closed door.

The note was brief; it alleged that some *Taíno* Indians still adored their idols veiled as saints and martyrs of the Holy Church in *La Habana*. The bishop remembered having a discussion with the governor at their last dinner together on this particular matter.

"You might not be able to control what the Indians are doing deep in the mountains, but let me declare to you that I wouldn't have that sort of thing going in the capital city of *La Habana*," the bishop had said. "I will use all the power of the church to uproot this kind of behavior."

The bishop examined the note carefully but couldn't recognize the handwriting. "This is indeed very interesting," he said to himself.

The afternoon heat smelled of the allamandas that covered the side of the terrace of his palace, which was connected to the cathedral via a passageway atop the sacristy. The bishop looked at the plaza from his terrace. The curved façade of *the Santa Catedral de La Habana* glistened as the sun bathed it in late afternoon golden light. The Carrara marble had been shipped from the port of Cadiz in Spain at considerable expense from his own fortune. His dearest friend, Juan Zúñiga y Valdevieso, had advised him not be extravagant. But it was on afternoons like this one that the bishop knew he was right all along. And he was very proud of it.

Bishop Javier Arrigoitía y Ramírez, grandson of the second *marqués de* Casablanca y Belladonna was overweight with skin thin as Chinese rice paper, a complexion he inherited from his mother, another Spanish aristocrat. His lineage could be traced back to San Sebastían in northern Spain. His father, the third *marqués*, also born in Spain, was the second son and wasn't expected to inherit anything. So his parents had sent him to Cuba to seek his fortune. There, he married the daughter of a Hatuey *Cacique* who died giving birth; the son survived. Soon after, news arrived from Spain that the bishop's father had become the third *marqués* after his older brother died in battle. He returned to Spain briefly to receive his inheritance and married a noblewoman from Seville. She loved her stepson deeply, as if she might have given birth to him. She encouraged his inclinations to become a priest; Javier's father opposed them. But just before dying a couple of years later, he gave his blessing. In his only trip abroad, Javier went to Spain to claim his title and to Rome, to become a priest. His stepmother became the overseer of Javier's material possessions. A year after returning from Rome where Javier was named Bishop by Pope Leo XIII, she died of pneumonia.

The bishop always thanked God for his true inheritance: his olive-shaped eyes, like the ones he once saw in his father's side of the family, the dark piercing gaze from his Hatuey mother, and the friendship of his schoolmate Juan Zúñiga y Valdevieso. Juan was the father of the bishop's only godson, Juan Francisco Javier. That weighed more than all the titles and money. Deep in his heart, the bishop didn't mind that the Arrigoitía y Ramírez line would die in the lavish family crypt just built in the Cristóbal Colón Cemetery.

A group of children entered the plaza from San Ignacio Street and startled the bishop from his reminiscence. He remembered the note in his hand. He sat in his rocker, exhausted by all the comings and goings of the day and the fateful note, and let the laughter and innocence of the children playing in the plaza take him back to his own school days at the monastery of the Jesuits outside the city.

The bishop's classmates were the cream of the crop in *La Habana's* elite. They were sons of the noblemen who came to govern these lands for the king or merchants of questionable roots who made the money in the Indies that financed the expansion of the church, which in turn educated their progeny along with the children of the poor.

Bishop Arrigoitía smiled as his memory took him back to the patio of the school where he was in fierce competition with his adored friend Juan. They were debating the virtues of the Sacred Virgin Mary as part of their final examination and the end of their formal education.

Juan was going immediately into his father's import/export business. Javier resolved to enter the Jesuits' seminary but hadn't announced it to his father yet, because he was afraid of his reaction. The bishop remembered that he got his break when Juan stumbled explaining the Immaculate Conception, and the prior declared Javier the winner.

"You will make a wonderful priest, young Javier," said brother Saagún, brimming with pride. "You have defeated young Zúñiga, a marvelous adversary," he added, embracing them both. "I should know, both of you are my most esteemed students."

Their competition wasn't only academic; it extended to physical feats as well. They were nearly equal in this area; they enjoyed fencing and wrestling together under the watchful eye of brother Saagún. According to St. Ignatius of Loyola, God needed an army to convert the New World, and it had to be physically as well as spiritually ready.

The memories, softened by the afternoon heat and the rocking of the chair, made the bishop nod off for a second, in which the note he was holding floated out of his hands and, fluttering, traveled the short distance toward the door. The monk, who was to remind the bishop to get ready for vespers, pushed the door open. The bishop opened his eyes wide as he remembered the note, but the monk only folded it and with downcast eyes, gave it to him.

"Your Eminence, you asked me to call you before vespers."

"Thank you. Please send a note to Sr. Juan Zúñiga and remind him of our dinner a week from tomorrow. He is so busy these days that he might forget."

"I will, Your Eminence," answered the monk.

Every three months, *La Habana's* port was bustling with the business mobilized by the flotilla as it prepared to go back to Spain. In the past few years, Juan had augmented his family's wealth as well as acquired a cadre of envious enemies and a few friends, including the Governor of Cuba, who competed with Juan Zúñiga in the shipping business. Bishop Arrigoitía was proud of his friend's accomplishments. They had dinner every other Friday, when the bishop's duties permitted. The other Fridays, the bishop dined with the governor, who was also the captain of the army. The bishop and the governor shared, by expressed command of the king, the administration of the island, which had been in political struggle since the revolutionaries started the push for independence at the beginning of the century.

II

On his way to his dinner with the bishop, Governor Don Faustino de la Cerda, took the route of the docks to check on politics, his business and the businesses of his friends and foes. His positions on class and race were well known. He thought, conveniently forgetting his own *mestizo* blood, that only white people should be at the helm of the government and society. The remaining indigenous people of Cuba were of no concern to him, unless he could use them.

"Stop the carriage!" he yelled as they were passing some market stalls. He jumped out and landed in front of an old Indian woman carrying some vegetables. After seeing the infamous carriage, she had tried unsuccessfully to hurry her pace.

“Papers!” demanded the governor, flanked by the two officers who always traveled with him. The woman reached into her vest and, as she was dragging out her parchment, her blouse opened revealing a silver and glass rosary and a triangular pendant made out of stone suspended from her neck by a thin, worn leather strap.

“What is that?” inquired the governor, pointing at the stone. The woman quickly tied her blouse together and straightened her vest. “Hmm, Teresa Zúñiga,” said the governor as he read the paper. “I have heard about you. Not only did your master free you before the emancipation, he also gave you his name. Too bad it won’t change the color of your skin. Let me see what is hanging around your neck immediately.” The woman hesitated for a moment. “Open your blouse, or my officer here will rip it off you.” The governor showed his disdain for the lower class position of the Indian woman; he wouldn’t stoop to touch her.

The woman showed the governor the rosary again, without untying her blouse.

“The leather strap! I know what a rosary is, old woman!”

The woman pulled the strap out. It had a pendant, a triangular stone with carvings on it. The Taínos called it a *“cemí,”* the god that lived in the mountains. “It is a present from my mother before she passed. If your Excellency, *vuesa Merced*, would kindly let me go, I need to prepare dinner for Don Juan and *mi niño*.”

“Yes, you can go home and cook,” said the governor. “But don’t let me catch you outside after the *toque de queda*, the curfew. If you do, I will arrest you.” He waited until she picked up all her packages and then he got back into the carriage. The guards resumed their posts and the carriage lurched forward, nearly running the woman over. Inside, the governor laughed and under his breath muttered, “I have got you now, Juan Zúñiga, I have got you now.” The carriage crossed the Plaza Mayor and entered the bishop’s palace gates.

“Your Eminence,” began the governor as he entered the receiving parlor. He started to bow when the bishop interrupted him.

"Faustino, leave the courtesies for the public. We are alone. Let Eustacio get you some wine and let us start business."

"Thank you," said the governor as he took his seat to the left of the bishop.

"Any civil matters that I should be aware of, Faustino?" inquired the bishop. His hand felt the folded paper in his cassock.

"None of interest to the Church, Your Eminence, the usual fracas among the people," said the governor with lack of interest. "A couple of complaints by some of the *hidalgos*, but those get solved quickly," he added.

"Who is involved?" The bishop eyes scrutinized the governor's face.

"The Souto family and the Gonzagas," replied the governor. "The whole situation started well. It looked like there might have been wedding bells sounding in the air, but it has deteriorated, economic matters."

The bishop sighed, "*Santa María purísima*, it will probably come to me. Do you need any help with the matter?"

"No, Your Eminence, they might scrape each other a bit, but everybody will return to normalcy within a week or so."

"And how is your business going of late?" asked the bishop, his eyes examining the governor's soul.

"Ever since I was appointed captain and governor by the King, I have not been able to devote as much time to it. I thought I had beaten Zúñiga by being appointed, but now I begin to doubt the wisdom of my move," confessed the governor. "Your Eminence knows that my son is still being educated and my wife can't conceive again. I am very distressed."

"Remember, my son, God has a plan for each one of us," the bishop said, patting the hand of the governor. "You know your dear wife isn't barren, and in good time you will have many children. Do not worry yourself sick, my son." He looked deeply into the governor's eyes again and asked, "Do you need confession at this juncture?"

"No," replied the governor, regaining his composure.

"Any business that I should be aware of?" the governor inquired as the dinner was brought in.

"Something is brewing," answered the bishop. "I received a note today. But I want to let things run their course for now, before I take any action. I need to investigate these allegations." The bishop's eyes measured the reaction of the governor, looking for any sign that he might know something about it. The governor moved uncomfortably in his chair. "The last vestiges of what had been a large Indian population have dwindled," the bishop continued, "and most of them have converted to the Holy Mother Church. But still, there are rumors that paganism is still practiced among them."

The governor looked at his plate, avoiding the bishop's intense gaze.

III

Juan Zúñiga's father had full understanding of the Spanish Canon Law. 7
He understood that it was a marriage between church and government that, if compelled, could overrule race. According to him, "racial lines were not strictly drawn in the sand that Cuba was settled upon," and he laughed about that remark. White skin, no matter which way it was acquired, was a status symbol of social superiority. Not all whites belonged to privilege, though, and a Mestizo in the right place at the right time could make things happen.

Don Juan Ramón consolidated a vast amount of shipping business and enough land revenues to have bought his son an aristocratic title. Many times he had boasted to his *compadres*: "I had the money to buy the title. Even better, I once had a *marquesita* begging for my favors. And you fellows know what that means!" He laughed and laughed. Everybody understood that it was a joke because Don Juan worked tirelessly for his money. He didn't have time for a wife. A mistress, that was another matter. The rumored *marquesita* wasn't the first one, but the most consistently mentioned. Nobody had evidence of the liaison. But one day, a well-known wet nurse who worked for one of the aristocratic families came to the docks.

"Where is Don Juan Ramón Zúñiga?"

A strong black laborer pointed to the spot where he was directing a load into his only ship. The woman stood in front of him and deposited in Don Juan's arms a handsome baby boy. She said with authority. "This is your son, and it is time that you take care of him." Her tone changed as she smiled at the boy and said, "*Tiene los ojos azules como el cielo en Sevilla, que mala suerte que heredó su nariz.* His eyes are blue like the sky in the port of Seville; too bad he got your nose."

The whole situation took him by surprise. While he examined the little face, he stopped at the pair of blue eyes and exclaimed proudly.

"This is my son, Juan. This is the happiest day in my life." No one ever questioned the paternity and Don Juan Ramón never revealed the name of the mother. He celebrated this child and in time instilled in him the same work ethic that guided his life. Don Juan made one concession to his confessor, Brother Saagún; he would let his child to be educated. He wanted his son to take the reins of the business when the right time came.

Because Don Juan Ramón worked on his business, *La Imperial*, with the fanaticism of a convert, Brother Saagún took special care of his son. Don Juan Ramón died of exhaustion 20 years later. His son inherited the business, added a new ship to increase revenues and got married to a beautiful Mestiza. She died in childbirth. The boy survived and even though his father was happy about that, the wound created by the death of his wife would never be healed.

IV

Juan returned home after a busy day at the piers, making sure that the shipment in his newly acquired vessel was in order. His son Juan Francisco Javier was tucked away in bed, his nana in a cot beside it. She was the same old Taíno Indian woman that had raised him. He would not think of anybody else to look after Juan Francisco. When Juan got home, the message with the bishop's rubric stamp was on top of the table. He knew it was a reminder of their next meeting.

Bishop Arrigoitía knew that Juan enjoyed their dinners. They matched wits every single time regarding religious and worldly matters, and the bishop got the latest information regarding the city and its business. He knew that Juan was respected and consulted by other businessmen, even some older than he was, a compliment in the bishop's eyes. Juan's visits made the bishop fidget with anticipation. He made preparations early every time and always served the best fish in the house.

The bishop would bathe and shave, things he didn't like to do much. This time, with the warm water running down his back and fragrant vapors emanating from the tub, the bishop recalled the last wrestling match at Jesuits' school. Juan had just pinned him to the floor, smiling broadly, as he knew he had won. A drop of sweat fell from Juan's forehead and landed on the future bishop's cheek. It was so close to his mouth, he could taste it. The heat of Juan's broad hands on his shoulders made him feel secure. He felt butterflies in his stomach and reluctantly pushed Juan away. As he was getting up, he feigned discontent and gave Juan one more gentle push. Juan said, "I have beaten you every single time, Javier."

The cooling water awakened the bishop from his trance. He was running late. After he put on his robes, he looked in the long mirror one more time, grabbed his belly gently, sighed, "OK, I am ready," and walked into the dining room where his friend was seated. Juan Zúñiga smiled broadly as he embraced his friend.

"Javier, *querido amigo*, how are you, my dear friend?"

"Very happy to see you, my Juan, too bad we can't wrestle anymore," he added as he tapped his midriff.

"I am too old for that now, Javier," Juan said, smiling.

"How is my godson behaving?" inquired the bishop. "You know the time is coming to start his education in the seminary," he added, looking into his dear friend's eyes.

"Yes, my friend, you will educate him but he will handle my business afterwards. There will be no seminarians in my family," Juan added with mischief.

"Ha, if the sweet Virgin is hearing my prayers," the bishop interrupted him, and both laughed.

Laughter and conversation filled the room, friends enjoying each other's company, the world turning outside at a different pace. Actual dinner started with a glass of Manzanilla sherry imported from Andalusia. Elevating the conversation, they debated possible themes for the bishop's homily at High Mass, the news from Rome and Spain and what Juan had heard on the docks about the Caribbean and the Philippines, the remnants of the Spanish colonies. After the first course, a claret wine was brought to the table; its fine purple color and woodsy aroma cleared their heads for more energetic intellectual pursuits.

The second course was brought in and they debated the emergence of the United States as a business power and how this was affecting the last of the colonies. Juan had heard that the gringos were going to send
10 a steamship to *La Habana*; the bishop was concerned about this and other political issues. The conversation turned to the political problems of Cuba. Even though José Martí had died three years earlier, the revolution was still going on. The bishop expressed his disapproval of the situation.

Then Juan turned the conversation to more familiar matters. "How is Brother Saagún doing?" The sadness was palpable in his voice.

"He is frail, but as I promised you, I will take care of him as he took care of us when we were his pupils," said the bishop with resolution. "How is your business these days? Are you ready for the flotilla?"

"Yes, I am. Why do you ask?" Juan was surprised by the question.

"You know, there are some people unhappy with your success, for which I pray to the Blessed Virgin every day. But you had better be careful. The situation is turning very serious." The bishop reached into his pocket and touched the note he received. "Maybe we should send your son to my friend Enrique Hernandez at St. Mary Star of the Sea in Key West. You know they have a good school over there run by the nuns of St. Claire," said the bishop very carefully, looking into Juan's eyes.

He laughed and added, "After all you might get your wish, and they will educate and return him to you; he can't be a nun."

"It is that serious?" asked Juan, suddenly grave.

"Not yet. I am investigating though; the sickness might be in our midst. I am telling you to keep your eyes and ears open."

The dinner ended as always with embraces and blessings from the bishop to his friend and a reminder of their next dinner in two weeks. As the door finally closed, the table cleared and everybody was gone, the bishop sat down, covering his face in shame. He always felt this way after Juan had gone; his heart ached and he couldn't help it. "*Santa María*, appease my soul and rid me of these feelings," the bishop prayed out loud and regained his composure. On his way to his bedroom, he put his hand in his pocket and pulled out the note. "*Juanillo,*" he said, "God and the Virgin bless you, because you are going to need all their help."

V

The next week started with bad omens. High Mass at the cathedral was interrupted by protests on the *Plaza Mayor.* The bishop was worried about the political missteps of the governor. There were rumors that the Americans were sending another ship to *La Habana*'s port on a naval courtesy visit. As the Mass was ending the voices from the plaza got louder.

"*¡Los gringos llegaron! ¡Un buque está entrando en la bahía!* The gringos are arriving! A steamer is entering the harbor!"

The governor, in his regular pew, looked at the bishop, made the sign of the cross on his forehead and quietly exited. The bishop hurried the end of the Mass.

The scene at the port was chaotic: some people were happy to see the biggest battleship they had ever seen before, others were protesting.

The governor expressed his disapproval. That morning he wrote a letter to the head of the Conservative Party in Spain, Don Francisco De los Santos Guzmán, expressing his opinion. It was Guzmán's job to forward it to the prime minister. The letter contained the following statement: "By the way, I have heard that the Americans are thinking of sending one of their warships to *La Habana*. They wouldn't dare it, as I am the governor-general captain." The letter would never arrive in Spain.

Another note was written to the bishop. The governor had to keep his other plot in motion if he wanted to keep his failing business afloat. This time, he didn't have time to have one of his officers write it, he penned it himself. Later that day at the harbor and in the middle of the fracas, the governor felt the parchment in his vest and remembered what he wanted to do. He pulled aside one of his lackeys.

"Take this note to the bishop's palace, and cover your face, don't let anybody recognize you, and don't give this to the bishop himself." The governor saw the man hesitate and shouted at him, "Do it, or I'll have your head on a platter!" The servant took off.

12 The bishop had changed his vestments and was busy at his desk writing a polite note to the US Consul in *La Habana*, Fitzhugh Lee, asking for information about the battleship. Eustacio came in with another note in his hand, again, without a wax rubric stamp.

"Who delivered it, did you see him?"

"No, Your Eminence, I couldn't recognize him," answered the monk, lowering his gaze.

"*Ay hijo,* my son, I don't know what I am going to do with you," the bishop said softly. "You are not cut out for the machinations of politics. Was it the same person that delivered the last message?"

"No, Your Eminence, of that I am sure." The monk was happy he got one answer right.

The bishop placed his ring on the melting wax on the folded parchment then waved it in the air to hurry the process. "Take this note to the American consulate and wait for a reply. And while you are waiting,

Eustacio, pray to the Blessed Mother that she sharpen your wits. Think hard and try to remember the face of the messenger. Now leave promptly. I have a very busy day."

The door closed and the bishop opened the note. It alleged that a free Indian woman performed rites and adorations to her ancestors' idols in one of the most important houses in *La Habana*. He recognized the handwriting on the note. The bishop was enraged. "Faustino, you have gone too far this time," the bishop said out loud. "You were playing with fire and you have gotten burned. You have forced me into action." He was so irate that he didn't hear the door; Eustacio was back with the reply from the consul. The bishop turned to see Eustacio standing still, holding the door open.

"How long you have been standing there?" His tone was so angered that the monk lowered his gaze and spoke in an inaudible voice.

"I just came in, Your Eminence," he hardly whispered.

"Speak up! What's wrong with you?" The bishop realized that he was screaming at the wrong person and apologized. "I am sorry, Eustacio, this situation is worse than I feared it would be. Now, did the consul asked you to wait for his reply?" the bishop's voice was soft and gentle.

"Yes," Eustacio said himself now.

Fitzhugh Lee requested a meeting at the bishop's convenience.

"Eustacio, *siéntate por favor*, please sit. I will answer the consul's note immediately and I will write a note to the governor. I want you to deliver them as soon as the wax cools." The bishop sat at his table to reply to the message from the consul. In two days, he would see him. He wrote another note requesting the presence of the governor in less than a week to discuss civil matters. The message read. "*Querido Faustino*, your presence is required to deal with the matter of faith and the Indian population that we have previously discussed. I have come across some evidence that is irrefutable. An arrest will be made. I would like to request the services of two of your officers as soon as possible." He read the message again and pondered his words. He didn't want to give the governor any hint that he had figured out the source of the rumors.

The bishop considered changing a word or a sentence, then rewrote the message on another parchment and sealed it with his stamped rubric.

"Eustacio, deliver these messages and pay attention to your actions. I will see you when you return and will inquire to whom you have spoken."

The next days were hectic. The presence of the battleship in the harbor had increased the protests and muddled the populace's actions. The meeting with the consul didn't go well.

The bishop had sent a message to Juan Zúñiga telling him to place his family under the Church's care and protection. He cited the latest events as an excuse. Juan was so busy making sure that his ship would leave for Spain that he complied with the bishop's request. The bishop had decided to send his godson to Key West as soon as possible. After questioning the Indian woman in private, he was assured in his conviction that the allegations were false and decided to employ her in his own household to keep an eye on her behavior.

The bishop was restless. He was awaiting the governor when word reached the palace that a riot had broken out. The "*voluntarios*," a group of home guard and sympathizers of the Spaniards, had attacked the offices of one of the revolutionaries' newspapers and the whole thing spilled out to the harbor. The governor sent a message canceling the meeting. Around noon the first explosion happened. This one caught everybody by surprise. The rumble that followed it rocked the city. The bishop thought it was an earthquake, but soon found out that the battleship had exploded. Three more explosions followed, and the city was in chaos.

Juan's son was in a room at the bishop's palace with the Indian woman by his side; neither of them had seen Juan since the day before. The bishop had sent Eustacio to the docks to bring Sr. Zúñiga with him when the third explosion shook the palace. The bishop rushed to the terrace. The afternoon had turned dark. The bishop came out to the terrace and tried to make out where the harbor was. He couldn't see it. All he could see was the dark cloud moving eastward toward the plaza. He was sure that some people had died, and he prayed: "*Santa María purísima, ténlos en tu Santo regazo.*" Blessed Virgin Mary, take them into your holy presence.

As the cloud moved, the bishop was still praying, open hands together, praying, making an offering of hands when a finch caught in the black moving cloud fell in his hands. It was dead. An old hymn crossed the bishop's mind:

"Una barca que se mecía
un gorrión cansado de volar,
y al temblor divino de aquella voz
florecía un aire de amor..."

His mother used to sing it, to him, to ease him to sleep. Today, the finch in his song and the finch in his hands were one and the same. He knew what it meant.

Eustacio, at the edge of the dock, saw Juan Zúñiga dive after a drowning sailor. The monk returned to the palace blackened, bloodied and confused. He told the bishop that Juan's oldest ship was moored near the battleship. When the battleship blew up, the ship caught fire. Eustacio related how the afternoon had become night and how he had to feel his way around. The monk reported that all hands on deck and all other available ships in the harbor helped with the rescue. He had seen Sr. Zúñiga from afar helping others get out of the sinking ships. He had tried to get near him, but there were too many people. It started raining flames and body parts. Wood and metal fell, too. The harbor was full of people and there were the bodies of the sailors from the battleship. Eustacio conveyed to the bishop how frightening the whole ordeal was. He told the bishop how a sailor had landed beside him almost in one piece and held out a note. It happened in what the monk described as the longest second of his life, and amid the chaos, he had the time to look down and grasp the note. The sailor died. Eustacio still had the note in his pocket. It was a letter to his wife.

Eustacio told the bishop that as the stern of the battleship sank, he saw Sr. Zúñiga go after a young sailor. The water was dark with the ashes and the oil spewing from the wreckage. Another man in a small craft went after them too. Eustacio told how Sr. Zúñiga came up for air and dove one more time, but did not surface again.

The bishop collapsed in his chair; his heart felt heavy. His eyes welled with tears but he suppressed them. It wasn't the right time or place. He brushed his feelings aside, concealing them enough to regain his poise and sent the two officers at his disposition to find out Juan Zúñiga y Valdevieso's fate. They returned just before dusk with his body. Juan had succumbed to exhaustion on the docks, his own ships lost. The governor had died, too, when a burning piece of debris fell on him after the second explosion.

The bishop mourned the death of his beloved Juan and buried the body in his own family's crypt at the cemetery. He cried in private and corresponded with his friend in Key West. Two weeks later his godson Juan Francisco Javier Zúñiga arrived in Key West to be in the care and protection of father Enrique Hernández at St. Mary Star of the Sea and the nuns of St. Claire.

THE LETTER THAT ACCOMPANIED JUAN FRANCISCO JAVIER ZÚÑIGA READ AS FOLLOWS:

Enrique Hernández
Párroco de la Iglesia
Santa María, Estrella del Mar
Key West, Florida
United States of America

Dearest Enrique

I sent you a cablegram last night telling you of my safety. I hope that it reached you before the morning papers, and that you were spared the agony of suspense and uncertainty.

It seems almost selfish to speak of ourselves even when so many hundreds are mourning the loss of dear ones. Still, I could only give you the brief statement that I was safe and unhurt.

I cannot tell you of the sadness that has descended upon me for the loss of my closest friend and compadre, Juan Zúñiga. The scene is still too terrible to recall, even had I the time. I will only say that I was in my room, waiting to meet the governor, when the ship blew up. Four explosions rocked the city and turned the mid-afternoon into night.

The whole ship was blown into the air, except the officer's quarters. Of all the people in the battleship, only 50 were saved, leaving about 250 dead. I cannot describe for you the horrors.

The question lingers whether the Spanish blew it up, or a mine, or whether it was torpedoed by the "voluntarios," to bring on a war–or whether it was one of these spontaneous explosions. We do not know. I cannot suspect my compatriots' garrison because their actions, sympathy and compassion seem to indicate that they are ignorant of the cause. For the present, we must put this matter in God's hands and trust His judgment. It is almost certain that the United States' Congress will declare war today, without waiting. I wish that this war could be avoided, but my good sense tells me that this is only a fantasy.

The mail steamer from the United States arrived today. It was anchored away from the docks, and I understand the precautions. I have chartered a boat to carry two people aboard that I love very much, to be put in your care.

The carrier of this letter is Eustacio Ramírez, my first cousin on my mother's side. He is my protégé but I know that he is not cut out for the travails and politics of the bishop's palace in La Habana. He has the heart and stamina of a good priest in a small parish like yours. I recommend that you put him to good use and enroll him in a good seminary within a year or so. Eustacio is accompanied by a boy, my godson Juan Francisco Javier Zúñiga y Valdevieso. He is the son of my best friend, Juan, who was killed in that awful tragedy that has fallen on Cuba and my house in particular. I am mourning my friend's death the best way I can, but I assure you, my friend, that my duties must be fulfilled and they will be. Don't distress yourself about any monetary concerns, I will provide for both of your guests as long as the blessed mother will allow me. I have also started judicial proceedings to ensure that young Juan receives the fruits of his father's honorable work. I will have to finish this letter now, since the boats are leaving in an hour for the steamer. Again, I wish that this letter would find you in the best of health, as it is leaving my person in a most anguished state.

Your dear friend in God and seminary companion,
Bishop Javier Arrigoitía y Ramirez
Marqués de Casablanca y Belladonna
La Habana, Cuba.
Finales de febrero 1898.

Eustacio also carried the letter that he got from the dead sailor. As it was not signed and he could not figure out who Cecilia was. The letter was found, with an English translation, among his personal effects when he died many years later.

[LETTERHEAD: NEW YORK AND CUBA MAIL STEAMSHIP COMPANY]
ON BOARD: U.S.S. MAINE
[HAVANA], FEBRUARY 13, 1898

Querida Cecilia:

Mientras te escribo esta carta, nuestro barco está entrando en el puerto de La Habana. Mi corazón está sumido en gran pesar por no saber qué va a pasar en los próximos días. Los oficiales han estado en reuniones a puertas cerradas por las últimas horas y por el barco corren todo tipo de rumores y teorías sobre las acciones que nos avecinan.

Mis compañeros [ilegible] tienen más preguntas que respuestas y todos estamos preocupados aunque seguros de que no hay otro barco más seguro que el Maine en estos momentos. El viaje las últimas noches fue un poco turbulento por la tormenta que encontramos en el Mar Caribe después de zarpar de Key West.

Querida Cecilia, no puedo dejar de pensar en ti. Y me da calma saber que tú estás a salvo con tu familia. Trato de batir mi pesar imaginando los planes que estás llevando a cabo para nuestra boda y a veces me divierto con estos pensamientos. Por favor escríbeme con estos detalles aunque son cosas que no me atañen, me darán paz y sosiego. Si no pasa nada, y nos dejan desembarcar, te escribiré con los detalles que te pueda contar sobre La Habana y sobre Cuba, yo tengo la corazonada de que todo lo que hemos estado leyendo en la prensa en Key West, no es completamente cierto pero tampoco tendré seguridad de esto hasta que lo vea con mis propios ojos.

Otra vez, te dejo en mis pensamientos, con una mezcla de pesar y agitación al no saber qué nos espera en los próximos días y ruego a Dios todopoderoso que tú y nuestras familias estén bien. Te extraño mucho y no sabes cuánto mi corazón espera verte.

Con cariño

Dearest Cecilia:

As I write this letter, our ship is entering the port of Havana. My heart is plunged into great grief of not knowing what will happen in the coming days. The ship's officers have been meeting behind closed doors for the last hours, and all kinds of rumors and theories abound about the actions ahead of us.

My friends [illegible] have more questions than answers about this situation. We are all concerned but confident that there isn't any other boat safer than Maine right now. The trip last night was a bit rough due to the storm we found in the Caribbean Sea after leaving Key West.

Dearest Cecilia, I cannot stop thinking about you. And it gives me great peace of mind to know that you are safe with your family. I try to undue my sorrow imagining how your plans for our wedding are unfolding, and sometimes I amuse myself with these thoughts. Please tell me about these in your next letter, although I should not bother myself with these details, they somehow give me peace and tranquility.

Juan Zúñiga y Valdeviso

If nothing happens, and we can disembark tomorrow, I will write you all the details and experiences in Havana and Cuba. I have a hunch that everything we have been reading in the press in Key West is not entirely true but I'll not be sure of this until I see it with my own eyes.

Again, I will take leave of you, my thoughts, a mixture of regret and agitation, not knowing what awaits us in the coming days. I pray to Almighty God that you and our families are well. I miss you so much. You have no idea of my longing for your presence.

Your beloved

A newspaper in La Habana carried only a small obituary of Juan Zúñiga y Valdevieso:

ZÚÑIGA DIES

Mr. Juan Zúñiga y Valdevieso died April 14, 1898, while helping those injured in the recent explosion of the battleship Maine in Havana Harbor. Zúñiga y Valdevieso owned the import/export business La Imperial. His two ships and some crew members were also lost in the fire. He is survived by his only son, Juan. Zúñiga y Valdevieso's remains were entombed in the family crypt of Bishop Javier Arrigoitía y Ramírez, Marqués de Casablanca y Belladonna in Cristóbal Colón Cemetery in Havana, Cuba.

The USS Maine entering Havana Harbor in 1898. Photo from the Monroe County Library Collection.

The wreck of the USS Maine in 1912. Photo from *The Key West Citizen* Archives.

According to Magdalena, this is the house her father bought at the end of 1933. It was built in 1906, but there are no records of the sale. The house faces North Beach Drive, today Eisenhower Drive, in a picture taken in 1965. Photo courtesy of the Monroe County Library Collection.

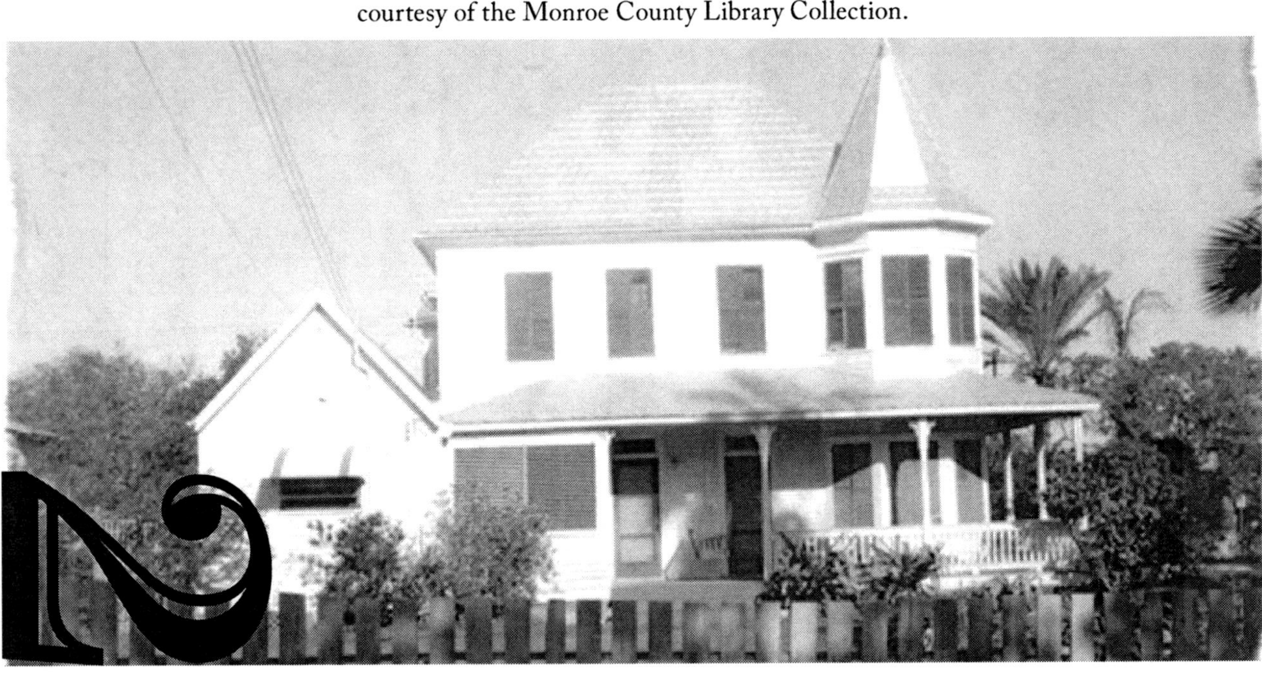

JUDGE JOHN ZÚÑIGA

Based on the recollections and newspapers accounts compiled by María Isabel Zúñiga, it takes place around 1930s.

Judge John Zúñiga was brought to the house that he recently bought on North Beach Drive. The upstairs room was well appointed with wood paneling all around. The massive bed was cornered against the windows. The judge's law books were all over the place. The scene was frenzied. Doña María Isabel Zúñiga was running about talking to herself and to Arturo Rivera, who had brought the judge home. The judge was swollen, blue and had foamed at the mouth.

Loosening the judge's shirt, Doña María Isabel admonished her husband, "I told you, I told you not to go. Arturito, what was he drinking?" She didn't wait for an answer. Turning around to put the cloth in the cold water, she noticed her eldest daughter standing in the doorway.

"Magdalena, what are you doing standing there like a zombie? Your father is sick and I don't know when you will be able to speak to him. Go downstairs with your sisters."

Doña María Isabel wasn't looking at her. She was too busy putting compresses on her husband's forehead. Damn, I can't take the ring off. His right hand was so swollen that his high school ring was buried beneath the skin. He loved this ring as much as he loved his wedding band that he wore on his left hand. Magdalena hurried downstairs. She looked older than her actual age.

The Depression gripped Key West, and Prohibition was supposedly in place. But the conch machine, the local's good ol' club, had deep roots in all aspects of the city politics and business. Governor Schulz married one of the local girls and visited the Keys regularly. Politics was the lifeblood of the coffeehouses, bolita palaces, dance halls, and cigar factories.

It was a hot, hot summer in 1932, and the first primary election had come and gone. Judge Zúñiga was the incumbent county solicitor; before that he was the Special Master in Chancery. He kept the title of judge even though his term has expired, as it was customary. This post was an elected one. This didn't particularly please the judge, who was trying to convince the governor of Florida to make it an appointed position. The county solicitor's job wasn't the most glamorous, but it had a hefty salary for the times and a lot of clout. The elections were held during summer in those days. The governor hadn't reached a decision regarding the post, so the judge came up for re-election.

The judge had locked horns with several of the island's entrepreneurs, arbitrated between rumrunners and the Navy, which was doing business at the same time it was patrolling the waters between Cuba, the Bahamas and Key West. Other cases were minor, but the powers that be wanted someone in the county solicitor's office with unquestionable loyalty to them. The judge knew this. Their candidate was Alyson B. Glare, a lawyer of questionable dealings and political machinations. The judge convinced his friend and protégé Arturo Rivera to run as an independent, trying to cut off Glare's possible victory. If his plans were right, a runoff election would have been called between him and Arturo.

But, in an unexpected outcome, the judge lost to Arturo Rivera, a recent graduate of Stetson University. The runoff election would be between Glare and Rivera. The judge wasn't beaten yet; he had a few months still in office and started an investigation of the board of elections.

The judge had agreed to help Arturo in the runoff. The judge said several times to his wife, "Judges shouldn't be politicians, *Los jueces no debieran ser políticos*." But that was the order of the times.

Back in the judge's room, Doña María Isabel was frantic. "Damned elections," she muttered to no one in particular. "Arturito, how many times did John say he was unhappy with the first round of elections?" She wasn't expecting an answer. "John thought that the Glare camp had tampered with the elections, thinking that you would be easier to beat in the runoff." She was looking for Arturo's reaction. "John wrote a few letters to Governor Schulz. Do you know where they are now?" she inquired impatiently.

"I don't know, Doña María," replied Arturo.

Judge Zúñiga and Governor Schulz exchanged a few letters that discussed the affair at length. The judge had little evidence of actual fraud, but it might have been convincing if brought out in the open. The governor didn't want to stir up the situation because he thought that nothing would come of an investigation. But he wanted to appease the judge. The last letter from the governor read, "If you feel that strongly about it, Zúñiga, why don't you see if you can come up with something? I will write Sheriff Landtrop and tell him to keep his eyes and ears open." The judge felt good about this development. He never thought that Schulz was going to give him permission to conduct such an investigation.

A week later the annual National Guard encampment in Key West began. Every year, for two weeks, the National Guard came to the island paradise to perform exercises dealing with water-to-land invasions and to practice how to repel such an attack. It was more a party than anything else; prohibition never affected the encampment. The same boats that practice how to land and repel were practicing their newly acquired tactics ninety miles away at the island of Cuba. They were smuggling the famous Bacardí rum and a couple of notorious *señoritas*. It was one of the governor's favorite times to come down from the humidity of Tallahassee. Rumor also had it that he was escaping the well-known temper of his wife. He arrived for the festivities and summoned Judge Zúñiga.

Doña María Isabel had advised her husband not to go. "I told him, Arturito, I told him today: John, tell the governor you will meet with him next Monday."

"I know, he told me when we met this afternoon," was all Arturo said as he was taking the belt from the judge's pants to loosen them up.

The judge didn't follow his wife's advice, which was unusual. Everybody knew how much he loved her. Even though she despised politics, she always found a way to give him her two cents' worth in any situation and he always followed her advice. He said many times that Mrs. Zúñiga had more common sense than the mayor.

Doña María Isabel screamed to Magdalena for more cold water; what was left in the basin was lukewarm. She continued her frenetic conversation.

"Arturito, and then he got dressed up. You know, he takes more time in that damned bathroom than any of my sisters."

She snickered and probably would have laughed out loud if it weren't for the gravity of the situation.

"You know how he likes to dress up. He is a sharp dresser. And you know that when he came out of that bathroom today, every single strand of his brilliantined hair had a place. He likes that everything matches from the tie to the shoes. And now, look at you, honey, let me stretch your legs out more."

Doña María Isabel continued her frantic ranting as she was trying to make her husband as comfortable as possible. She was a small, determined woman. She put her arm gently under the judge's broad torso and lifted. Arturo was there trying to help, but mainly he was there listening to her.

"When he moved to the mirror, the one that is on the back of the door, to pin his favorite tie, I told him. I told him, 'John, I know those people, and you will drink. You better be careful of who is around you.'" It was almost a matter-of-fact comment. She didn't know it was their last conversation.

"He called me *Mami*," she started again. "You know, Arturito, he called me *Mami* whenever he wanted to get away with something," she said as an afterthought. '*Mami*,' he said, 'I will be very careful. I have to show these people that I am not afraid of them,' and then he added, 'Anyway, you can't say no to the governor.' Just be careful, I told him, before kissing him goodbye.'"

She was looking at him tenderly as he painfully tried to breathe and she lowered her cheek to his forehead. A small tear escaped her eye and landed gently on his temple. He moved his head slowly, eyes wide open, and his hand touched hers.

II

At the encampment, the festivities were just getting started. The governor and his staff were mingling with the National Guard and the locals. Arturo Rivera was there too, with other friends of Judge Zúñiga. They were keeping tabs on what the Glare supporters were doing. People exchanged stories from one tent to the other. They squared debts, asked for favors and traded gossip. This was the way things were done back then. Nobody thought anything about it. There was no Sunshine Law and no disclaimers.

In one of the tents a Cuban lady was singing. The boys had gathered around her. It was so hot and she was belting out "Let's Do It." She was sitting at the table and one of her legs was perched in the next chair. Her voice had the raspiness of Andrés Segovia's guitar. One of the soldiers was standing behind her with a harmonica. It was quite a sight and Judge Zúñiga, on his way to the governor's tent accompanied by Arturo, stopped and savored the moment. His cigar moistened by his lips, let out a very small and elegant puff before the last note came out of the singer's mouth. He winked at her. She nodded, accepting the compliment, and he said to Arturo, "She sings beautifully, but you have to hear her singing in Spanish. It would grab you by the belly and never let you go." He puffed his cigar again, now like a true Cuban.

When the judge made it to the governor's tent, the two of them separated. The governor was dressed in a dark blue suit with a red tie. The judge was dressed in his brown suit with a crisp white linen shirt. He wore his fedora to the side; it was easier to tip it to the ladies when he was walking down the street. The governor was taller than the judge, but it was Zúñiga who looked the more dapper. The governor put his arm around the judge's shoulder and gestured to his friends in the tent for everybody to see.

"*Zúñiga, deja las cosas como están*–leave everything the way it is now, drop the investigation. Some people will get hurt," the governor warned.

"Some of your friends?" returned the judge.

"And some of yours."

As the judge's face darkened, he loosened the governor's grip subtly. It wasn't a brusque gesture, but a firm one. The judge had few convictions, but they were solid. They were walking in step now, and the judge said, "Your friends are not my friends and I think that Rivera has a good chance of beating Glare. I will not drop the investigation now."

"I just want you to think about it," said the governor as he tried one more time to put his arm around the judge's shoulders.

They came back to the tent where their table was the center of activity; it was alive with conversation and laughter. The lieutenant colonel from the National Guard, Rivera and Glare were seated. Arturo observed everything with keen eyes, as Glare talked and laughed and just enjoyed the moment. They knew how to have fun. The soldier with the harmonica pleaded with the Cuban lady to sing "Crazy Blues," but she refused, saying that she wasn't Mamie Smith and that the blues were not suited for the celebration.

Another of the soldiers turned one of the tubs that held the iced drinks upside down and started drumming on it. He started an Afro-Cuban beat: four short, two long. The soldiers got around him. The clapping hands gave tempo to the beat. The lady extended her hand to the nearest soldier and began to dance. Her hips were moving in cadence with the beat four short, two long. A *tambora*, a Caribbean version of the tambourine, joined the beat. The tent came alive with music, shouting and dance. Everybody enjoyed the performance.

Beer and rum were brought to the table, among more cheers and laughter. All the bottles were tightly sealed except the bottle of rum that was placed in front of the judge and Arturo Rivera. Arturo didn't drink rum, and because they had come to the encampment to check what the Glare camp was up to, he wasn't drinking beer either.

It was two o'clock; the two ladies sang and danced everybody to a great time. By six they all were merry and the conversation cheerful. Glare made his way to the governor's side and they exchanged a few words, not noticing that Arturo and the judge hadn't left the table.

"Is HE dropping the investigation?" Glare asked the governor as he looked at the judge.

"No, he isn't," replied the governor, concerned. "Glare, listen, I want you be very careful about this. Don't forget that I have given him permission to do it. It was in a personal letter, but nonetheless it's binding."

Glare lowered his gaze and was going to speak when he noticed Arturo's presence. He laughed out loud, "That's a great story, governor! Can I use it privately?" Then they separated.

A few minutes later, the judge complained of stomach pains. The lieutenant colonel asked that a cot be brought to the tent. He asked the judge to lie down for a few minutes. "Maybe the judge had one too many," said the lieutenant, elbowing Arturo and laughing. Arturo wasn't amused. The judge dozed off for half an hour. He sweated profusely and was obviously uncomfortable.

Arturo nudged him; "Juan, it's time to go. You are not feeling well, and I have the information that I came for. Glare is in cahoots with the governor, but I am not going to give up without a good fight. We still have Senator Sears from the county on our side. He will plead our case in Tallahassee; he told me so a couple of days ago."

The judge got up with Arturo's help and great effort. Arturo tried to get away from the tent as fast as possible without generating mistrust. He thanked the governor for his hospitality and assured him that he would take the judge back to his house safely. The governor insisted on sending for his car, and a member of his staff was dispatched to get it. After a couple of polite refusals, Arturo relented and told the governor that they would meet the car at the end of the road so the judge could get some fresh air away from the booze and the cigar smoke. Arturo thanked him, and after a short walk they waited for the car.

"Juan, you look pale. Are you okay?" Arturo asked when they were seated in the back of the shiny black Packard.

"I'm not sure," answered the judge. "The pain comes and goes. I think I need to lie down in my own bed." The drive to the house on old North Beach Road was long and silent.

III

When they arrived, Mrs. Zúñiga was already at the doorstep, hands on her hips. She was wearing a dress printed with flowers and bright green leaves. It was around six-thirty; the sun was setting. The door behind the judge's wife had beveled leaded glass that reflected the sunlight. It gave her the appearance of an aura, much like the one the artists put around the *Vírgen de la Caridad del Cobre*, the patron saint of Cuba, or the *Vírgen de la Guadalupe*, the patron saint of Mexico. The judge already had a hue of blue tinting his face, but he was still the Latin lover when he addressed his wife and said, gesturing, "*Mami, eres la viva imagen de la Sagrada Vírgen de la Caridad*; dear you are the vivid image of the Sacred Virgin Mary."

She was waiting for them; another staff member had telephoned Doña María Isabel saying that the judge wasn't feeling well. She smiled and said angrily, "You better get your prayers straight, because when I am done with you, you are going to be sorry." She knew something was amiss, but she couldn't figure out what.

"Arturito, how many drinks did he have?" she asked as he passed her en route to the bedroom upstairs in the turret.

"Probably a couple," he answered from the staircase.

"Rum or beer?" she asked, following them.

"Rum," Arturo responded as he pushed the door in.

"John *mi'jo* that's going to be the death of you."

She removed his shoes as Arturo was taking his jacket off. "You are so conscientious about your health, why would you do this to yourself?" She was already loosening the buttons of his shirt. The judge lay down on the mattress. He was very uncomfortable.

"*Ay Madre mía*," she exclaimed as she looked at the judge's face. "Your forehead is purple!" Doña María Isabel screamed to her daughter from the top of the stairs. "Magdalena! Telephone Dr. Delgado or Dr. DeKlerk, whichever one answers first. Tell them it's important."

It was close to eleven o'clock when Dr. Delgado arrived. Since no one called Dr. DeKlerk back to tell him he wasn't needed, he showed up at midnight. Judge Zúñiga was howling in pain. Dr. Delgado said, "Maybe the judge had too much to drink and stretched his bladder."

Mrs. Zúñiga was exasperated. "He is not drunk. He's sick, you moron!" She was all over the judge; as she tried to soothe the judge's pains with compresses.

Her outrage took Dr. Delgado by surprise. He looked at Dr. DeKlerk, who continued without saying anything. Dr. Delgado apologized.

"I am so sorry Mrs. Zúñiga. I understand what you are going through."

Doña María Isabel picked up the basin. "This water is warm. I need to go downstairs and get cold water." She didn't wait for an answer and took off. The doctors drew another blood sample.

"This doesn't look right! I can't figure it out!" Dr. DeKlerk was upset.

"It is too thin and the color isn't consistent," concurred Dr. Delgado.

"That and the color of his skin. I know something was given to him, but what was it?"

"Julio, this doesn't look good." Dr. Delgado and Dr. DeKlerk didn't have a good prognosis.

"Ralph, I am calling Chester Porter, maybe he can help with these blood specimens," Dr. DeKlerk said as he went downstairs to use the phone. Dr. Porter arrived around one-thirty in the morning; he couldn't figure it out either.

Magdalena stood by helplessly while her mother kept coming and going with the compresses. Mrs. Zúñiga sent her down with her sisters one more time and kept talking to her husband as a way of not thinking about the situation, trying to reassure herself that everything would be all right by sunrise.

Arturo waited until everybody left. Mrs. Zúñiga, exhausted and hoarse, finally gave in and sat in the brown leather covered chair that the judge kept beside his bed with a reading lamp, the comfortable, weathered chair he had refused to give up when they moved into the new house. The patina and the wrinkles gave it character. Mrs. Zúñiga looked the same way. She nodded off for a few minutes, and Arturo brought her a glass of cold water. He touched her hand so gently that she hardly looked up to him. He was almost whispering when he said, "Do you want me to stay, Doña María Isabel? I can sleep here with the judge and you can go to bed. You are going to need the rest."

"No, Arturito, you go home to your wife." Mrs. Zúñiga regained her composure, drank some of the water and placed the glass on the small table on the other side of the chair. It sat for a minute on top of the open morning paper the judge had left there. She quickly removed it, folded the paper and placed the glass on top of it. She took Arturo's hand and stood up, patted his shoulder and added, "I spoke to her earlier, when the governor's aide called me to say that John was coming home sick. She knew you would be here for a while."

Arturo looked puzzled. "Did the aide say anything else?"

34 "No, I don't recall that he said anything else, only that the judge wasn't feeling well and that the governor had ordered his car to bring both of you back here. I said to myself, that is so thoughtful of the governor," she said. "No, go home, I still have to put the girls to bed and call María Eugenia, my sister-in-law. No, maybe I should wait until the morning to do that."

She was thinking out loud as they went downstairs toward the small foyer. "I am so confused right now. I can't think straight. Give Evelyn my love, dear, and thank you for all your help. You know John thinks so highly of you."

"I will be back in the morning to see how the judge is doing," Arturo said as the door closed.

Mrs. Zúñiga turned around and walked into the front parlor. It had a tropical flair to it with the plants and the light-color furnishings. The Judge favored the heavy wood carved furniture that he remembered from his father's house in *La Habana*; she liked the lighter ash wood furniture that was in vogue when they married. She looked around and carefully located each of her three daughters. Carmen, the youngest one, was curled up in the small settee at the far end of the parlor. Her black hair was as coarse as the judge's but straight as her mother's. María was lying on the opposite settee; her skin was milky and thin. Neither of them looked like Doña María Isabel, they were more like the judge's side of the family. Magdalena was half asleep in the rocking chair.

Doña María Isabel knew that her daughter wasn't going to be tall, but she had a commanding presence. All the screaming that they usually had between each other disappeared in moments like these. Doña María put her hand on Magdalena's shoulder and the girl jumped out of her skin without making a sound. Her eyes grew wider as she came out of her sleep.

"Shush," said Doña María Isabel, putting her index finger in front of her lips. "Help me put your sisters to bed. Please carry Carmen, and I will take care of María; and be quiet, your father is asleep in his room."

IV

By the next morning, Mrs. Zúñiga knew what was coming. She called her sister-in-law, María Eugenia, and explained that she needed help with the children. When María Eugenia arrived, the judge's daughters were gathered downstairs in the front parlor.

"Honey," Tía Eugenia looked at Magdalena, but she was addressing all her nieces. "Until your father gets well, you will stay at my house on Division Street."

Mrs. Zúñiga ushered the children upstairs, where their father was laboriously breathing. They said their goodbyes, not knowing that Judge Zúñiga was already unconscious.

"Mamá?" Magdalena asked, inaudible to everybody but her mother. "Is Daddy going be OK?" She didn't want her sisters to hear the question.

"Of course he will be all right, honey," Doña María Isabel assured her daughter.

The judge never regained consciousness. Dr. Julio DeKlerk called in the middle of the afternoon. "Mrs. Zúñiga the circumstances of your husband's death are suspicious. But none of us could figure out what he ingested."

"Arturito said that he drank rum," said Mrs. Zúñiga.

"Whatever the substance was, it interacted with the alcohol in the rum. We don't have the laboratory facilities in Key West to figure it out. None of us have the expertise or the equipment to deal with it. The death certificate will list 'acute hemorrhagic nephritis, profuse bleeding of inflamed kidneys' as the cause of death." They exchanged a few more words and the call ended.

Two days after the judge died, Mrs. Zúñiga called Veritas Insurance. She knew the judge had all his insurance policies with this agency. A secretary answered the phone, "Mrs. María Isabel Zúñiga? I will take your name and whatever policy number you can give me. An agent will call you soon. I can't tell you which because I don't know which agent handles your policies. But someone will call in a few days."

The next day the agent phoned. "Mrs. María Isabel Zúñiga? I have reviewed all the paperwork that we have pertaining to the policy numbers you have given me. We have a problem. It is my information that all the policies were liquidated."

"Are you sure of what you are telling me?" Mrs. Zúñiga tried to contain the mixture of emotions that were boiling inside her. "I feel overwhelmed right now. I need to make some phone calls; may I call you back?" She hung up and called Arturo Rivera.

Her breathing quickened when she heard the voice on the other end of the line. "Arturito, I have no idea how to ask you this question."

"Doña María Isabel?" He couldn't recognize her voice.

"Yes, yes, it is I." She was speaking so fast that Arturo couldn't keep up with her. She blurted out questions about the insurance policies.

"Doña María, please calm yourself. I can hardly understand what you are saying." It was all he could get in before she started again.

"I cannot believe it;–if this is true I'm destitute. My daughters, my daughters, I have three daughters!" The staccato slowed to a whisper; the whisper turned into a very soft sob.

"Doña María, please, he did mention the possibility but I didn't know for sure that he had done it. Please don't forget that he wasn't planning to be dead, he was planning to stay on as the county solicitor. The salary is not bad, and it was a gamble. You know better than I that the judge was a determined man." Arturo never referred to the judge by his first name to his wife. She wouldn't have allowed the familiarity. But she called him Arturito because he was young enough to be her son and because the judge had loved him so.

Doña María Isabel became destitute and tried to use some of her connections to solve the problem to no avail. She moved her family out of the house on North Beach Road to live with her mother on Catholic Lane. After a few years, she rented and later bought a small house on South Street. The judge's two sisters helped in every way they could, and the girls finished their education with the nuns at St. Mary Immaculate Star of the Sea.

Over dinner one night Doña María Isabel discussed a few things with her relatives. She convinced her mother that she needed some time to sort things out. She said to her sister-in-law, "María Eugenia, I am very thankful for what you have done for the girls. I also want you to understand that I don't resent my husband. I know he would have told me about the insurance. I believe that he didn't have the time to discuss it with me. He wasn't sick and his death wasn't an accident. And the worst part is that I know I can't prove it." Mrs. Zúñiga was determined to find out what happened and who was responsible for her husband's death.

Her friends and relatives advised her not to be too candid about the situation. Her husband had told her several times that evidence without facts was circumstantial, and she knew she had circumstantial evidence.

The only thing left for her was to enlist the help of Arturo Rivera. He wrote a letter to Senator Sears in Tallahassee. Sears passed on the letter to the governor, who replied that he didn't have the people or the resources to tie up in an investigation, given the political and economic atmosphere. During those years, every time that the governor visited Key West, he paid a visit to Mrs. Zúñiga. Maybe it was guilt, or maybe he just wanted to know if she had any more information.

V

A few days after Judge Zúñiga's death, Arturo called Doña María Isabel. He was so upset that he stuttered. "Doña María, the governor replaced Judge Zúñiga with an interim solicitor to finish the term, George Hernández, a recent graduate from Stetson University."

"Son of a bitch," said Doña María Isabel. "You know what he is going to do? He is going to eliminate the elections and close the case!"

She decided to take matters into her own hands, despite the advice her family and friends had given her. She wrote directly to the FBI. In 1932, the Federal Bureau of Investigation (FBI) was known simply as the Bureau of Investigation.

Mr. Clyde Tolson, assistant to Director J. Edgar Hoover, inspected everything before it got to Mr. Hoover's desk. He wasn't surprised that people would write directly to the director; but he hadn't seen such a beautifully handwritten letter in some time. The penmanship and the parchment envelope got his attention. He opened Mrs. Zúñiga's letter and enjoyed every word of it. The letter was so passionate; the story moved him in such a way that Clyde showed it to Mr. Hoover. Clyde mounted a keen speech that convinced Edgar to look into Mr. Zúñiga's case.

J. Edgar Hoover dispatched two agents to Key West. They investigated the incident for four months. They concluded that the web around Judge Zúñiga's death was so tangled and so far reaching that an investigation would affect the upper echelons of the state government in Florida. After consultations with President Herbert Hoover, the director decided to leave the matter unresolved.

One note from the agents caught the director's interest. Among the strange occurrences recorded were a number of meetings. "The subjects met several times in a darkened club downtown called The Black Angus, where homosexuals dressed as women mingled with politicos and family patriarchs." The address and the hours were recorded dutifully. Hoover took a piece of paper from his desk, jotted down the information and deposited the whole dossier in a file labeled "unresolved" in a locked cabinet that sat beside his desk.

J. Edgar Hoover picked up the phone, dialed Clyde's personal line and said, "Clyde, we are taking a vacation. Please book us first class on the next available train from Miami to Key West."

The vacation never took place. The bureau became interested in another, juicier case. In December 1932, a Ford automobile, which had been stolen in Pawhuska, Oklahoma, was found abandoned near Jackson, Michigan. In September of that year, it was discovered that Clyde Barrow and his paramour Bonnie Parker drove the car to Pawhuska. Agents learned that another Ford had been abandoned there, which had been stolen in Illinois. A search of this car revealed a man and a woman, indicated by abandoned articles therein, had occupied it. A single piece of evidence linked the two cars. Two prescription bottles, found in each car, filled to "Mary Joe Barrow," led special agents to a drugstore in Nacogdoches, Texas. The investigation disclosed that the woman for whom the prescription had been filled, was Clyde Barrow's aunt. Hoover's attention shifted toward these developments. Bonnie and Clyde were more important to Hoover than a small political squabble in the little town of Key West.

Assistant Clyde Tolson's personal line rang a few hours later. "Clyde, please cancel the vacation to Key West, something had come up," and almost in a whisper, "I'm sorry, I know you were looking forward to this."

"Don't worry Mr. Hoover, there's plenty of time." Clyde Tolson had been instructed to address Edgar as Mr. Hoover whether he was in public or private.

The Key West Citizen published the following about the interment of Judge John Zúñiga:

FUNERAL RITES FOR JUDGE JOHN ZÚÑIGA SERVICES CONDUCTED AT LÓPEZ CHAPEL YESTERDAY

> *The funeral of Juan "John" Zúñiga, who died last Monday, was held yesterday afternoon at 5 o'clock, with services conducted at the López Chapel by the Reverend Shuler Peele.*
>
> *Members of the Elks and Knights of Pythias, of which the deceased was an active member, attended the funeral and performed duties as pallbearers. A large number of sorrowing relatives and friends joined the funeral procession, which extended for several blocks. Internment took place in the family plot in the city cemetery.*
>
> *The mayor and other city dignitaries attended.*

Arturo Rivera submitted a Memorial Resolution to be recorded in the minutes of the Criminal Court of Record of Key West, Florida regarding the Hon. Juan Francisco Javier Zúñiga. (*The Key West Citizen* published it in its entirety a week later.)

MEMORIAL RESOLUTION PRESENTED ON BEHALF OF THE CRIMINAL COURT OFFICIALS OF THE CRIMINAL COURT OF RECORD OF KEY WEST FLORIDA IN RELATION TO JUAN FRANCISCO JAVIER ZÚÑIGA.

> *The Bar Association of Florida and Monroe County has sustained a great and serious loss in the death of Hon. Juan Francisco Javier Zúñiga. Mr. Juan Francisco Javier Zúñiga was a native of the Republic of Cuba;*

he became a citizen of the United States shortly after arriving in Key West in his early childhood. He was educated at Saint Mary Immaculate Star of the Sea school. Mr. Zúñiga was studying pharmacy when he decided to take up the study of law. He read law and was trained by some of the most illustrious lawyers in the city. Mr. Zúñiga attended Stetson University and graduated from the Law School with honors. He returned to Key West and began the practice of law. He handled many intricate and bitterly fought cases not only in our local courts but also in the Supreme Court of Florida and in the Federal Court of Appeals at New Orleans.

Mr. Zúñiga was elected to the position of Police Justice of the city of Key West and occupied that position for three terms. He presided with dignity and fairness and administered justice to all violators with equality. He was afterwards elected to the Florida Legislature and served for three terms. He was elected County Solicitor and was performing the duties of that office when he died.

He married Miss María Isabel Haskins of this city. He leaves his widow and three young children, Magdalena, María and Carmen, to mourn his loss. Mr. Zúñiga was a good citizen, a distinguished lawyer, a patriotic public official and loving husband and father. The Monroe County Bar has therefore sustained a loss not easily regained.

It is, therefore, respectfully moved that the Bar Association of Florida and Monroe County extend to the widow and family of Hon. Juan Francisco Javier Zúñiga its sincere sympathy, and that a copy of this tribute be furnished to the press for publication.

Respectfully submitted by
Arturo Rivera, Esq.

Around forty years later, *The Key West Citizen* published the following article, in remembrance of Judge Zúñiga.

POLITICIANS SHOULD ALL REMEMBER JUDGE ZÚÑIGA

Citizen Staff

"Remember Judge Zúñiga!" That's a deep, dark warning known and recalled among many of the veteran conchs in political circles. It was 40 years ago this month that Juan Zúñiga, judge of the city police court, died a painful and horrible death in his home on old North Beach Road.

His widow, María Isabel, a native of Key West from one of its oldest families, still lives here quietly, in a small, neat home, with her pets and cartons of old photos going back to those days.

Those were the days.

Judge Zúñiga, a smartly dressed man, was a political thorn in the side of the reigning "machine." Against the advice of his wife, the judge went to the National Guard's annual "encampment." It was something like a mini-American Legion convention—all good fellows getting together, swapping stories and playing politics. There was no lack of liquid refreshments, Mr. Volstead notwithstanding.

Judge Zúñiga left the house that Sunday at noon and returned around 6:30 p.m. and went straight to bed, according to his wife's recollections. Mrs. Zúñiga, her three daughters, and a family friend stood bedside helplessly. Several local doctors were summoned to the house, but they could not do anything.

The judge died in severe pain after going into a coma, Mrs. Zúñiga said, and one of the doctors suspected poisoning, but he couldn't prove it.

Post-mortems were not exactly the rule of the day in those early years, but some attempt was made. His kidneys and internal organs were sent to Michigan, not to Miami, and it was never actually clearly established what was the cause of death. The organs disappeared and no chain of evidence survived. There is no autopsy report in existence.

Mrs. Zúñiga worked furiously after that to find out precisely what happened to the judge and who was responsible. She contacted everybody she knew, and through some contacts in the government she finally reached the late director of the FBI, J. Edgar Hoover, who dispatched two agents to Key West who interviewed some parties here.

Nothing was ever actually settled as definite proof of wrongdoing, however, and the matter was dropped.

Only recently, the warning "Remember Judge Zúñiga!" came to life– it was at a cocktail party given for some local politicos by another politician, and opposing factions were invited. One man worried about going, and his mother told him: "Remember Judge Zúñiga!"

The Judge and Doña María Isabel loved each other deeply. There are many examples of this kind of love among the mausoleums and family crypts that populate the Key West Cemetery.

Another dedication reads:

I thought of you with love today but that is nothing new.
I thought about you yesterday and days before that too.

I thought of you in silence, I often speak your name.
All I have are memories and your picture in a frame.

Your memory is keepsake, with which I'll never part.
God has you in His keeping, I have you in my heart.

3

According to Magdalena, this is the house where she was born in the 1920s, before they moved to the house on North Beach Drive. The statues were added later.

CÓMO HAN PASADO LOS AÑOS
IT'S BEEN TOO LONG

The life and times of Magdalena Zúñiga, a songstress who lived in Key West during the 1940s.

For Stephen

Regina always put on eyeliner. Going on the street without it was like going out naked, exposed, eyed by everybody. She got up every morning, switched on her outdated coffeemaker, and cleaned her face with cold cream. She always said, "Soap has never touched my face. *Ése es mi secreto*, that's my secret." And then she painted that languid line across her lower eyelid.

After applying her makeup full power and *con to' los hierros*, she stood in front of the armoire and took out a carefully preserved box.

"No," she decided, putting it back where it had been. She picked up another one and opened it the way a priest opens the holy place where the host resides. The room filled with the smell of cedar and mothballs as she lifted the dress out of the box. Regina put her finger on her nose, avoiding the Armageddon of a sneeze.

"Ahh, everything in its place," she said.

She opened the paneled window and hung the blue taffeta dress from the sill to air it out. She reached for her coffee cup, picked it up and sipped.

"It has been such a long time." She sipped again and the words mixed with the coffee.

Regina's apartment in the Meadows was small, but orderly. She didn't need much space. She had come from a well-heeled family whose fortune was lost. She didn't mind that, because she had tired of money and its pressures early in life. By the time her sexual flights of fancy came to light, the money had dwindled and the reputation of the family was irreparable, so no one really cared. Regina liked it that way.

Her inheritance was spent, so most of what came her way was antique furniture from her mother's side of the family. She sold whatever didn't have sentimental value. The pieces she kept were treasures in her heart: grandmother's lace, mother's rocking chair, father's wedding band, an aunt's armoire, pictures and a couple more furniture pieces.

Regina was not the model child. She understood that people in her circle lived the way they wanted as long as they didn't "rock the boat." Regina's relationship with her grandmother had been great; Amaw told her that she was *una niña especial*, a special girl.

Regina used to have a lover, a Colombian woman. That relationship went down in flames a few decades ago. She thanked the fairies that her parents, and specially Amaw, passed away before the whole affair came to light. She moved to the southernmost point, Key West, where she hid from her relations, from the stuffy life regimented by rules in which she didn't believe and social graces that choked her. She walked away from a trust fund set up by her distant mother and controlling father.

In Key West, she tailored clothes, taught piano, violin, gave voice lessons and worked part time at the convalescent center on Stock Island. She had taken care of her great aunt before moving to Key West, so she had experience. That kind of work grounded her. Regina enjoyed working with elderly people. She was also like her father, a powerful and despotic stockbroker, in that she enjoyed command. She was General MacArthur leading her armies, and most of the residents of the center were good soldiers.

Her music students were no different than the seniors at the center. She weeded slackers out early. Regina would take a student and, ten minutes into the lesson, knew whether the pupil was going to succeed or not. Sometimes she stopped the lesson and talked to her young students as if they were adults. She would pose the radical question: "You didn't agree to this, did you?" The students would pour their hearts out, not because they felt that Regina was a warm person, but because she did something no one else had done before and they appreciated it. Then Regina would pick up the phone, call the parent and explain very succinctly that there was no "spark." If the conversation with the student was deep enough and Regina knew the parent, she would suggest an alternative activity, whispered in her ear by the student, wink to the parent at whatever moment they showed up; and both parties left her apartment feeling privy to a secret and happy about each other.

Then one summer many moons ago, a Cuban woman knocked on her door. She was neatly dressed but not in fashionable clothes. Regina knew these kinds of people. Regardless of their origins, they were reliable. She liked these clients. They paid on time, kept up with their kids' lessons and trusted the teachers. A scraggly young girl probably seventeen, maybe older, stood behind the Cuban lady.

"Miss Regina, I heard about you through the ladies at Mary Immaculate. I am not rich, but I can afford lessons. This is my niece. I have taught her piano and everything I know about singing, which is not much. I think she needs training because *tiene buena voz para cantar*, she can sing. If you don't mind the imposition, I would like you to test her voice and tell me whether it is worth your time or not. I will trust your judgment."

"Excuse me, please come inside. Your name again?"

"Oh, I'm sorry. I'm María Eugenia Busto. This is my niece, Magdalena." Regina led them to the small, well-appointed living room. On the opposite wall, a standing piano proudly dominated the wall. Its rich, dark mahogany was polished to mirror shine, a sign of the care and love of its owner.

"Mrs. Busto, even though I can teach voice, I am mostly a piano teacher, Mr. Pickett on the other hand…"

"Yes, I know about Mr. Pickett, but I want a female teacher. My family doesn't believe that a man should be teaching music to a young lady. You certainly understand that. My niece is talented, and you won't be disappointed. She is a tad disorderly given the fact that her dad died a few years ago."

Regina understood. She extended her hand to the girl and the teen took it. Regina felt the spark. She drew the hand closer to her and Magdalena moved forward.

"What is your name?" Regina asked. As she looked intently at the young woman, the aunt seemed to fade into the walls of the small apartment.

"Mi nombre es Magdalena. Tengo diecisiete años," said Magdalena, I'm seventeen. Regina and Magdalena knew why they were standing in front of each other at that moment in that room.

Magdalena grew insecure, among strong women. She started drinking around high school, hiding from the nuns at Mary Immaculate. She experimented with different drugs, to quiet the voices in her head. The one that bothered her the most was her father's. She didn't want to forget it, but she couldn't bear to hear it. Regina's imposing character fascinated and scared her.

II

Magdalena woke and stretched in her cot and the cat jumped from the pillow to the floor, its hair standing up. The humidity had long since started to peel the paper off the walls; the sun had already discolored most of the furniture, and whatever it hadn't, the cat had scratched. In the bathroom, there was a unique array of panties and pantyhose drying. Under the sink, the drips from the pipes had damaged one of the patent leather shoes she had bought a month ago at The Salvation Army. The refrigerator, which never worked properly, was leaking again.

"Joaquín, *desgraciao*, usurer, just fix these fucking apartments. For what you are charging us for this *pocilga*, this pig's sty, you'd think you'd have a little more compassion."

She picked up the damaged shoe and threw it out the window, knowing exactly where it was going to land.

"Magdalena, go to hell, you fucking whore, let me sleep." The voice answered the throw and the shoe zoomed back in through the same window. If Magdalena had not moved, it would have hit her. But the damned shoe landed on the cat's tail and it went into another hissing fit without knowing the exact reason for it.

"Your fucking mother is a whore," Magdalena answered. "Oh, I forgot, you don't know who your mother was, you bastard. And if you hurt my cat again I will crack your balls and feed them to that flea-infested thing you call your dog."

"Let me sleep, *cabrona*," and the window slammed closed.

"*Ay bendito*, oh god, look at the time. I will miss my rehearsal because of this son of a bitch," Magdalena screamed, knowing he could still hear her. She looked at the phone, thought about it for a minute, and dialed. Magdalena didn't like to call Regina. She didn't like to be obligated to her. Before Magdalena could hang up, Regina's voice was already on the other side like an incantation.

"Regina *es* Magdalena, *¿cómo estás?* How are you?"

"It is about time. I was just going to call you, *haragana*, lazy bum." Regina always scolded Magdalena with a mixture of doom and ecstasy in her voice. "*No me digas que te estás levantando a estas horas.* Don't tell me, are you just waking up?"

"*No hace horas que estoy despierta,* I have been up for a few hours," lied Magdalena. "I need your help; I don't have anything to wear for the show."

"*Para acá ni mires,* don't even think about it. My clothes don't fit you and I am sure that I am not sewing you a dress. *Ese va ser un día muy frío en el infierno*, that will be a cold day in hell."

"Don't jinx my chances," pleaded Magdalena. "I have been waiting for this break; fortune is knocking at my door and I don't have a thing to wear."

"*Déjame ver qué podemos hacer.* Let me see what I can do about it later, the show is not tonight, anyway. Now, about rehearsal, did you call Enid yet? And clean up your act if you haven't yet. I don't want you around me if you are using," Regina snapped, not waiting for an answer. Dial tone... Magdalena stood there puzzled and enthralled at Regina's ability to read her like a book even when they were in different places. She shook her mind (and heart) and hung up the phone.

III

Enid heard the clock and cursed in her head—she never cursed out loud. Beside her, Armando snored placidly. He hadn't heard the clock in years. She kissed him lightly on his shoulder and got out of bed.

Even though they didn't work nights anymore, they kept the habit of sleeping in the afternoon. The rehearsal brought back memories, like her conversations with Magdalena about her complexion. "You will turn into a prune if you don't take care of your body." But Magdalena never paid attention and Enid stopped saying it.

Enid stretched out that thought; those memories had been dormant since the club was closed. She furtively ran her hands over her body, not wanting to know what was obvious. As she walked toward the ratty kitchenette, she said out loud, "It's not too bad," answering her own question. She sang out a note. It came out rusty. Enid never stopped singing but she had stopped training when the money ran out.

"Enid, where are you? Give me a *buchi*," came the voice from the bed.

"Where are these two that no one is calling to set the rehearsal? I'm coming, I'm coming, *ya voy, ya voy, viejo*. What, do they think that we have been practicing the last few years?" She was talking to herself. When she came near the bed with the demitasse cup, she looked at Armando as if looking at something new and old at the same time. He was still good-looking, very handsome, and a smile came to her lips.

"What are you looking at?" He smiled back at her and wrapped his arms around her waist. Then he let go, turned and said, "You should have left me a long time ago."

"*Déjate de esas cosas, viejo*. Let the past alone, honey, things are improving... be happy for once." He buried his face in her waist, let out a long sigh, and inhaled her aroma. She kissed him on the head and pushed him away.

"*Deja viejo*, leave me alone, the girls will be calling soon to set up the rehearsal and you have things to do. Go get ready while I iron your shirt."

IV

It pained Enid to remember how they took away the liquor license. That was the only way that all those *envidiosos* could get back at him, the ones that envied his success and a couple of bums that became enemies for no reason at all.

In her mind these were the same people that never understood that in order to enter the Flamingo, a person needed the right clothing and a bit of education, "*un poco de educación y cache.*"

Armando had opened the only club in town where anyone could have a decent meal, dance to slow music and have the best mojito, just the way Hemingway liked them. *Only lo mejor*, the best, came to the Flamingo to see and be seen. So the bank, the envious, the gawkers, the usurers, and the vultures took the dream away and that almost killed him. They concocted false charges that the club was selling liquor and drugs to minors. A couple of corrupt inspectors shut the club down. It destroyed his ambition. Soon enough, the club changed hands and names. The clientele changed too, *pa' peor porque nunca fue lo mismo;* it was never the same.

She remembers still, when the pianist left. Regina followed him because she couldn't deal with the new atmosphere. She was a singer not *a mujer de la calle*, a streetwalker. She had her standards. Magdalena started showing up drunk. That was the best case, because otherwise, she showed up with *un bamboleo que se la llevaba el demonio,* hopped up, and no one could deal with her. No one but Regina; she knew how beautiful Magdalena's voice could be. She remembered that it was only because Regina convinced Armando to hire Magdalena, in the first place, and only Regina could control Magdalena *como un general del ejército* and make her deliver that beautiful raspy voice that made men pee in their pants and want more to drink to hide it.

At the time, Enid noticed the strange hold Regina had over Magdalena but always chalked it up to *cosas de mujeres de las que yo no me quiero enterar*, women dealings that Enid didn't want to know about. The problems continued, but Enid stayed with Armando when the money ran out. They moved to a worse neighborhood. She didn't mind that; then they sold the good furniture, and she didn't bat an eyelash.

One day, depressed and with a few drinks under his belt Armando said to her, *¿Por qué no te consigues a alguien que te pueda dar lo que tú te mereces?* Why don't you get someone that could give you what you really need? I'm old and broken. I'd understand if you did."

She turned on her heels, looked directly in his eyes and said, "I'm not here for your things or money." She kissed him on cheek and added, "*Te debiera dar una bofetada que te haga comer los dientes*, I should slap you hard enough to knock your teeth out." And left the room.

At first, Enid continued going to the club to keep tabs on Armando, once the proud owner, now only the bouncer. She saw how the paint was peeling off the walls and how the colored glass of the windows shattered as bottles and stones were thrown through them. Then Enid stopped going to the club.

The wooden chairs broke or rotted and sometimes were replaced by metal and folding chairs. The waiters left without returning their uniforms. The broken floor tiles weren't repaired and the parquet dance floor died, splintering and screaming.

The reddish mahogany bar was painted purple and the drunks carved their faint hearts and their *bellaqueras*, their unfulfilled desires, into the wood. The mirror in the background became a gray painting that didn't give back reflections. At that point, Armando gave in to the alcohol and the shame that consumed him. He hated the new owners and they fired him and never let him inside again.

V

The only thing left in the club from the old times was Magdalena. She was part of the furniture inherited by the new owners, she and the tab she had run up for so long that no one really knew exactly how much it was. The bartender started diluting her drinks with water and she started turning tricks soon after they fired Armando. She wore the same old dresses and carried the same jeweled purse that was missing half the stones. She had the only cushioned bar stool and started using opera gloves so no one could see the tiny red dots at her fingers and her elbows.

When she was so stoned that she melted off her chair, she screamed, "*¡Esto es una mierda*. Shit, I was a singer, *¡yo cantaba en el Club Flamingo!*"

One of the men would catch her on her way to the floor and try to prop her up on the stool, barely holding back his laughter.

"Maybe you were the flamingo," he said and laughed out loud as roars and laughter filled the room.

"*Hijo de puta, apuesto que ya ni se te para, cabrón*, son of a bitch, I bet you can't even get it up, asshole. You don't even know what the Flamingo was because they never let you in," she would reply hissing. "You don't even know what a real flamingo is, even though you are as dumb as one of them."

There would be laughter in the room again, and she'd stand up as well as she could, straighten up her dress and tumble out of the bar, triumphantly pushing everybody out of her way. When she reached the door, she would survey the room and flip the bird to everyone, slam the door, and weave her way two blocks down Petronia Street to her cubbyhole.

Finally, the club became too run down even for the bums, and it closed. Its death performed a sort of miracle. It resurrected Armando's ambition. Enid knew that he wanted to reopen the club. He did everything with that purpose in mind. Some of the old clients and friends promised to invest, but the majority didn't have the resources to help them. For most of them, the club had become part of their memories, part of the good old times.

VI

One afternoon Armando came in a bit earlier than usual, white as a sheet and gasping for air. "What's wrong, *Armando pareces un fantasma*? Have you seen a ghost or something?" He slumped on his chair still holding the copy of *The Key West Citizen*. "*Habla, hombre, que me llevas el alma en vilo*. Say something—you are driving me mad!" Armando handed the paper to her. Enid scanned it quickly, not knowing what she was looking for. Armando finally said, looking at her like a kid who has been given a bag of candy, "Read it out loud, please." Enid started, "Police found the mayor's son and an older woman in the parking lot of Faustos..."

"*Eso no*, not that, look underneath the picture." Armando said, a bit exasperated now.

She started again "Corruption in the City Commission, FBI investigating Commissioner Toño Laguirre. Arrest imminent." He was elated; she was puzzled. She knew Toño and Armando didn't like each other, but not the extent of it. After all these years, Armando was coming out of his nightmare. Enid didn't know what had happened fifteen years ago one night in June. Toño Laguirre, then the city attorney, came to the club already drunk. He had a few more drinks. Toño liked to throw his weight around and brag about this or that case he was working on. Armando listened, uninterested until Toño started bragging about the women he'd had sex with. The girls came out to sing their second set and Toño wouldn't shut up. Armando heard Toño talking about Magdalena, then Regina. Armando leaned closer to Toño and quietly but firmly guided him through the back door so as not to disrupt the performance. Toño started laughing uncontrollably, put his hand inside his pocket and pulled out a wad of money.

He said to Armando. "*¿Cuánto quieres?* How much money you want to let me have Enid?"

Armando roughed him up a bit and reminded him that it was a club, not a whorehouse. When Enid came outside, everything was over—she thought. But Toño decided then and there that he was going to put Armando in his place and began the vendetta that didn't stop until the club was closed.

VII

Today was a day of triumph. Enid held Armando's face in her hands. She knew he was ready. He jumped out of the chair and made the calls needed to reopen the club.

Enid was in the kitchen still, but glued to the wall listening to the phone calls. She figured out that some of their friends were very happy to hear Armando's voice; others thought his voice came from the underworld. They thought he was dead. Most of the reactions were lukewarm. Enid knew the original location was out of the question, but she had heard that some of the properties around the 900 block of Duval Street were up for sale. Maybe the owners would be happy to rent a vacant storefront with an option to buy. Enid made a mental note to talk to Armando about it, when she heard him discussing possible locations with Don Silvio Marxuach. Don Silvio was in his eighties, one of the old regulars who later became a friend. He treated Armando like a son, and they had a couple of inside jokes that Enid didn't care to know about. Don Silvio told Armando that he wasn't getting around much anymore. Enid's heart skipped a beat when Armando told her about their appointment at Don Silvio's house the next morning.

Enid got up early. She knew that Armando hadn't even closed his eyes the night before. "*Pareces una nena el día de su quinceañero*, you are acting like a debutante the day of her party," she told him as she handed him a cup of strong coffee. He had shaved and showered two hours beforehand.

As they made their way toward Don Silvio's house; Armando said, "*Estoy en el quinto cielo.* I'm in seventh heaven." Enid gave him a little push to knock on the door of the beautiful house on Pearlman Court. Armando stood there for a minute and then knocked. The door opened and they were ushered into a gleaming library. Don Silvio was seating by the bay window beside his son. The meeting went on for a couple of hours; strategies were laid out to get back the liquor license and to rent the vacant property with an option to buy it. Don Silvio looked at Armando and his son and in a strong tone of voice said:

"I want two things out of this deal. First, that neither you nor Junior here nags me about drinking and smoking the night of the opening. Second," he turned around and carefully took Enid's hand, "That the girls sing 'It Has Been a Long Time' for me." Enid said, without missing a beat, "Your request is granted, Mr. Marxuach."

VIII

Magdalena was still pleading with Regina about the dress and the drugs.

"I just came out of rehab, I'm clean as a whistle, and I have been doing the voice exercises that you taught me, you want to hear me?"

"*Déjate de musarañas*, stop talking nonsense," thundered Regina on the other end of the phone line. "I hate when you waste my time. If it wasn't for the dammed Toño Laguirre, he put all that *porquería* in your body and your mind. I hope that he burns in hell now that the FBI has him. He has a lot to answer for, and I hope that they throw the book at him." She was pacing. "And about the rehearsal, I want you there on time and ready to sing. Do you understand? I won't put up with any crap; you know me better than that."

"Yes, Ms. Regina," Magdalena answered, as if she were still seventeen years old. A chill went down her spine.

"I'll call Enid, and we'll meet two days from now at noon. That's all the advance notice I'm giving you, and show up clean or I will make sure that you are. *¿Me entiendes?* Do you understand me?"

Magdalena got to the nearest chair in her cluttered apartment and sat down. She was sweating and shivering at the thought of Regina's hands on her body. The line on the other side had gone dead a couple of seconds ago but Magdalena was still holding the receiver.

Regina paced some more, trying to remember what it was that she was going to do. Talking to Magdalena always unhinged her. "Ah." She remembered her beautiful, unruly hair, her olive skin and her smell. She hadn't forgotten that afternoon when she opened the door, and there was Magdalena with her aunt. She had felt the spark the moment she touched her hand.

"*¡Dios mío, quién lo diría después de casi quince años!* Oh shit, after fifteen years, she still gets to me!" Regina heard her own voice. "The taffeta dress... shoes, I don't have any shoes." She was trying to get hold of herself. She stopped and breathed deeply. She paused in front of the armoire's mirror. "What am I going to do with my hair? I look like the night of the living dead." She stopped again and grabbed her waist. "I look like a tank," she said, even though she knew she was in decent shape.

Her mind drifted again to the afternoons spent polishing Magdalena's voice and manners. Their conversations ranged from literature to social mores. It had been a joy too painful now that it was over. She didn't want to admit it at the time, but she was in love with Magdalena. When the girl started going out with Toño, "that sorry excuse for a man," she said out loud, Regina couldn't contain her rage. *Solo podía cantar y sacarse la rabia de adentro.* Regina could only sing to get her rage out. When Regina and Magdalena sang together it was a duel in the middle of a duet.

"*¡Ave María purísima si mira la hora que es!* Jesus! Look what time it is." Regina picked up the phone and dialed Enid's number.

"Hello, are you cooking? Don't worry, honey, I just wanted to confirm the rehearsal date and time. OK, in two days at noon? Sure I will be there. You haven't heard from Magdalena? I've spoken to her; we'll be there."

IX

The original pianist was dead, so they contracted the young man from the Brown Derby. He had a spinet that he moved to Enid's apartment.

Magdalena, as usual, was late and looked at the staircase suspiciously. In her mind she was about to scale Mount Everest. Sweating profusely, she reached the top of the stairs and struggled to open the door, con *un bamboleo*, besieged which demonstrated her latest trip to the land of the stoned and the unconscious. Eduardo, the piano player, turned toward the door and lifted his hand from the clavinova. Regina automatically turned her head in the same direction.

"You are not only late, but stoned. *¿No te da vergüenza?* Aren't you ashamed?" Regina grabbed Magdalena by the arm and sat her down.

"You have to stop doing this shit. OK, put your head between your legs, honey. *¡Respira carajo, respira hondo!* Breathe damn it, deeply, breathe!"

"Enid, bring me a glass of cold water." Regina commanded. "No—forget about that, where is the bathtub? Turn on the cold water."

Magdalena tried to fight. In her mind, she was fighting and swearing but nothing was coming out of her mouth; her body was clay in Regina's hands; her body had given up. She never fought Regina. Regina's hands made her body tingle, and her mind tried to resist her feelings. But now, Magdalena was at Regina's mercy *indefensa y sin darse cuenta*, defenseless and motionless. Regina didn't do anything but give Magdalena a good shower. Enid watched the scene with a mixture of pity and guilt. If Magdalena was in a rough spot, she earned it herself. She always thought about Magdalena's beautiful voice. But Enid didn't have time. She made tea for Magdalena, who was coming out of the shower shamed but with her voice intact.

Enid was a bit off key, not because she couldn't sing but because she hadn't adjusted to the fact that they were going to sing again. Regina and Magdalena were caught tying loose ends in a spiritual catharsis, *un despojo espiritual.* Enid noticed how skinny Magdalena was.

X

The group started rehearsing daily. Magdalena tried very hard to keep herself in check, but it was pointless. The junk took over her mind, though she tried to be ready for rehearsals. Regina promised her a cold shower every time she showed up stoned. Every time that Magdalena thought of her limp body in Regina's hands, she sobered up in thirty seconds, *compuesta y pa'l baile en treinta segundos.*

Enid let Regina take care of the rehearsals and focused her energies on Armando. He was busy getting the new location ready. Don Silvio and Junior were there every step of the way. Armando slowed down only when he couldn't get little details as perfect as they had been at the original club.

"Honey, don't worry about it," Enid came through the doors of the new building looking directly into Armando's eyes. "If the chairs are not exactly the ones you had at the old club, the world is not going to stop spinning." She started humming one of the songs.

The name of the new club was *La Nochebuena*. It was a double meaning;
in Spanish it means "Christmas Eve" and "the good night." All the paperwork and licenses were in place. *The Key West Citizen* announced the opening but word of mouth had spread like locusts in a rice paddy. Everybody that needed to know knew.

The rehearsals were fine. Eduardo was already in tune with the singers and Magdalena was singing her usual repertoire that included songs like: "Ain't Nobody's Business if I Do," "I Got It Bad and That Ain't Good," some jazz and blues. It was only when she was singing, "The Man That Got Away" and "It's Been Too Long," that her hands trembled and she sobbed as she sang. Regina sang the Spanish torch songs such as; *"Salomé," "Ausencia," "Mentira"* and *"Perfidia."* Enid decided that she was only going to do second voice and harmonies with the girls.

XI

Everything was right. Enid would be beside Armando when the club opened. Then Armando would go to the bar to take care of his A-list and, finally, he would go around to all the tables welcoming everybody.

It almost seemed as though time turned back fifteen years. Enid came around from the stage and saw how Armando greeted every guest who came in, and examined every waiter, waitress, every tray with food, everything that was in motion. She smiled; Armando was happy; destiny had played all its cards in this one game.

Don Silvio, in his wheelchair, came in with what was left of the old gang, cheering and smiling with a cigarette in his lips. He shook Armando's hand. Armando signaled a waiter who brought a round of drinks. Don Silvio took the first one and passed it on to his son. Junior clicked Armando's glass and said: "*En honor de papá*, in your honor, Dad."

XII

In the dressing room, Enid was pacing. Regina, wearing her blue taffeta dress, was glued to the mirror examining her makeup. Magdalena hadn't arrived yet.

"Did you call her?" asked Enid.

"Yes, dear. No one answers at her apartment," answered the face in the mirror.

"I don't know why we bothered with her," Enid muttered, not wanting Regina to hear her.

Regina's eyebrow went up in front of the mirror; she looked at herself, sized up her figure and approved. Enid, looking at Regina, moved in the sphere of the mirror and was going to say …

"Yes, it's been a long time." Magdalena's voice came from the doorstep. She stumbled in, undone. She dropped the dress that Regina had given her on the floor. A small trickle of blood oozed out of the crook of her elbow.

"Here we fucking go again," raged Regina, pulling Magdalena into the room. "You won't let go of that shit, will you?"

"Don't touch me, Regina." She reached to Enid. "Enid, help me sit down." But it was too late, Regina had already sent the bus boy for a bucket of ice and before Magdalena knew it she was in the middle of Alaska.

"*Carajo*, shit, let me go, get me the fuck out of here! Enid, Enid, help me!"

"Honey, you were warned. *Tú mismita te hiciste la camita, ahora, ¡acuéstate!* You made your bed, now lie in it!" Enid turned around and let the scene roll on as scheduled.

The buzzer in the dressing room sounded. The show was beginning.

Since Magdalena wasn't ready, Regina sang a couple more songs. She vented all her rage, and as always, she sang with such feeling that she charmed the audience, getting from them tears and smiles. Even Enid did a couple of her standards to give Magdalena time. Regina went back to the dressing room. Armando looked at Enid, puzzled. She winked back at him. He understood.

Eduardo wasn't happy, but he was warned about the situation. Regina made sure he understood that Magdalena might be a junkie, but she had the voice of a cherub and it was worth all the money of the audience and all the time she would take to deliver it. He played a solo and received some applause.

Enid went back to the dressing room. Regina had asked for more ice water. Enid stood there, just looking, without interfering. Regina was massaging Magdalena's body very tenderly. And softly Magdalena came out of her insides. Slowly, her mind began to clear. Still in the small dressing room and regaining consciousness, Magdalena gripped Regina's arm. Her eyes were wide-open and shiny brown. Regina knew the reaction; Magdalena was back. "Good," she said.

"*Déjame*, leave me, I'm OK, I'm OK," said Magdalena. She stood up getting away from Regina's hands.

Enid took what was left of Magdalena and stuffed her in the dress. Magdalena gave Enid her worst look in her arsenal. It was all she could do.

She stood up, ironed her creases with her hands in front of the full-length mirror and gave in. She took a minute to readjust her bra, Enid noticed. Again she was in her teens, and Regina was in command.

They went toward the stage, Regina in front, holding Magdalena's hand. Enid was walking behind, just in case.

Magdalena walked to the stage and waited in the wings. Holding on to the side curtain like it was the only lifesaver from a faraway ship in the sea.

"I need air," pleaded Magdalena. Enid opened the stage door and Magdalena walked toward it. Magdalena took her last pill from her brassiere. Regina didn't notice, and Enid didn't say anything. At the door Magdalena inhaled all the available air in one breath. She turned around and her face was bright and beautiful again. She was OK; she was very well. The world opened up to her.

They took the stage. Magdalena, beside the piano, was the center of the world, and she knew it. Everybody was waiting, and when she started singing "The Man That Got Away," they weren't disappointed. The thunderous applause, the cheers almost drowned the song, but she continued; her voice carried over it all. Her notes touched the sky. Her leg trembled a bit; Enid stepped slightly forward, Regina signaled the pianist not to stop and moved to block his view. When the song finished the magic was complete; there was a beautiful second of silence and the applause started again. Enid scanned the room and figured out where Don Silvio was parked.

Magdalena looked at Regina, smiled and signaled the pianist to start, "It Has Been a Long Time." The notes coming from Magdalena were fluid, melodious, her timing was impeccable and the lyrics caressing. She was enjoying the song even more than the audience was, and for once, nothing else mattered. Magdalena was radiant. Don Silvio pulled on Armando's arm and said in his ear, "You got a hit. It will be all right."

The girls went to the dressing room. Magdalena was walking on air. She was holding a yellow rose someone in the audience had given her. When Magdalena stepped into the dressing room, Enid hugged her. Regina took her face gently between her hands and kissed her on the forehead.

Then Magdalena sank down, and everything that was radiant turned pale. Her friends watched in shock, as her smile became a grimace, her eyes rolled back and a trickle of bright blood came from her nose. The world escaped like sand through her fingers.

The front page of *The Key West Citizen* carried the following:

SINGER AT NEW DUVAL STREET CLUB DIES

Citizen Staff

After completing her signature song on the stage of the recently opened La Nochebuena, singer Magdalena Zúñiga died in her dressing room. Zúñiga, described by her fellow performers as a recovering alcoholic and drug addict, died of an overdose. Several attempts by the paramedics to revive her were unsuccessful and she was declared dead at the scene.

Club owner Armando Cortés described Zúñiga as "a melodious singer with impeccable timing and a velvet voice." Zúñiga teamed with Regina Vachon and Enid Cortés to form the vocal trio The Gardenias.

The Zúñiga name is well-known on the island. Her father was Judge Juan Francisco Javier Zúñiga, who died under suspicious circumstances more than a decade ago. She is survived by two sisters: María Arteaga (widowed, son Raymond) and Carmen Dávila (husband, José Juan). Zúñiga also leaves behind two sons Manuel Zúñiga and Elías Ramírez. At her request, her body will be cremated and interred in her family plot in Key West Cemetery.

The site of the former Viva Zapata Restaurant in the 900 block of Duval Street has been vacant for years. *La Nochebuena* nightclub would have easily fit in this spot.

4

The Grotto at Saint Mary Star of the Sea Basilica in Key West depicts the Virgin Mary as she appeared in Lourdes, France. It is believed that as long as the Grotto stands, Key West will be spared a direct hit by a major hurricane. Siña María shared that certainty with the people of Key West.

SIÑA MARÍA

The disappearance of one resident from an assisted living facility near Key West around 1950 creates an unpleasant situation for her son.

To Lynne Smith
and Miss Florence

Mrs. María Arteaga was poised at her usual table, all made up and dressed, as she was every day at nine in the morning. This part of the facility was constructed with the exposure to the sun as the centerpiece, and the residents enjoy its warmth.

Today though, Mrs. Arteaga was busy writing, seated straight up because she always said that age is not an excuse to lose your good posture. The sleeves on her dress were fluttering above the paper; the printed lilacs were pouring their purple dye all over the table. They were taking over the table, the writing, the air. Their perfume took over, infusing the room with its aroma.

Occasionally, she paused, gathered her thoughts, and judged the overall effect, always proud of her penmanship and ability to communicate precisely what she wanted in writing. She paused again, scrutinized the paper, almost talking to it. She caught herself almost thinking out loud, looked around to make sure nobody was aware of her, of her letter, smiled impishly and continued.

Across the room, the orderly, fussing with a wheelchair and positioning it so that Mrs. Bauza, another resident, could face the morning sun under the royal Poinciana, asked, "Dear, what are you writing so thoughtfully?"

"Just a note to someone." There is something different about today, she thought, as she inhaled the morning. The walk was going to be long, but she was ready for it.

A few hours later, before the orderly figured out she was missing a resident, Mrs. Arteaga had already shown up at the Salvation Army. She was tired but exhilarated. She picked out a pair of ragged jeans, a flowery shirt, a wide-brimmed hat and a pair of beat-up sneakers and asked the attendant if she could wear her new ensemble. Even though it wasn't the first time the attendant had heard the request, he squirmed a bit and said, "Don't you want to wash it first?"

For just one second, it all came back; her perfectly white little hand, no wrinkles, no blemishes, not a pore out of place on her face; then she swatted the thought away, putting it in its right place. The reply came fast: "No, I'm quite content with it. I'm just going to put my dress and my shoes in a bag, if you don't mind." The note flawlessly folded in a parchment envelope was peeking out of the front pocket of her dress.

"Suit yourself, ma'am."

The crisp air hit her outside. She remembered the perfume of the lilacs in the dress, now neatly folded in the bag she was holding. She remembered the first time she wore it, to a winter picnic at the house of a friend of her son, on Whitehead Street. Was her name Connie? Anne? Sheri? She couldn't remember, but the air had been just like today. The tables had been set in the small, pleasantly untended garden. She had looked across the street to one of the stately manicured white mansions and thought that everything was in its place. The crisp air hit her again; she paused and looked at the trashcan beside her. The thought was alarming, joyous. She felt the bag as if to say goodbye, her fingers stroking the thin plastic. She smelled the lilacs, felt the note in her pocket, sighed, and just kept walking.

She wanted to sing but, not wanting to attract attention, walked on silently. The sun felt good on her skin; she even smiled at the thought of getting browned by the sun. Her new self didn't care about the warnings of the UV rays anymore; she kept walking. This would not have crossed her mind a few years ago, a few days ago, a few hours ago. Her spine tingled. Her whole body tingled. The sun browning her skin, the song in her head—it almost got out this time—she caught it. She focused carefully on what she was doing, her thoughts so different from a few hours ago. Her feet inside her sneakers, her own sneakers. She smiled. Why didn't I wear these before? The thought of her sensible black pumps trapped in the plastic bag with the lilacs gave her great pleasure.

Her feet brought her to the vicinity of St. Mary's. Her new thoughts pulled her away, as if it was condemned, but a sudden impulse compelled her to the Grotto. The afternoon had turned warm. She looked at the whole structure for the first time in all those years. She thought of the history in each of those stones, she thought of the nun's hands that put them in place. She thought of the faith of those nuns and she was amazed. She looked at the Grotto again and noticed the edges, felt the edges. She never touched them before. She went around to the back, and felt the stones again. She was at peace with herself, finally at ease. She touched the bag for the last time, smelled the lilacs from the dress. It was OK.

She looked at her hand, as she placed it inside the bag. It looked a bit different, it wasn't perfect anymore, and she liked it better. She glanced at it for a second and went directly to the pocket, pulled out the note and placed it in the flowery pocket of her new shirt. It felt safe there, and she put the bag on the ground. So far, so good.

The smells of the soup kitchen, the one she volunteered at so many times a few years ago, called her. She was hungry! She felt hunger. Her new self was happy for those feelings. She fell in line with the others and soon her turn came.

The volunteers seemed a bit more stressed; today there were more people than usual. Someone shoved a cardboard tray with a plate into her hands. She welcomed it. The mashed potatoes arrived first, unannounced, on the right side of the plate. With a quick and clean swipe, some rice and beans to the left, a piece of chicken to the front, neatly arranged. She knew the maneuver quite well, had performed it many times herself. Today, it didn't matter which side of the table she was on.

When she raised her eyes, her cheeks flushed at the sight of Marta Ramirez's round face. She had forgotten that the wide brim of the hat shadowed her features. Anyway, Martita, as she used to call her with affection, didn't have time to look at her. There weren't enough volunteers, and plenty of people needed a meal.

María was very fond of her, of Martita, who wasn't happy with her place in this life. She tried so many times to comfort her pain, but the trappings of her life kept Marta tightly in place. She raised her hand to touch Martita one more time, to comfort her. She looked at her hand. She retrieved it, took hold of herself; the fact that Martita might have recognized the hand or the gesture threw her into a panic. She almost screamed, but the line kept moving, and Martita didn't give any hint of recognition. She had blended completely with the group.

II

It was all in the headline: "Resident disappears from Seashore Manor." The police were stymied, and Ray Arteaga's reaction was quick.

"What do you mean, you can't find her? Excuse me, how big is this island? How come you can't track her down?" He yelled.

He separated the phone from his ear, covered the mouthpiece, and mouthed to his assistant Scott, "Can you believe this shit?"

"No, no, you don't understand. We're talking about my mother here! That picture that I gave you was taken only two months ago. She should stick out like a big sore thumb in this town." He was thinking of her features, her milky white skin. When she had met his father, she loved his wavy, jet-black hair and his olive skin. Ray wasn't thinking about the sun changing his mother's skin. That wasn't possible in Mrs. Arteaga's family mindset years ago. Ray's grandmother, always aware of her family's economical position, approved of Mr. Ramón Arteaga's wealth but wasn't very keen of his shade of skin. It didn't mattered to María; she was in love. Ray inherited his mother's good looks and his father's skin tone.

"When will you call back? OK, I'll wait then." He said as he hung up the phone.

Raymond's thoughts were diverted to the task at hand, the planning of the Navy Officer's Charity Ball at the secluded Von Phister Street estate of a gay couple. A few years before, he worked with a catering and fundraising organization called Bon Fetes. Not because he needed to work, since he had money of his own. The owners who were good friends and he was connected to some important and interesting people.

He discovered that he enjoyed the business, learned the craft and opened his own catering company called Circus Maximus. His contacts, which had grown exponentially since then, and his reputation for the right "touch" made him successful. He took a long time in getting things just the right way. The way his mother had taught him.

He put together a small office that was tastefully decorated without being overdone. His favorite furniture was Mission or Shaker style. "Nothing beats their clean and simple lines," he said. The walls were painted ecru, "bright white always bothered me." He had some pieces of art, "but not overloaded." His favorite was a Cuban painting, which he knew his father had liked. "Nothing particularly important about it, maybe the colors," he said the last time he tried to describe it to anyone. It was a surreal landscape with several fish that looked like cucumbers in it. The head of a bald woman with big red lips was in the upper right corner. The moon or the sun was in the top center. "I always thought it was the moon; the moon governing the tides and water movements makes more sense than the sun," he observed once. The waist and the butt of the woman were on the left side. "The same one?" He used to ask, as if trying to make a joke that never worked. Around the center were lemons, roses or tulips, and one breast. "Where's the other?" He quipped, trying the joke again, unsuccessfully. The teeth of the fish were in the bottom right corner of the painting. He attempted describing the picture, jokes and all, several times without success. He covered the office floor with an off white Italian tile. It was almost pale yellow or lime color, the contrast with the walls had a cooling effect that Raymond enjoyed.

The affair at the Von Phister Street estate was one of the many fundraising events Circus Maximus was organizing. The pressure was on and he knew it. "I can't screw up this one," he said aloud.

His mother had been gone for two weeks now. He couldn't really sort out his emotions. Was he happy? Was he sad? All those years of living together had pre-empted his feelings toward her. She was old; she was in good health.

I haven't talked to her in such a long time, he thought. There were all those years of politely living with each other, stealing little secrets and silences from their daily routine. She had stopped loving Dad, but she stuck by him from the time when he became sick until he died. He had been too young to die. He fell ill, but as he was accustomed, he didn't seek any medical help. It happened so fast, and caring for him was her duty. She shielded me, her only son, from that ugliness. That was her duty too. "Yeah, she loved him once," he said out loud. "I loved him too," continued the soliloquy; "but I couldn't talk to him, tell him what was eating me inside. Did he ever suspect it? Probably. I was just a kid, but I knew about love and beauty and he was so gorgeous. Every time we touched, my hands, my heart hurt."

He shook his head, trying to dispel his thoughts. He thought of Toby his collie of 11 years. The one thing around the house he wouldn't let the help take care of was bathing Toby. And every time after the bath, the dog shook his head to get dry. He thought of the image of shaking these unpleasant thoughts, like his dog, and he half-smiled. He thought about his mother again, all those years, sacrificing their lives so they wouldn't step on each other's toes. His skin was as silky as his mother's, though tanned as his dad's has been. He was well built though not muscular. He didn't like gyms; he didn't have time. He had her features and his father's wavy hair.

Don Ramón Arteaga died such a long time ago. After he died, he left them everything; Raymond repeated himself and figured that he was thinking out loud. "We were well off."

It wasn't lack of love. She knew I loved her. We didn't have to say much to each other. That's it. They will find her. How can they lose her on a two-by-four-mile island? Nah, he thought looking down at his desk. The paperwork in front of him was calling loudly; he brushed it aside. The phone rang. He rushed to it, expecting it to be the lieutenant.

"What?" It was the restaurant that usually helped him with some cooking. He especially liked to serve some of their desserts. With less than two weeks to the ball, they wanted to cancel the order for dessert. "I'm sorry, but you promised, and I have to hold you to that promise. You can't backtrack now...you know that I talk to a lot of people...." He paused, collected his thoughts for a second, and said: "I'm pretty sure you can fix this conflict that you have." He was in mid-sentence when he noticed the assistant coming. "Pick up line two," he said.

"Can you hold on for a minute?" he said and without waiting for an answer he hit the red hold button on the machine.

"Do you know what the lieutenant is going to say?" Nod from Scott. "Have they found her?" Negative sign from the assistant. "I can't talk to him." He gestured with his hand and pushed the hold button again.

Another week went by with no sign from the police or Mrs. Arteaga. Raymond had undertaken other aspects of the Von Phister project. That was the way he liked to work, putting his fingers into various cooking pots at the same time. He equated himself to a chef preparing several dishes. He wanted to create as much noise and chaos around himself as possible, to drown his thoughts, his feelings. He wanted to quiet his mind; he wanted to silence his heart. He looked up at the painting for a second, and he thought the black woman was screaming at him: "They haven't found her. Don't you care to know where she is right now?" He looked up, to figure out who was speaking to him. The painting stared back at him. He shook his head; the crazy thoughts went away.

His various pots were all boiling. Sometimes when he was stressed out he felt these little centers of pain in his head. It was as if someone were sticking pins through his skin. He usually stopped whatever he was doing for just a second, put his thumbs on his temples, pushed hard on them, and the pain ceased.

He couldn't control it this time. "Get out of my freaking mind!" He said it out loud, looking down with a gaze that transcended the paperwork, the desk, and the floor itself. He was going through the earth looking for hell or heaven. He didn't want to think anymore. He wanted everything to stop and everything to move in fast forward. Scott sat down; he cleared his throat, letting Raymond know that he wasn't alone.

"Oh, I'm sorry," Raymond said. "Look, I'm not feeling well. Why don't you go ahead and leave for tonight? I'll catch up on some of this paperwork and maybe call the lieutenant to see if they have done anything at all." Offering the usual comforting words, Scott left. Raymond was left alone in the small office.

Another week passed. The police were dumbfounded. They couldn't find her. The lieutenant wasn't giving excuses anymore. This exasperated Raymond. But he didn't have time to deal with it. "A fine freaking time you have chosen to do this to me," he shouted to his mother, to the air, or to whomever wanted to hear him. The phone rang; the assistant lifted his head heard the now-usual outburst. Without flinching, Scott said, "Mr. Arteaga is unavailable to take your call right now. May I take a message?"

All of Ray's workers knew about his imperious attitude and behavior. Some of them even liked it. His behavior had turned sour in the last month. His frustration at the police ineffectiveness about his mother's case and the pressure that he had put himself under were too much to handle. Still, amid all the chaos, the preparations for the ball had gone forward. Some edges were smoothed; some needed work. For the sake of the business, he was willing to deal with all these difficulties.

The night before the ball, the search for Mrs. Arteaga entered its second month. After his usual afternoon shouting match with whoever was chosen by the police lieutenant to endure the diatribe, Raymond had two piles of papers in front of him. The left one was a pile of police reports and notes on the search. The attorney's papers and bills regarding the lawsuit against Seashore Manor and the city were also in that pile. The right pile was the paperwork for the ball, almost finished.

He wasn't feeling well. He felt compelled to look at the painting.

"Really?" he asked out loud. The fish started moving; the fish started swimming out of the painting, with their colors spilling all over the place as their scales fell on the light colored Italian tiles. The eye of the bald orange woman looked at him ominously from the top right corner of the picture, like he was a Martian or an apparition. She seemed to be running away into that corner, her big red lips quivering with fright.

He felt the first pin go through his head, and then next, and the next. He stopped what he was doing, put his hand on his temples, pushed hard as he tried to sooth his pain, but the red-lipped woman's presence was all-engrossing.

¿Sabes dónde ella está? "Do you know where she is?" The orange woman asked from the canvas, over and over. He started to reach out for the phone to call the lieutenant. As he was extending his hand darkness took over the room.

He was found the next morning at his desk, slumped over his notes and numbers for the party. A massive aneurysm had inconveniently interrupted his work. One hand was resting on his lap, palm up, as if he had tried to undo his silk tie or maybe the buttons on the shirt. The other was on top of the desk. The movement of the arm was clear. It had glided across the papers, knocked out the ink well for his Montblanc pen. His mother had always told him that good penmanship and a good pen are the accoutrements of a gentleman. The ink had run opposite to the hand movement, had flowed towards his head. It had fused with Raymond's dark wavy hair, giving it the highlights of the blue that would melt the most ice-steeled look of any woman, or man for that matter, around. But the ink had run under his hair to the side of his face, blemishing that extraordinary olive silky skin his mother had envied so much. It also created a great deal of trouble for the funeral's parlor's cosmetician. She managed to hide the stain as best as she could.

The gay newspaper published a few lines accompanied by a picture that Ray didn't like in its next issue:

> *Mr. Raymond Arteaga Zúñiga, a very quiet soul according to all who knew him, shunned the spotlight. He was becoming the power behind the throne of Key West charity society. After working for a few years at Bon Fetes where every event that*

> *he touched was blessed, he started his own company, Circus Maximus.*

That was as much as anybody knew, and still knows, about him. If you got him even to consider the subject of his persona, he would brush it off with the usual "I'm a very small fish in a very small pond" remark. He neither denied nor admitted his beginnings in this town. He always laughed when the question arose, and some said that maybe he was from Charlottesville—it sounded classier to him than the hospital on Stock Island—he wasn't sure how this rumor started but he never stopped it.

III

> *Key West, Florida*
>
> *Dear Ray:*
>
> *I have thought long about this letter. I don't want to start off on the wrong foot. Lately, we have not been speaking to each other. We have not been doing anything at all. I guess that if I disappear you will feel better. There is nothing wrong with you; there is nothing wrong with me. Maybe we have been together for a long time and you still have not figured out that like you, I was once a very sheltered individual. Position and money controlled my life. I'm changing this. There is something inside me that compels me to go through with my plans. I have to figure it out on my own without the shelter that has become my shroud. Am I scared about changing my life so radically at my age? No. You are still young. Your father would have been so proud of what you have done with your life. But I have the feeling that when you grow as old as I am now, you will feel the same burden. We're so much alike. You are part of my past now; my bit is done. Go now; let me be with*

my future.

Yes, I have thought about what others might think. Oh, you little devil you, ... you were the one who told me not to think about what others might think, ... but you are the one who does. You were the one who told me to live the moment because it might fade way... I am going to take your word for it. You warned me about this, you warned me about that; you have sanitized your life so well that I don't fit in it anymore. Thinking about it, maybe I don't want to fit in it anymore.

I now have something to give. I have recently discovered that, selfishly, I always wanted what was yours. But in the last few days I have resolved that it wasn't yours either. I have always had an excuse to keep you and to love you. And now, I don't need one to give you up and to keep you away.

Love,

Mother

Mrs. Arteaga took the letter out of her pocket. She hadn't read it since the day she wrote it. She had been so busy with her new life that some days she forgot it. She read it again, folded the paper carefully and searched the other pocket in her blouse, taking out a small picture of a child, the one that was no longer hers. She ironed it out on the opposite side so her hand wouldn't touch the glossy side. She kissed the picture and gingerly put it on top of the letter, and placed them both with the utmost care in a parchment envelope that she had gotten from the post office, and tossed out the original now tattered. It was the most beautiful envelope she could manage at this point in her life. Not having everything at the tip of her fingers felt good. Who knew I would treasure something like that, she said to herself. She looked around and focused on her cart.

"Yes, I have a cart now, and I stole it from Fausto's. Does that make me a felon?"

The question popped up in her mind out of nowhere. She hadn't felt this childish in a while. Her laugh made others aware of her. She didn't like that, so she turned inward again.

"Remember never to attract attention to yourself," she told herself, making sure the notation she made the morning she disappeared hadn't been and wouldn't be forgotten.

She looked around again, consciously following the task she sidetracked a few minutes ago. She took a big banana leaf she had gotten off the curb. A building was being demolished for a parking lot, so all the shrubbery was laid on the sidewalk. Lovingly, she tied the only ribbon she possessed around it, an almost-clean purple one she had dug out of the garbage in the store behind the Carter's family compound on Southard Street. She sighed in relief, knowing her most treasured possession was safe for now. She stuffed it between her newspapers.

"Who would think about looking among newsprint?" she thought.

She put the whole bundle under her head, waved goodnight to a couple of passers-by, snuggled up, and settled in for the night. A homeless man came around and respectfully asked her if she had any food. They all knew who she was. They called her Siña María, "*Siña*" short for the Spanish title *Señora*, lady of the house. She had in fact been the lady of a very elegant house once.

They all respected her. There was a wall of respect around her. None of the homeless, whom she fed out of her cart with whatever she could get her hands on, ever mistreated her. Not the drunks; she scolded them, softly. Not the prostitutes whom she befriended by hearing their stories patiently and giving the best advice she could.

Not even the slow ones for whom she had a warm spot in her heart. Even the one they all called Juan Diego; Siña María took special care of him. Nobody knew how old he was; he just acted like a teen. The police considered him harmless and steered him away from trouble when they could. When the police had to intervene with Juan Diego, they took him to their facilities on Stock Island, but they never booked him. Once the officers figured out that this old lady was taking the load off their shoulders, they were relieved and made sure of her's and Juan Diego's safety. If anybody had looked at the way she treated him, they would have thought she had known him since he was born. But they all knew who she was. She was Siña María.

"*Ay m'hijo no me queda na' coge este peso y vete a La Dichosa en la calle White, Don Paco te dará un café.*" There was no translation needed. He understood perfectly that she was giving him the only dollar she had to go to White Street to La Dichosa bakery where Don Paco will give him some *café con leche* and maybe some bread if he mentioned that Siña María sent him. They all knew that a penny given to them by Siña María wasn't going to be spent on booze or drugs. Some of them did it anyway, the ones that didn't know, the ones that she would take special care of, until they figured it out. She always took care of everybody and someone always watched over her.

IV

Ray's funeral was one of the city's best shows in years. Not since the Archer's (you know, the family that has the school, the firehouse, the baseball park, and the street near a major avenue all named for them) had the town so completely shut down to mourn, to sightsee and to gawk. It was phenomenal. He never wanted it to be.

Wilhelmina Harvey was a good friend to Ray; she was also at the beginning of her political career. She looked for something to do to memorialize him. Not sure whether Ray was born on the island, she decided to "conch" him, to make him an honorary conch at the wake. Hence this long tradition was born. Ray wouldn't have cared one way or the other.

A young newspaper person apprentice, on vacation with his newspaper publisher father from Alabama started his own tradition at that funeral. He took pictures of himself beside the coffin. He tasted the power of the candid photograph. This fascination with the dead and the notorious will take a hold of him for the rest of his publications and his life. From that moment on he would be known as the "colorful photographer." Ray wouldn't care for that either. The paper wrote a front-page article about him. He wouldn't care for it either but might have enjoyed the fact that its editor, who didn't know who Ray really was but felt that he had to write something, misquoted him and had his age and last name wrong.

The city commissioners met that week. Commissioner Spear, another friend, shook Commissioner Napps out of her normal stupor, and proposed naming the corner of Atlantic Boulevard and First Street for Raymond Arteaga Zúñiga. It was such a prominent corner. The debate became spirited. At the end they agreed on principle and decided to revisit the issue in the next meeting for a final vote. And there was Patrick "Pat" O'Celacanth.

Pat was one of the founders and owner of Hypnotic Quests, a tour guide business. It was an opportunity too good to pass. He wanted to show what he called his innovative leadership. Because history was as malleable as clay, he made his tour guides change their routes and their speeches-to-be-dispensed-to-the-tourists to accommodate the newly renamed corner. For lack of what to say, Pat cited Ray's lineage, tracing it to the Spanish origins of the Island. This action had re-written what Ray's father tried so hard to erase—the "*mancha de plátano*" that plantain stain that denotes the Hispanic origins of the family by giving his son a gringo's name and baptizing him at St. Paul's Episcopal Church. He did this against his wife's open and outspoken disapproval.

Thus, swiftly, Ray became one of the founding fathers of the island. He wasn't remotely related to the founding Indians and he probably wouldn't have cared to be part of a concocted, contrived historical discourse that served only to entertain the tourist, and fuel the coveted aorta of the business that feeds the Conch Republic.

The crowd was packing into St. Paul's Church, spilling into the street. Someone saw an old lady pushing a cart among the crowd. She had become a "well-unknown." Everybody recognized her, but no one knew much about her. Some knew that she loaded up her shopping cart at the soup kitchen in St. Mary's and distributed food to the homeless and the drunks on her way around the island. She was the only one not taking part in the show. It was part of her route. She stopped for a brief moment and figured out that it was a funeral. She didn't know whose it was but, as it was her custom, she mumbled in Spanish, "*Dios te haya cogido confesao.*" The old ladies in the corner of Eaton and Duval knew what she said; "I hope that you were in the grace of God when death came." And at the same time they all crossed themselves in the Catholic custom. She pushed her cart forward making sure she wasn't trampling anybody.

The next few days the papers were full of it, the opulent funeral and the details, or lack of them for that matter, of the will of Raymond Arteaga Zúñiga, read a few days later. Siña María kept her route and chores for one more month, pushed her shopping cart around the island feeding people and talking to anybody who wanted to listen to her. She was found dead a few days after the commissioners had agreed to name the corner of First Street and the Boulevard after Ray.

None of papers could agree on her story, but all of them tried. A young reporter wrote a short piece about her.

HOMELESS WOMAN FOUND DEAD

Citizen Staff

Siña María, one of those well-known colorful characters of Key West, was found dead on her favorite corner, Ramón Arteaga's Blvd. and First Street. The police interviewed a few of the homeless people but received no leads. Everyone spoke highly of Siña María, and none could think of anybody who wanted to harm her. One of the homeless, the one that they call Juan Diego, said "Siña María was a very nice lady who was once very rich and helped my family." The police dismissed this testimony on account of Juan Diego's mental disability.

The coroner determined there was no foul play. After the preliminary investigation was finished, the body was moved to the Alvaro-Obregón Funeral Home, which donated its services.

The investigators are not discussing the contents of her shopping cart. The chief of the police is withholding this information pending an inquiry about a letter found in the cart addressed to Raymond Arteaga Zúñiga.

The back of the Grotto at the Basilica Saint Mary Star of the Sea in Key West, where Siña María found the right spot to leave behind the trappings of her previous life.

5

Carmencita and José Juan could have bought a house like this one to restore. Still today, among the beautifully renovated houses of Key West, there are homes that have not changed much since they were constructed except for the ravages of time.

EL OLOR DE LAS AZUCENAS
THE SMELL OF THE LILIES

Hospital and police records helped piece together this part of the story. Be careful what you wish for, because you might have to deal with it. The action centers on the 1960s.

They grew together, like those couples in the Harlequin novels. *¡Ave María!* Who would have thought it! Pretty as flowers. The families lived one beside the other and since the two of them met, a mysterious link happened and grew stronger. Of course they went to school together, and they didn't lose track of each other, *¡ni pie ni pisá!* What year? I don't know, well, it was when the Navy Base was still around. José Juan got a good job fixing their expensive machines. He was even sent away for a few days to get special training on some important boat parts. Everybody was so proud of him. His picture was on the front page of the paper.

Carmencita's mother wanted her to wait. "*Eres una niña todavía*, you're still a girl," her mother once said. But there was no change in the young lovers' minds. Their parents winked, thinking that maturity and the school of hard knocks would cool them down. José Juan would go out *de parranda* with his friends, Carmencita would look shyly at the other boys at Bayview Park on Sundays, accompanied by her friends, and everybody would be happy. Someone said that they made some kind of a love pact, like Bernardo and María in *West Side Story.*

Their relationship continued, and everybody knew them as the *noviecitos*. No one expected it to last. Everybody thought that after adolescence they would be wiser. But love, or the devil, would have his way and they didn't ever separate. Resigned to the inevitable, their parents eventually arranged everything. When you saw the way they held hands, you knew what they meant to each other.

The mothers, already best friends, were delighted *as consuegras* and happy because neither of them had to deal with the problems that come often with children's spouses.

A few days before the wedding, Carmencita's mother had the usual conversation with her daughter. They laughed and cried and Doña María Isabel told her stories of her own wedding day and night. Different than her sisters, Carmen had another sense of what marriage, and for that matter, life was all about.

"*Mamá*, I really don't know how to feel. Everybody tugs at me one way or the other. I don't know if I am cut out to do this. I don't want kids and I don't have all these expectations that José Juan has. If we could only be together without anybody else. That's all I want, to be just the two of us. No family, no friends. *Los dos solitos.*"

Doña María Isabel brushed off the whole thing, "*Déjate de tonterías niña*, stop the nonsense. You just have butterflies in your stomach. They will disappear soon enough. *Las mariposas siempre vuelan con el viento nunca encontra de él.* Butterflies fly along with the wind, never against it."

The happy day came; Carmencita was more beautiful than ever and José Juan, there were no words to describe him. He was so handsome, intelligent and ambitious; he was the most desirable, and had the best future among the boys in the neighborhood.

"Carmencita, I will love you forever. If I lose you I won't be able to live," José Juan said to her on that day. "But there is something very important that I would like to promise you. Although my parents love each other very much, they also like to argue a lot." He was looking at her with such tenderness that she came closer to him.

"I want to promise to you that we won't argue like that. But if it ever happens I will walk away from it. Not because I don't care about you but because my parents arguments are very difficult to endure. Do you understand what I am telling you?"

Carmencita thought that the pledge was odd, but it was so romantic that she kissed him on the forehead and lingered there for a few extra seconds. José Juan sighed like something had been taken off his shoulders.

The wedding was one of the neighborhood's blissful days.

II

They bought the little rundown house on the corner of Catherine and Royal streets. It was a shotgun house but they didn't want much. The house needed some repairing and José Juan spent a good part of that summer getting it just right. Carmen was right by his side re-doing the inside. The house had a good cement foundation that was part of the front porch and José Juan built a wooden door for it. José Juan carved diamond shapes into the wood panels to make it more inviting and covered the floor with Spanish tiles. He discussed the possibility of fencing the yard, but Carmen wasn't sure about it, so he didn't do it. José Juan replaced all the wooden slats from the front that were weathered, sanded them and painted them shiny white, and then he painted the window frames blue. The porch wasn't covered and José Juan built a roof that gave it the look that is part of the architecture of Key West. He also painted the inside of the roof of the porch blue.

"Why are you painting the porch blue? Carmen asked.

"To keep the spiders and the wasps from building their webs and hives inside the porches, to make them think it is the sky. You didn't know that?" José Juan answered, surprised.

He bought the cast iron pillars that finished the porch and hand carved wood gingerbread adornments that connected the rafters with the iron. He repaired the rest of the perimeter fence and gave it the same coat of shiny white paint. On the windows on the east side, he installed aluminum shutters so the sun wouldn't shine directly into the back bedroom and the kitchen, and he planted a beautiful *flamboyán*, a royal Poinciana tree. It was mature already but not full-grown. The lot on their west side was already occupied by a two-story house, which took care of the afternoon sun. The neighbors had already started planting purple *trinitarias*, bougainvilleas that were growing fast and thorny.

"Those colors are so deep and beautiful," said Carmen that afternoon. She loved the deep purples and reds. José Juan planted some that were pink and peach.

When fall arrived and the weather started to cool down, José Juan started on the tin roof. He replaced all the rusty panels and buffed them by hand.

"These days, people just slap some paint on their roof panels and it doesn't look the same." José Juan said to Carmen, "That's wrong."

José Juan was very industrious with his hands and very passionate about his new wife. He couldn't wait to get his hands around her waist, spin her around and plant a long kiss on her lips. José Juan kissed Carmen this way one afternoon in front of his mother who was visiting. Doña Margarita fired one of her famous scowling looks at her son and *mirándolo de soslayo* she told him. *"Deja de hacer éso en público, parecen dos lapas*, to stop doing that in public because they looked like two leeches." Carmen pushed him playfully toward his mother, José Juan kissed Doña Margarita on her cheek and went with Carmen to the back of the house to help in the bedroom.

The inside was Carmen's domain. But José Juan laid tiles on the floor, helped her bleach the walls and move the furniture several times until she was happy with the arrangement. They painted the kitchen a very light green, built new cabinets and bought new white appliances. The families and friends contributed whatever was needed. But Carmen kept turning around and looking and turning and saying that there was something missing. She went out for a walk along Truman Avenue and found her answer in the front window of a dressmaker shop. There were *azucenas*, fresh lilies, in a beautiful glass vase. That was the missing piece. After that she had fresh lilies in the little white house.

Things started to change. Carmen could not conceive, and José Juan wanted an entire baseball team or, at least, one basketball team. One of their wedding presents was a bottle of brandy called *Duque de Alba*, very expensive stuff. It is one of those customs that the family kept from the time before they came to Key West. José Juan kept the bottle *pa' bebélsela* to drink with both his father-in-law and his pai on the day that Carmen said that she was expecting. The bottle, *diz que,* was *añejo,* twelve years old. It matured many years more.

III

In twelve years, they never argued and Carmen never heard words of reproach from José Juan's lips. He never spoke about children after that; even though seeing kids playing in the street, he felt that a thorn of a key lime tree had been placed in his mouth. But he never said a word.

Carmen would get all dolled up every day to wait for him to come home after a hard workday at the Navy base. She was meticulous and the results were impeccable, even perfection. Her hair, that mallet of black hair, was sometimes in braids, sometimes all up: she looked like one of the *modelos* from the *magazínes* that she used to collect and keep around the little wooden house all the time. She would always be *empolvadita* with only a hint of rouge in her lips; she didn't need anything else. The table would always be set and ready so when José Juan arrived, *cansao* and hungry, he just needed to freshen up and eat.

Carmen became a porcelain doll. The house was always very clean and fragrant, although she had stopped putting fresh lilies, *azucenas frescas,* in the kitchen and the living room.

After a while, José Juan stopped doing his usual stuff in the outside of the house. The *trinitarias* started growing wild and the grass was growing all over the place. The paint started to peel on the outside walls and the aluminum shutter in the bedroom window on the east side came off its hinges. Carmen asked José Juan a couple of times to fix it and then she stopped asking and hung a cream-colored valance in front of the lace curtain. She started to mask the little house problems that José Juan wouldn't get around to fixing. When the ceiling in the kitchen started showing water spots, she bleached them with a bucket and a brush.

A couple more years went by, and somehow Carmen had a glimpse of hope that José Juan would come out of the slump that seemed to have taken over him. They learned to tolerate each other's unspoken pain. It was a mystifying bond. Every so often he would come around her chair, caress her fondly on his way to bed. Or sometimes she would not sleep until his breathing became easy and she knew he was fast asleep. On those nights her kiss would descend like a butterfly, hardly touching his cheek. She would cry herself to sleep, but he never heard her.

Sometimes she caught him looking at her, *de soslayo* sideways. "Is there something wrong?" she asked one day. He didn't answer.

IV

One day José Juan came home early. He didn't notice that the table wasn't set. He sat down without changing his shirt, his face ashen.

"*¿Te pasa algo*, is there something wrong?" Carmen asked, avoiding looking directly at him.

"No, nothing… well… yes. On Monday they will close the mechanics part of the base. They say that are taking it *pa'* North Carolina because here they lose a lot of money." He put his face on his hands and just stayed there slumped over the table.

"Don't worry, *Viejo*, we will get by," she said.

A couple of days went by. José Juan didn't seem to work too hard to find a job. His dejection deepened, and he spent more time in the house. She came in to tell José Juan something important, but when she found him slumped in the same chair, she got exasperated.

"Are you going to get up out of that chair and find a job?" she argued. "Or maybe it is time that I start looking for a job. How that's going to sit with your family and friends?" She waited for his reaction.

Slowly he turned his face toward her. His rage was unavoidable. "*Mi mujer no trabaja para nadie*, my wife won't work for anybody."

She kept going at him; she couldn't stop. "Well someone has to work around here. How do you think we are going to eat? What will happen when we have kids? She threw the question like a dart at him, not expecting his reaction.

He got up like a wasp had stung him. She moved closer to the back door. "God damn, you are going to throw that at me now. I can't hold a job and I can't have a kid. Say it, say it, I'm not man enough for you."

Carmen had never seen him like that; she thought he was going to slap her across the face. He was charging toward her.

"*Piensa bien lo que vas a hacer*, think carefully what you're going to do," she said her voice trembling. Her left hand was barely holding to the doorframe. He came closer and brushed against her as he barreled out the back door. In her panic she let go and very quickly lost her balance. She thought she was in one of those slow moving dreams. Her legs hit the bottom of the stairs, her breast hit the first step and her stomach hit the second, hard. A sharp pain went up her spine. She thought she might have broken something. She laid there in shock and confusion and held her stomach. A single thought formed in her mind, "the baby!"

José Juan didn't look back; he just went off, walking as fast as he could. His feet pounded the earth the way that he would have answered her attack. His temples were throbbing. He went down Royal and reached Truman Avenue and headed toward North Beach Drive. He reached the shoreline and walked along the beach.

Two hours later, the sand that had gotten inside his shoes was rubbing against his skin. It made it raw but he didn't care. He turned around and started toward home. He knew he had failed his promise and wouldn't forgive himself for the rest of his life. This dull feeling of failure would take him to the grave; there was nothing left.

Carmen had heard the back gate slam shut. She wasn't sure, at first, whether he had seen the fall; now she knew that he hadn't. She lay on ground for a few minutes more, and then struggled to pull herself together. Getting up sent stabs of pain up to her shoulders. She reached the back doorframe and pushed herself in. Grabbing a chair, she plopped herself in it and tried to breathe. She didn't know what to do; she didn't know how to react. She just sat there, stunned. An hour and a half just passed her by. She stood up slowly; her feet seemed leaden, and she stumbled. By the time she reached the bathroom the throbbing had moved into her pelvis. She struggled with her dress. She sweated, and the fabric stuck to her skin. Every effort to shove up the dress seemed endless. She finally worked her underwear down to her thighs. "Good enough," she thought. She sat gingerly on the toilet seat.

In her confusion, an unfamiliar feeling got a hold of her belly. It felt like a bowel movement, but it was different, strange. She felt she was draining. Extraordinary amounts of liquid seemed to leave her body. The heavy liquid smelled of a combination of overripe bananas and paint thinner. She couldn't avoid looking at herself in the mirror from the other side of the small bathroom, struggling with her own blood. Her stomach muscles were moving independently from her thoughts. The lack of control was something Carmen wasn't used to feeling. But she knew she must let the process finish. Something finally dislodged itself from her. She sighed with relief and heard the front door open and close.

The porcelain doll came out of the bathroom all dolled up. José Juan was in the living room wrestling with his mind. They didn't speak for days. The incident was never mentioned.

Things turned from bad to worse. José Juan didn't find work. Every time he got an interview, he was told that he was overqualified; they couldn't pay for his expertise. Someone suggested that he should go to North Carolina and get into to the base there. He discussed it with Carmen. They almost did it, but his mother was dying in the hospital on Stock Island. José Juan took care of her for most of the year. Neither he nor Carmen left her side.

V

The neighbors said that eight months to the day José Juan's mother died, she returned to look for her old man. The neighbors argued about the circumstances; some were sure that José Juan's father died of a heart attack; others said later that he died of *tristeza*, of longing for his beloved wife. *La curandera*, Doña Purita, the *santera* priestess told one of the neighbors, "The ghost of Doña Margarita came and carried her old man away last night. It was so hot and humid that you could cut the air with a knife. I saw it with these eyes. *Yo lo vi, yo lo vi con estos mismitos ojos. ¡Que se me caigan los ojos aquí mismito, si les miento a ustedes!* I saw it with these eyes. Let them fall out of my sockets if I'm lying to you!" The neighbors nodded in agreement.

It was around this time that José Juan began hoarding medicines. He felt tired, empty and without *chavos*, money, because all the savings were gone. Between sickness and funerals the little money left to him by his family went to the doctor's and the undertaker's bills. By this time Carmen's mother had died, too, but there was no money, only a few debts.

José Juan's mood didn't change; he still couldn't find work and when someone tried to help and offer him some relief or a *chamba*, a chance to work, he either didn't show up or refused politely. He stopped going outside during the day. Carmen didn't know what to do. She kept herself busy taking care of him and the inside of the house. She couldn't do much about the outside, other than keep the grass from swallowing the front porch. She watered the plants. She tried once to trim the *trinitaria* but the bougainvillea scratched her, so she left it alone. The money was running really scarce, so she hardly ran any water and kept the electricity to a minimum, which suited José Juan's mood.

Carmencita wasn't feeling well. Her abdomen was bothering her. Several visits to the pharmacy didn't offer any relief. Mr. Cobo, the pharmacist, intervened. "Carmen, I know you don't want to hear this, but you should be checked by a doctor. I have talked to Dr. Cabañas and he would help you." He handed her a paper with all the information. After a couple of exams, the results were in.

That Saturday morning, she left the house without waiting for the mail carrier. As José Juan was reading a letter in the living room, Carmen arrived from her appointment. José Juan looked at her; there was something wrong. Carmen's face had a mixture of anger and pain that he couldn't ease or heal even if he wanted to.

"What is that note?" she asked without changing her expression.

"The bank is calling the mortgage," he said.

Without a word she handed him her test's results. Her insides were all wrong, that's why they couldn't have children and it was getting worse. She had cancer too, and there was nothing the doctors could do. All those years came back, all the pain; it all washed ashore in a wave. He looked up; there was a tear in her eye. He extended his hand; she placed hers in his, and very gently she sat in his lap. At the seashore, the wave came in carrying the butterflies. "*Las mariposas siempre vuelan con el viento, nunca en contra de él.*" She heard her mother's voice one last time. And as he kissed her, all the bitterness, all the resentment, the old pain, and the new pain of the last few years, it all melted down with the receding wave.

VI

They discussed the pact matter of factly; it was theirs alone, unspoken all these years. They had agreed to it. She looked at him, he saw the eyes of the young girl and the smile that he had almost forgotten returned to his lips. The bottle of pills rested on the nightstand. She wasn't sure what he had taken, probably the morphine pills. His mother loved those pills; they really took the pain away. She used to smile softly after taking them and then float away.

"*Aquí tienes*, here drink this," she said handing him a glass of dark liquid. He propped up a lucid moment brought by the aroma of the añejo.

"*¿Duque de Alba?*" he asked, even though the bottle was still in her hands. He gulped the liquid down, and Carmen watched as José Juan drifted away. The house smelled of fresh lilies once again, and they fell asleep breathing them, hugging each other in the clean house that now would always belong to them.

Carmen coughed and woke up. She had sweated a little because of the chill of José Juan's embrace. She ironed out the creases of her dress with her hand. Looking at him, she thought and hoped that he might be at peace at last, and then she called the police.

She couldn't join him. It was too much for him to ask, and after building her life around his unspoken guilt and depression, she couldn't mourn him. She had taken good care of him; now she had to find out if she had a chance. She had to grasp that last straw of hope. She was hoping that the doctors could do something. Maybe if she could get to Miami. Following him blindly this time wasn't an option.

The bank foreclosed on the little house and tried to sell it. But no one wanted it. It really went downhill. There were too many rumors in the neighborhood about it being haunted. The wood rotted and one of the limbs of the *flamboyán* decided to come through the roof in the bedroom. The neighbors say it was José Juan's arm trying to embrace Carmen. The floors gave in to the termites and water damage.

The Key West Citizen published the following:

POLICE DECLARED DÁVILA'S DEATH SUICIDE

Citizen Staff

After a short investigation, KWPD has declared that José Juan Dávila, resident of Key West, committed suicide at his home on Catherine St.

The autopsy showed that Mr. Dávila, unemployed at the time, ingested an undisclosed amount of morphine tablets before going to sleep. His wife, Mrs. Carmen Dávila Zúñiga, was unaware of the situation and found her husband not breathing and unresponsive the next morning.

After receiving an emergency call from the residence, dispatchers alerted paramedics who arrived at the residence within minutes. Efforts to revive Mr. Dávila were unsuccessful and he was declared dead.

Mrs. Dávila declared that her husband was suffering from depression after losing his job, his parents and then their home. She added that she was unaware that Mr. Dávila was hoarding medicines and morphine tablets prescribed to his mother who died of cancer.

Investigating officer Landtrop corroborated some of the facts and in his written report stated that there was no reason to doubt Mrs. Dávila's testimony and the matter warranted no further action. Mrs. Dávila was cleared of all suspicions and will be seeking treatment for an undisclosed illness in Miami. The couple had no children. Mr. Dávila has no known family members and was interred in Key West Cemetery.

VII

Carmen went to Miami to the university hospital and got herself listed in medical trials and attempted everything that the doctors advised her. She instructed the staff to turn away any visitors and endured massive amounts of chemotherapy and other new medicines. The treatment almost succeeded, but the cancer returned rabidly *como un perro rabioso.* By that time, her body was very weak. She endured a couple more treatments of chemo, because she was told about this new operation to scrape her insides. The doctors hadn't wanted to perform the procedure but she insisted. It was her right. It was her battle. She wasn't going to let go. She died on the operating table.

The hospital published the following notice in the *Miami Herald. The Key West Citizen* picked it up:

KIN OF MYSTERY WOMAN SOUGHT

The Miami University Hospital is looking for the next of kin of a woman who died last week. She was registered as Carmen Dávila with no known address in the Miami area. If you have any information about this patient please call the hospital at 305-555-5252 or this newspaper.

Hospital records showed the following information:

In October, Dr. Manuel Zúñiga, resident of the city of Key West, Florida, requested possession of the cremated remains of Ms. Carmen Dávila. Mr. Zúñiga demonstrated kinship to Ms. Dávila by form of affidavits and other documents that showed that the deceased was his aunt. The hospital's legal department, after corroborating the authenticity of the documentation, released the remains to Dr. Zúñiga.

Key West Cemetery records showed the following information:

November, Interment of cremated remains of Carmen Dávila Zúñiga on the Zúñiga family plot. No ceremony was performed.

6

The iguanas, like the chickens and the cats, are a bone of contention among the residents of Key West. Iguanas are considered an invasive species and a source of superstition, anger, awe and scorn. This young one is sunning itself on a particular cool afternoon at the cemetery.

IN HELL'S CIRCLE

Old pictures, guided the writer toward a dark pathway of the family's history. The action occurs during the late 1970s and early 1980s.

And when they pass the ruined gap of Hell
through which we had come, their shrieks begin anew.
....
And this I learned, was the never ending flight [of]
....
Love, which permits no loved one not to love,
took me so strongly with delight in him
that we are one in Hell, as we lived above.
Dante: The Inferno
Canto V

Two friends met after a long time. They embraced, asking themselves why they hadn't talked before. They looked at each other and tried to find traces from the past. David looked younger; he died first. Elias followed six years later, after all appeals to his death penalty sentence were exhausted. He didn't want to pursue them, but his attorneys insisted. He had lost some hair and gained a few pounds, but he still had the same handsome features that had attracted David in the first place.

"It's been a long time, hasn't it? I thought that everybody had forgotten about it," David said with a sad smile.

"Well, some might have forgotten, but I didn't forget," said Elias. "Oh well, I am here anyway, I didn't fear oblivion. You were the one who didn't want to face death, but you died anyway."

Doña Mariana, the street's mouthpiece, had just finished sweeping the little piece of Ashe St. that runs in front of her house. She went in and turned the TV on as usual; she heard the newscast that interrupted her Telenovela, dropped her jaw, and screamed through the open window to her neighbor Doña Rosa.

"*Ave María purísima*, Rosa, Rosa, come quick, the police found a head...." She didn't finish the sentence because Doña Rosa, as usual, was waiting for the signal to cross the street and dish it out with Doña Mariana over dark rich coffee and crackers.

The broadcast continued. *In Little Hamaca City Park, Key West police made a gruesome discovery Saturday: a murder victim's head wrapped in a bed sheet. This case has taken a few weeks of hard work and good old detective work, but the pieces are falling in place and an arrest is imminent, according to unnamed sources.*

The investigation started after a South Florida water-management district employee, who was checking a floodgate, found a headless body early last week in a Homestead canal. The remains were identified later as those of David Findley of Key West. Mr. Findley, who was identified from fingerprints, had been beaten, probably with a bat or a hammer, police said. But authorities did not indicate where or when they believed the murder occurred or what was used to sever the head. An autopsy showed that Findley died from injuries probably caused by a blunt instrument.

Elías expression changed because he remembered the fight; his eyes became dark with memories. "Will you ever forgive me?" he added almost in a whisper. David didn't answer, as usual.

They went out walking, like they used to. David, as always, started the arguments, the criticizing, the nagging, the recriminating, fighting the same tiresome fights. He was feeling the same bottled anger that hadn't let him die in peace. Of course, after the bitching started, things always got out of hand. Elías was the same. For him there were two kinds of people in the world: the ones he could use, and the ones he couldn't use. He used the ones he could, then tossed everybody else away.

The transmission carried on: *David Findley had recently moved to Key West with his partner Elías Ramírez, who returned to Key West a few years after the death of his mother. The few people who were at Little Hamaca Park Saturday afternoon were shocked when they were told what had been found there earlier in the day.*

"A head—that's horrible!" said a woman fishing for blue crabs in the salt ponds near the park.

"It's unreal," said her fishing companion, a lifelong Key West resident. "It's way out of character for this part of town. Since I've been a kid, this place has been safe. Away from the tourists, it's a place where kids can come and feel safe and comfortable. Unfortunately, someone chose to use it as a dumping ground. What can we do about it other than complain? This town is going to hell quicker than a speeding bullet," he concluded, shrugging his shoulders.

"David," Elías said, "you knew I couldn't get rid of it, the anger. I have cut my anger loose so many times, with so many lovers. It fills me up. It is like rearranging their minds and souls, working them up; and when they rebel, when they begin to figure it out, I give it to them; I try to bring them back in line. It was the same with you. And if after the first beating you don't get back in line, I try harder. Maybe you hadn't gotten the message yet: you have to change; otherwise you are going to suffer more."

"Elías, you haven't changed a bit. Always living in the past," said David "*¿En dónde carajo estamos?* Where the hell are we?"

The news voice interrupted. A two-lane winding road reaches the park from Flagler Avenue through the mangroves. By day, it is a place where youngsters play and people fish or walk their dogs. But at night, when the gates are closed, it transforms into a homeless hangout and is also notorious for homosexual activity, near-by residents say.

"I don't understand why the police aren't doing more. All those homosexuals and crack cocaine-snorting thugs should burn in hell," said another exasperated resident who didn't want to be identified. As we were putting together this footage, she came around and talked to us. She was short and stocky, dressed in teal shorts and a red polka dot top. She approached the crew with her dog, a mixture of a Chihuahua and a miniature pinscher, dressed the same way. "Every time that I walk Fifi in the park I find needles, prophylactics; yesterday I came out around midnight, and I found them there like two iguanas melting into each other," she added, disgust reeking out of her expression. When asked what she was doing walking her dog after midnight, she spat on the ground, cursed and walked away. "We will continue to watch this investigation closely, watch our six o'clock broadcast here on channel 4."

"I don't know," said Elías, a bit bothered, "but I hope this isn't eternity, because to spend the rest of it with you is the worst thing that could happen to me."

"Don't worry. We'll find a way to avoid it."

The voice from the box came back. More on the ongoing investigation of the murder of David Findley. Police pieced together the following series of events, starting with a routine criminal-mischief report, which led to the arrest. Last week, a resident of the Petronia Street Apartments told police that he had seen a man, later identified as Elías Ramírez, puncturing the tires of a Chevy Carprice parked illegally on the street. The man then drove away in a 1980s Honda Accord.

The Accord was gone when police arrived, but it was back on Petronia Street later that week. Police impounded it after determining that the damage to the tires of the neighbor's car was enough to make the crime a felony. Officer Bubba Landtrop, grandson of Sheriff Landtrop, ran the vehicle's plates and found that the car belonged to Elías Ramírez. Law-enforcement department technicians found blood residue in the car's trunk and front passenger's seat.

The whole gruesome scene replayed itself. David was sleeping in the bedroom. Elías entered in a rage, hammer in hand. David grabbed his head after the first blow. The pain returned easy, slow, and everything came back as if he were coming out of amnesia. The fight about returning to Key West, the insults, the complaints, the frustrations, the unrealistic desires that turned to ugliness and contempt. The drinking, the drugs, the nights spent dancing in a drug-induced trance at The Monster. The mornings spent in the small rooms of the Island House. The little stuff, the big stuff. Elías grabbed David's throat. He was trying to get free of his anger, but he couldn't stop. The liquid gaze, the only omen that David couldn't decipher that night before the storm of blows that killed him, wasn't in his eyes anymore. In addition to this nothingness was the fury of having to leave life behind before the time to leave had arrived, without being asked, without wanting it. David remembered that, while his head was spinning in circles and exploding, he did land a successful blow to Elías, who tried in vain to shield his face. But it was too late; a trap door opened and David fell in, unintentionally, because there was so much unfinished business.

Elías could laugh and leave David on the floor gasping for air and black and blue, footprints on his skin. Elías knew the necessity of continuing the beating, of causing David pain, of looking at David's face shrouded with fear, weeping and swollen; of discharging the restrained resentment. Elías felt satisfaction and left the body slumped on the floor. David unexpectedly opened his eyes and Elías saw the defiant spark that he knew so well, and started kicking again. Elías needed to kick again, again, until he felt that David wasn't daring him. Every one of the muscles in his body ached but he tasted relief. It was an exquisite purge. Elías looked at the body for a minute, touched his forehead and after one second of pure fear and confusion decided what the next step was.

The transmission came in, one more time. *The police couldn't find Elías Ramírez. A neighbor told them that he left Key West for parts unknown but later that week, police got a tip that Ramírez had returned to his Petronia Street Apartments and found him there. Ramírez confessed to the murder and was arrested without incident. First-degree murder charges were being prepared against him during the weekend, said a source from the courthouse on Whitehead Street.*

Elías, driving back to Key West after disposing of the body, had been confused; time had jumbled in his mind. He wasn't sure of how many weeks or days or hours or minutes or seconds had ticked in place.

He was talking to himself and asked, mechanically "*por favor, perdóname baby*, please, forgive me." Promising that he wouldn't do it again. "Honey, it won't happen again." Explaining, "The anger took over my body, I didn't understand how." Weeping, "I love you, *te quiero mucho*, I love you very much, a lot, please, don't feel bad, please, forgive me. *Perdóname otra vez, por favor.*"

And he repeated the same thing over and over. Elías looked at David, which he had placed in the front passenger's seat. The bed sheet didn't cover it anymore.

David said, "Don't worry baby, I love you too."

Elías hit the brakes so hard that they screeched. He was back on Petronia Street in front of his mother's apartment building. Dawn was coming.

David spoke again, "Honey, can you take me to Hamaca Park? Just like the first time we came to Key West?" Still in a haze, Elías restarted the car.

The next thing that Elías remembered was being back at the apartment. It was mid-morning. He felt safe. Known things, comfortable things, surrounded him; he had the afternoon to read a couple of old newspapers and was aware of the situation. He selected a few pictures from a wooden box on top of the coffee table. One of his mother, a young and beautiful woman; another of him and his brother, happier days in Key West. The last one of him and David in Chicago before the grim pull of Key West grabbed hold of them. He examined the pictures for a few minutes, picked up the phone, and after reaching a voice on the other side of the line, he said, "Yes, I just want to report that I saw Mr. Elías Ramírez walking down Petronia Street a couple of hours ago." And after a short pause, "No, sir, I don't wish to identify myself, just a concerned citizen. Thank you and have a good afternoon."

Half an hour later, the knock on the door sounded. Elías Ramírez answered, now at peace with himself.

The broadcast was over. Doña Mariana and Doña Rosa looked at each other and complained how the times have changed. "It's in their blood," Doña Mariana said with contempt, "Did you know that his mother was a drug addict?"

Judge Reneé Hutchinson had only one question for Elías the day of his sentencing.

"Mr. Ramírez, why did you sever the head of Mr. Findley?" Elías had kept his head down during the proceedings. The judge tried again. "Mr.

Ramírez, this court is addressing you, answer the question, why did you sever Mr. Findley's head?"

Elías answered almost whispering: "I needed to talk to him."

The day of his appointment with Sparky came; while he was led down the corridor in shackles, Elías Ramírez looked down at the floor. He had not spoken for a few years; if anything, the guards heard whispers and they didn't mind. He didn't utter a word during his appeals. He never smiled. The guards were used to his silence, to his lowered stance. They had to literally drag him everywhere. This time was no different; the guards were helping him walk down the corridor. He hadn't requested a meal; he hadn't eaten; he was weak.

Then, his head bobbed up. The guards stopped and looked at him. He was standing straight up. The guards let their grip loose and Elías started walking by himself, as the shackles on his feet permitted it, steadily toward the chair. He saw a figure already seated in his chair. As Elías came closer, he noticed that David's scars had healed nicely. Elías winked, David smiled and extended his left hand to touch Elías' cheek, his right hand to help Elías sit down. No one heard David's voice: "*Ven siéntate a mi lado, tengo algo que decirte*. Come here and sit by my side. I have something to tell you," and it was, for now, over.

Two friends met after a long time. They embraced, asking themselves why they hadn't talked before. They looked at each other and tried to find traces from the past.

Six years after his sentence, *The Key West Citizen* published an item buried on the left hand corner of page 3.

RAMÍREZ DIES IN THE ELECTRIC CHAIR

Citizen Staff

On Dec. 22nd, six years to the date of his guilty plea, Elías Ramírez, 36, died in Florida's electric chair for the murder of his partner David Findley. The Findley family declined to attend the execution. Only the required state staff and the deceased's brother, Manuel Zúñiga, attended. The body was cremated and the ashes will be interred beside his mother, famed local songstress Magdalena Zúñiga, at Key West Cemetery.

Elías Ramírez met David Findley in Chicago where Mr. Ramírez moved to follow a career in modeling and acting. They moved back to Key West in 1975 and both worked in the service industry.

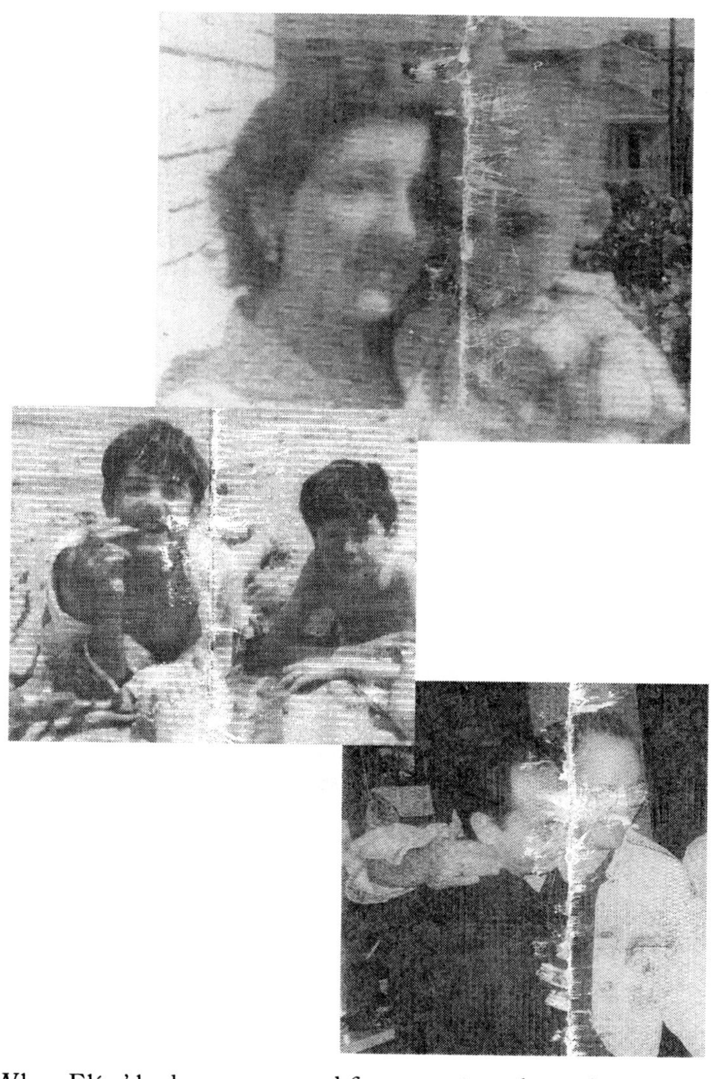

When Elías' body was prepared for cremation, three photographs were found folded in his shirt pocket. They were damaged but they seem to be, top: Magdalena and Elías, left: Elías and Manny, right: Elías and David in Chicago.
Photos from Zúñiga Family Collection.

7

Angels are the most common sculptures used at the Key West Cemetery.

THE SPOT ON THE WING OF THE ANGEL

"La vida no es lo que uno vivió, sino lo que recuerda, y cómo la recuerda para contarla." "Life is not what one has lived but what one remembers and how it is remembered in order to recount it." *Gabriel García Márquez*. This story takes place between mid 1980s to mid 1990s.

For Eliana Martinez to whom Elton John never dedicated a song.

When Steven Carmichael and Manuel Zúñiga brought Angelita to their house for the first time, after all the paperwork and all the red tape, Steven put the baby in his lap and examined every single pore in her skin. The first thing he noticed was those big black eyes and the mat of tight curls growing on her head. Steven knew all the possibilities, but his instinct was that everything was ok, and it always would be ok, that nothing could go wrong. Now, a couple of years later, he didn't have time to think about his instincts. With the tip of his fingers, he turned back the sheet, took his sandals off and lay in the hospital bed. He took Angelita in his arms and rocked her a while, humming to her what would become her favorite lullaby. It was also Manny's favorite, his mother used to rock him to sleep singing it.

"Una barca que se mecía
un gorrión cansado de volar,
y al temblor divino de aquella voz
florecía un aire de amor..."

It was very early in the morning; Dr. Manuel Zúñiga was walking down the hall at the Lower Keys Medical Center when he heard the voice of Nurse Díaz behind him.

"Dr. Zúñiga, what's that in your pocket?" asked the nurse, a little confused after she saw the ball of gray hair peeking out of the corner of the pocket of his white lab coat, the only one that was clean after the last three days. "You look ragged!" she added. "How many days will you work without sleep? Your shift is done. Why don't you go home and sleep a little?"

"Don't worry about it, Ms. Díaz. Has Dr. Ocasio arrived?"

"I'm going to check with the receptionist right now." He didn't reply. Shrugging she started to walk away.

"Oh, this." He grimaced, trying to check his pocket without taking out the furry thing, "Angelita gave it to me so I would take care of it for her."

He started his rounds quickly, passing between the beds taking temperatures, shinning a penlight in the eyes that sometimes didn't react. He went up and down the corridor, run, run as a soul in pain that couldn't move backwards. Forward, fast-forward, he stood in front of Angelita's room and felt helpless for the first time in his career for the first time his life.

As he entered, the glare from the small window blurred his vision and his mind went away to

> *Central Park in New York City in the middle of the eighties, wandering. Somewhere in the park, a famous artist would be giving a free concert to collect money for Angelita. He should have been singing a pretty song that he had re-written for Angelita. The fans would be hearing this and their hands would be in the air swaying like one wave. Candles and disposable lighters would be raised in the air. The singer and the public would become one in song.*

But this particular concert had never taken place. Angelita wasn't Ryan White and Elton John has never heard of Angelita.

Silence was everything in the small room in the hospital. One wall was full of cards. In an uncomfortable armchair was Steven, watching the monitor. The screen didn't show a half-hour comedy, or a soap, or a film. It showed a single green line that jumped once in a while. It was constant and irregular at the same time. Much like the roosters in town, on Eliza St. where Angelita lived with her two dads. The roosters there sing every morning, they never fail but they never sing at the same time. It was Angelita who pointed this out to them one morning; but neither of them had ever paid any attention to it. Today, it became very clear.

For three days the flowers dropped and dried in the vase on the table, ugly yellow flowers that Steven brought in because one of the custodians gave them to him instead of throwing them in the trash. He no longer had time to leave the room unless it was in the mornings.

"Honey," Manny said a bit loudly, coming out of his wandering in Central Park. "Why don't you go home and sleep for a while. Angelita's situation won't change today. Please go rest so you can be strong for her."

"Manny, don't scream at me please, you are going to wake her up. And if you do, all hell will break loose. I assure you!" Steven's voice came through his teeth in slow spurts. He really wasn't angry with Manuel, but something had to give.

With a stern look but loving touch Manuel took Steven's face in his hands. He blew softly in each of his eyes and with the lightness of a butterfly, placed his lips on his. "I love you more than ever," he whispered just in time before the first round of nurses opened the door to start the day.

The routine was the same. Steven left the room once a day to let some hot water run down his back, change his clothes, drink a *buchi* and eat a bite of something so his stomach wouldn't grumble so much. The nurses entered and changed the sheets. They also changed Angelita's position to avoid bedsores and to massage her body a little bit. They all sang to her, touched her, so she knew that her friends were there. They all wore disposable clothing over their uniforms, rubber gloves, and a paper bootie on each shoe. The nurses always apologized to Steven.

"You do understand that we don't want to offend you? It's hospital policy." Steven had heard it so many times. He knew that it was important to them, so he always answered the same way.

"I know darling, I know. You do what you have to do." But he didn't use any of those things.

The administrator told Steven that if he didn't wear all that stuff, he couldn't see Angelita. "You are the biggest jerk this side of US 1," Steven answered and called his lawyer.

At the courthouse on Whitehead Street, Judge Rivers, without thinking too much, read the administrator the riot act. Since that day, Steven wore what he pleased and left the hospital only once in the morning.

After the nurses bathed and changed her, Steven told Angelita the things that had happened the day before. Sometimes, he invented something, not to bore her with the same stories. He made sure that Angelita was dry and combed her hair. This was the hardest part of the morning, to comb that bristle of hair with a hairbrush that didn't work anymore and that Steven wasn't going to throw away anytime soon because a lot of memories were part of it.

Steven always cut Angelita's hair short, but after her first birthday, she had a hissy fit any time that Steven brought the scissors near her, so he decided to let her hair grow. As it grew he had second thoughts. Every morning Steven seated her in front of him and the ritual began. The hairbrush went in and out, and Angelita shouted as if someone were killing her. "Angelita, for god's sake, don't shout so much. You want the neighbors to think that I am murdering you?"

Now, the same brush lifted and tugged the girl's hair with smooth sweeps and Steven wanted her to shout like that, to shout so hard and wake up the neighbors. And he sobbed softly while he combed it and he touched the great soft tufts. Then Steven put a red bow in Angelita's hair and rocked her some more and thought out loud about her weight. The ounces she loses, the half ounces she gains: it was akin to a metronome sideways. The sight of Steven and Angelita replaced the image of Central Park in Manuel's mind as he entered the room. "And how is the light of my eyes today?" he asked forcing a smile.

He looked at Steven in the same corner where he was the last time he checked.

"And how is the best partner in the world doing today?" He squeezed Steven's shoulders and kissed his forehead.

"You see, Angelita hasn't complained in the last few days," Steven answered as he turned his face to the window.

"You hear what your daddy said, Angelita? Tell him it's not true," Manny said doing the routine check-up. His ear got closer to the half-opened small mouth, as if she were talking softly to him. The pen lamp didn't arouse any response, but Manuel kept talking anyway.

"What did you say? OK, I will tell him. Honey, Angelita has told me to tell you not to worry about her too much. She is breathing well and she just told me that she might grace us with her presence today."

Steven turned from the window and looked at his lover. Manuel didn't have to guess; Steven's mood wasn't good. Manuel went behind the armchair and as he gave Stevie a smooth massage in the shoulders he breathed a sigh. Manuel caught a glimpse of Nurse Díaz going down the hallway; he told Steven, "I need some analysis done," and left chasing after the nurse. Manuel wanted to check the last T-cell count.

Manuel got to his office and just collapsed in his chair and laid his head on the desk. The nurse entered with the normal noise of her white starched uniform. She saw him, assumed the position of a sergeant of the army and growled:

"Doctor, if you don't leave and rest I'm going to call Dr. Ocasio so he'll force you out for the night. For three days Angelita has been in a coma, and you haven't slept. You already know that you can't do anything."

"Ms. Díaz, thanks for your concern, but I don't need my partner and you acting as my mother at the same time." He lowered his head again. The nurse placed a glass of orange juice on the desk and left, followed by the rustle of her starched skirt.

II

Dr. Zúñiga had attended Angelita's birth, and when he saw her for the first time, she was all eyes and hair. In that childbirth, in that sterile room, there was a feeling of injustice so great, of a lack of God that worsened when the mother didn't even want to see her. Dr. Zúñiga just stood there with the baby in his hands; the mother's reaction caught him by surprise. He came out of it when the attending nurse raised her voice almost to a scream. She needed to bathe and prepare the baby. Later the doctor checked with the nurse. Nobody had come to see the infant in the ward. Two days after Angelita was born, her mother checked herself out of the hospital and disappeared into the wind. When the Department of Children and Family Services came to fill out all the paperwork, including the birth certificate, they didn't know what to write down on it. Manuel had a short conversation with nurse Díaz.

"Ms. Díaz, check all the paperwork, the name has to be somewhere." Dr. Zúñiga was impatient.

"Aha! Here it is!" Ms. Díaz was happy. "It's Rodríguez, but that's probably an alias. I'm sure that they are not going to find her." She said to Dr. Zúñiga, "Why don't we call her Angelita, it means little angel in Spanish. And who will deny that she isn't an angel? Any complaints, bring them to me!"

"Ha, Ha," laughed Nurse Lakisha Saunders, an older Conch from Bahama Village and Díaz's best friend. She was big and sweet as the molasses color of her skin. "Calling all personnel: Nurse Díaz is on the war path, make way or be crushed by the Puerto Rican justice machine, ha, ha. Out of her way, I'm telling you, children, get out of her way."

Nurse Díaz had a strong constitution, broad shoulders and muscles as thick as her Puerto Rican accent. Through her hard work she had become the head of the neo-natal ward. When she was upset, she spoke only in Spanish. When she was happy, she spoke English almost with a Welsh accent. She was raised by the nuns of the Sacred Heart in an orphanage located in Santurce, Puerto Rico, where her favorite teacher, who taught her English, was from Wales.

"What is the procedure now?" Dr. Zúñiga asked the caseworker.

"DCF will try to locate the mother," he answered like a robot. "People don't know that they can't be charged with abandonment as long as they leave the kids in a hospital or a firehouse. If she is an illegal alien, we will never find her," he added sadly. "The child will become a ward of the state, then the long process of foster parents and adoption starts."

"*¡Yo no quiero tener problemas con la DCF!*" Nurse Díaz said rolling her 'r's.

"*¿Qué dijo?* What did you say?" It was the code phrase that Dr. Zúñiga always used to let Díaz know, that she was in Spanish mode and no one heard or understood a word she said.

"I don't want to have any problems with the DCF!" she said with a suspicious look.

"I've decided to foster her. We are certified as foster parents by the state." Dr. Zúñiga was looking at the caseworker. The guy saw the parting of Red Sea and plunged forward to the Promised Land.

"I'll be more than happy to start the paperwork. My regional director is going to be so happy!" He started scribbling; Nurse Díaz wasn't paying attention to the exchange and continued her conversation with the doctor.

"Ok," she said and added, "if DCF comes after me, you will be paying child support!"

"My dear, sweet nurse Ratchet, if they come, I'll promise to marry you!" Dr. Zúñiga exclaimed out loud to the whole nursing station. Everybody laughed.

"That would make my mother, very, very happy!" Díaz was roaring as she rolled her 'r's. The whole station laughed.

The DCF caseworker was pleased and finished his business quickly. He said that he would advance the foster application procedure, knowing that Dr. Zúñiga and Steven Carmichael had two other foster children. The department was happy with them fostering children because they took good care of them. They had good jobs; they had good healthcare insurance to supplement what was mandated by Florida, and a house in Key West.

Immediately Dr. Zúñiga convinced Steven that they could be the foster parents, and maybe later adopt her. Even in this political and social climate, Dr. Zúñiga thought that they might get away with it. It was time to try the adoption path; he had read so much about it lately. The newscasts were full of it; even Oprah had expressed her favorable opinion on the matter. Steven was reluctant but he agreed.

When the results of her blood examination arrived positive for HIV, Steven cried a little; he felt some resentment. Not at Manuel, not at Angelita, but at the forces that were capable of so much lack of affection. At their unfair and unwanted judgment of an innocent child.

"Steven, these things don't have an explanation," Manuel said to him with a lump in his throat. "We can't abandon her now." They didn't have time to think about what could happen or how hard the whole ordeal would be. The rage in Steven's eyes said everything. That night they became, without knowing, without wanting to, without being asked, Angelita's champions and activists.

III

Six months after her first birthday, a spot appeared on Angelita's back. It was Karposi's sarcoma, a form of skin cancer related to AIDS. Later that year pneumocisistis carini appeared in her lungs and Angelita had to be hospitalized. Díaz stopped Dr. Zúñiga in the hallway that morning.

"I heard about Angelita," she said.

"Yes, those are clear symptoms that AIDS is progressing faster than what we thought. I can't leave her without protection now." He bowed his head for a minute. When he looked at Nurse Díaz again, she was weeping softly. It was the first and only time that Dr. Zúñiga saw her cry.

Steven and Manuel knew what was coming, and after another battery of tests the hospital became a second home for the family. When Steven and Manuel had time, they took Angelita on walks, and showed her things so she wouldn't forget them: an ant, a yellow anole, a chicken family, a six-toed cat and a hummingbird. When Angelita heard it up close, she clung to Steven's neck even though she couldn't stop watching it.

Angelita started to wither. Through the whole ordeal she showed the behavior of a child older than her age, a child who knew what was coming down the pipeline. The day of her second birthday, the nurses decorated the waiting room a little, and the custodians Damián and Antonio hoisted the hospital bed and set it in the middle. Although the nurses took Steven shopping for presents, half an hour was all he could stay away from the room. He bought another present that Manuel was supposed to give her, but Manuel went down to the lobby and bought a stuffed kitten for her. Coming back into the room, he said to Steven, "I know it is a bit selfish, but I wanted to give Angelita my own present." When they lit the candles on the cake, Angelita's eyes illuminated and while they sang, she embraced the kitten. It was the last time that Manuel saw Steven so happy. A week later Angelita gave Manuel the kitten before one of her tests. She didn't want it to be cold, so she placed it in the pocket of his lab coat.

IV

Manuel and Steven tried in vain to adopt Angelita. The state of Florida had taken a thorough stand against gay adoptions. "It's ironic," said Sarah Smith, the couple's attorney. "In the application for adoption there is a checklist and one of the questions is whether you are a homosexual. If you mark 'yes,' the instructions inform you that you have not met the criteria for the department of Children and Family Services. If you mark 'yes,' to whether you are a felon or a drug-addict, however, you can proceed with the application process."

The judge wasn't impressed. The attorney charged again. "There are couples lined up waiting for healthy white babies from private agencies.

My clients don't care about color, sex, age, or health, they just want to give a child a chance to have a real place to call home and be loved."

Judge Rivers replied with sarcasm, "So you want me to punish these couples because of the way they think?"

"No," replied the lawyer. "I want you to recognize and reward my clients for their compassion and because they have a positive effect in a system that is characterized as ineffective and corrupt by the media and other agencies."

The judge continued the case for a couple of weeks. Before going back, Manuel, Steven and the attorney discussed the strategy at the dining room table.

"We need to boost your profile more," the attorney said. "Which case worker do you guys like the most?"

"I guess Nana," answered Manuel. He turned around and looked at Steven for approval.

"Ok," said the attorney, "the judge has to meet her, and Angelita too."

"No way," said Manuel. "I am not putting Angelita through this. Nana is ok but not Angelita." Steven, who had stayed quiet through most of the conversation, stepped in. "Manny, this might be the only way that we can change that moron's mind about the whole thing."

When the day came, the judge interviewed Nana. "Can you summarize your opinion of these foster parents?"

"Yes," Nana started her testimony. "This couple has taken in children that have been abused, some that are mentally sick, but mostly HIV positive children." Nana shifted in her chair. "Most of these children are rejected by other foster families who are in the system looking to adopt a healthy 'all American' child."

Angelita was seated beside Steven in her favorite Winnie the Pooh jumpsuit, very poised and straight looking at the judge in his eyes. The judge lowered his gaze. Nana spoke for half an hour more. When she was finished, the attorneys presented more arguments. Opposing counsel argued, “It is in the best interest of adoptive children, many of who come from troubled and unstable backgrounds, to be placed in a home anchored by both a mother and a father.”

“I can’t believe this argument, your honor!” charged Smith, “I can’t understand how we can live in a state that has spent in excess of $350,000 of the taxpayers’ money to prevent this couple from caring for and loving kids that are rejects of the same system that is supposed to take care of them. Don’t you think that it would be more productive to use that money to keep these children alive?”

“The State of Florida has the right to legislate its ‘moral disapproval of homosexuality’ and its belief that children need married parents for healthy development,” countered the state staff attorney.

Smith wasn’t going to let him have the last word. “Your honor, counsel has presented to you the real issue here. It is not the ‘best interest of the adoptive children’ that we are discussing; it whether or not the state of Florida can use the constitution to assume that sexual orientation has anything to do with good parenting.”

The judge stepped into his chambers. When he came back, an hour later, he delivered his decision. “This court is very cautious when asked to take sides in an ongoing public policy debate. It is the decision of the court that to rule that the legislature was misguided in its decision is one of legislative policy, not constitutional law. The law is very clear, gay couples can foster a kid, they can’t adopt.” Steven was crushed. “I can’t believe that he ruled against us.”

V

“Zúñiga, come to my office. We need to talk,” said Dr. Ocasio without looking at him. “I just arrived and Díaz told me that you haven’t slept in three days. You cannot burn out on the ward. I understand what you are going through, but pediatrics is full and we need you.”

“I know, I know,” he grumbled. “Today I rested in my office. I’ll bet you Diaz didn’t tell you that?”

"How many hours? One, two, or was it until Diaz saw you so she wouldn't pester you anymore?" Dr. Ocasio asked, looking at him.

"I don't know," was all he could say as he turned to start rounds again.

"If you don't go home tonight, I don't want to see you tomorrow."

Manuel gave in and decided to go home and rest. On his way to see Angelita one more time, Díaz came running down the hall, "Dr. Zúñiga, she is awake!" He rushed to the room, and Dr. Jiménez was already there with Steven, who had Angelita in his arms; she had come out of her coma. She was so small she looked like an infant. The readings of the monitor were irregular.

The tiny child spoke clearly to Steven, "Daddy, sing me a song." Steven was sobbing and singing at the same time,

"Una barca que se mecía
un gorrión cansado de volar,
y al temblor divino de aquella voz
florecía un aire de amor…."

Dr. Jiménez pulled Dr. Zúñiga aside; he didn't have good news. Manuel stepped behind Steven and Angelita, and she extended her arms to Manuel and he took hers. She smiled sweetly at the kitten in his pocket; she had put it there before one of her tests and forgot it. The line on the monitor became flat. Manuel started to sing as Steven said to him, "Let her go, Manny, let her go."

The next morning officials from DCF came and retrieved Angelita's body for interment. Steven looked at Sarah Smith. "Can you ask the department if they would let us pay for the cremation?"

"We can try; we can use the argument that they will save some money. They probably won't resist that." She answered as she opened her cell phone. After a few minutes she was furious. "I hate to deal with bureaucracy! They won't let us have the body or pay for the cremation. They don't want to set a precedent for others to follow."

"Can we sue them?" Manuel asked. "I can't believe that they won't let us bury her." Sarah Smith tried unsuccessfully to turn the department around.

The memorial was held in Manuel and Steven's living room. The room was decorated with balloons and Angelita's pictures. Manuel tried to break Steven's anger and depression, tried making the situation as bearable as possible. "Honey, I didn't know we had taken so many pictures, remember this one?" The nurses from the hospital and the lawyers were all present.

"Where is Nana?" asked Steven as someone opened the front door; in came Nana dressed in a yellow suit and sensible pumps. She was as loud as the dress, and she was smiling impishly.

"Are you stoned or something?" Steven was a bit bothered and intrigued. "What are you carrying?"

"Isn't it beautiful? Suzie DePoo made it for me." She placed the delicate box on the shelf beside a picture of Angelita. It was a gold leaf metal box with gold threads that seemed like filigree. Sitting on top was a metal and wood angel holding one of its broken wings. "Can you guess what's inside?" Manuel and Steven looked at each other puzzled. "No," said Manuel.

"It's Angelita." Nana had the expression of a child that has gotten away with something. "I know the regional DCF director, and I called in a couple of owed favors, and … here she is."

VI

The next November, Sarah Smith filled out some miscellaneous paperwork and a couple of appeals that she was hoping someone else from the ACLU would take on to continue the fight against DCF. She was exhausted and looking forward to returning to Chicago and putting all these emotions behind her. She had packed her bags that afternoon and she had paid her bill at the B&B on United Street. It was a relatively new establishment called 'Black Onyx' owned by a lesbian couple and a few other investors. Sheri Gilbert was one of them; she was a chosen member of the Zúñiga-Carmichael family. Her stake on the new venture was to secure the liquor license and run the bar, called Club Pacific Ocean. She had flaming red hair and a penchant for dark haired women.

"Hon, have you tried the new bar yet?" Lori, one of the owners, asked Sarah. "It's still kind of rough back there but once we are finished with it, it will be a lovely tranquil place for gals to meet without pressure and loud music. And besides, Sheri is a great gal with a healthy sense of humor."

"A good sense of humor is what I need right now!" Sarah said, "Like a fish needs a bicycle or a hole in its head."

"Oh, oh," replied Lori. "Grumps alert! Grumps alert!" And picking up the phone she dialed the bar. "Sheri, dear, I'm sending you a blond in need of a good talk and a drink, which is on me."

"What's your pleasure, sis?" asked Sheri, and after taking a second look, "Are you ok?" The bar was empty and it was early.

"It's almost six o'clock," said Sarah, "turn the TV on any of the network news. No, turn it on the Court TV Channel." And just like a well-oiled cuckoo clock, the newscaster was discussing the intricacies of the case. "Oh dear, I have completely forgotten that this was going on. And you were in that mess." They talked for the rest of the night while Sheri tended the bar, and Sarah ended up in her room. The next morning as Sarah was getting ready to go to the airport she said to Sheri:

"Didn't you tell me that you were into dark haired women?"

That day Sarah went to Chicago for the last time. She quit her law firm, made sure that her pending cases were taken care off and packed her clothing. Her Chicago friends were surprised. One in particular voiced the group's concerns. Silvia has been Sarah's best friend since college and together they have supported each other in good and bad times. "Sarah, you have always been careful about everything in your life, it's not you to do this. What happened in Key West?"

"To tell you the truth, I'm not completely sure yet. Key West is a weird place, but weird in a good way. This case opened my consciousness; I can do something good down there. I don't know what yet, but I can try. I also met someone. And you know more than anybody that I've sacrificed that area. Maybe is time to give it a try."

"And if it doesn't work?" Silvia said.

"I'm not letting this one get away. And if it doesn't work, I'll be back pestering you!" Sarah said with a smile.

"Oh no missy, not to be bossy, but you're not thinking this one through and I'm a bit worried. You know that I spend my life worrying."

"Silvia, if I don't try it, I won't know. And you can come and visit."

"You know I hate heat," Silvia added.

"You will come in the winter. We can start a new tradition. We can celebrate New Year's together, every year."

Sarah found an apartment she liked on Catherine Street. It was small and expensive compared to what she rented in Chicago. That was her first shock about living in paradise. Sarah was used to buying everything new. Everything had to match; Pottery Barn and IKEA where her favorite stores. She went to the Salvation Army and decorated the place in an eclectic style. None of the dishes matched, she did the same with glassware. The coffee table will double as the dining table. A pullout sofa will harbor guests as they visit. This simple situation gave her a sense of satisfaction that she hadn't experienced before.

Sarah came to Key West with a few contacts from her ex-boss but her mind was made up to work with the ACLU in some capacity. Sarah started working on that and on Sheri with the same zest that she applied to other areas of her life. One difference; there wasn't a clear plan.

VII

Dr. Zúñiga reported back to work at the Medical Center a whole week before he was due. Dr. Ocasio had forced him to take a month off after Angelita's death.

"Dr. Zúñiga, though it's a week early, I'm glad you are back," said Dr. Ocasio. "Are you doing ok? How's Steven holding up?"

"Oh, he is doing well. As well as he can with all the litigation and the kids' school and his business. I guess we are doing ok. I need to start my rounds again. Thanks for your understanding and the few weeks off," he said.

"What is that gray thing in your pocket?" Dr. Ocasio was looking at the gray fuzzy head that was peeking out of his colleague's lab coat.

"It's a kitten 'Beanie Baby.' Angelita gave it to me."

The Key West Citizen published the following:

ANGELA RODRÍGUEZ DIED DUE TO COMPLICATIONS OF THE AIDS VIRUS

Citizen Staff

Angelita, the Department of Children and Family Services foster child who captured the hearts of the state of Florida, died last Wednesday of complications due to the AIDS virus, with which she was born. Abandoned by her mother at birth, her father unknown, Angelita was placed in foster care with the openly gay couple, Manuel Zúñiga and Stevie Carmichael. The couple's move to adopt her was blocked by DCF, which claimed that the only safe place for the little girl was a straight household "anchored by a mother and a father," according to agency spokesperson, Lisa Cortez.

The case was heard by the 11th District Court of Appeals in Atlanta, which ruled against gay couples trying to adopt children. In Key West, the case sparked a support organization and events to help her foster parents and two other couples of gay and lesbian plaintiffs cope with the mounting lawyer's fees. The Florida ACLU stepped in to take the lead in the case.

"All we wanted was to give Angelita the love and care that she needed. Even though she is no longer with us, our legal battle continues because the position of the state of Florida makes no sense and in fact, denies adoptive children access to loving, caring households," said Zúñiga and Carmichael. When asked if they would foster other children, they answered in the affirmative noting that at the present, they are fostering two boys, Eric and Tommy.

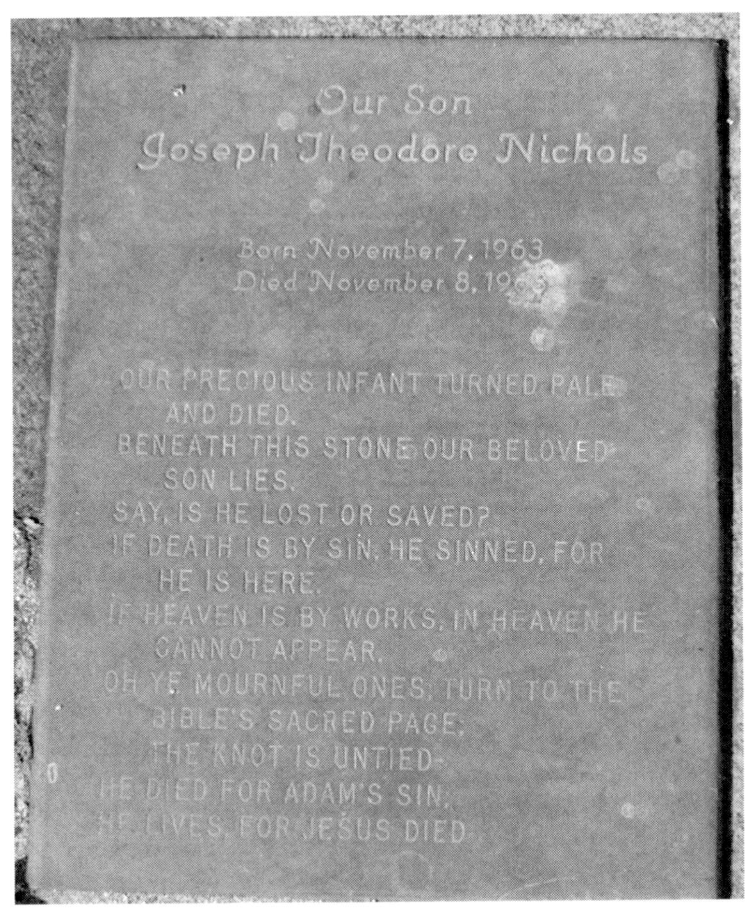

The death of a baby is the most traumatic experience for his/her parents. This epitaph found at the Key West Cemetery expresses that sorrow and pain: "Our Precious Infant turned pale and died. Beneath this stone our beloved son lies. Say, is he lost or saved? If death is by sin, he sinned, for he is here. If Heaven is by works, in Heaven he cannot appear. Oh Ye Mournful Ones, turn to the Bible's Sacred Page; the knot is untied, he died for Adam's sin. He lives for Jesus died."

As a young man, Adam Arnold's dream was to become a pilot.
His resting place is always adorned by an airplane.

Angels also symbolizes resurrection and the rejuvenation of life.

MARÍA DE LOS ÁNGELES ZÚÑIGA CARMICHAEL

> "Someone who wins a Pyrrhic victory has been victorious in some way; however, the heavy toll negates any sense of achievement." Most of the time, a lost battle is the bridge for an uncommon solution. This story starts in the late 1990s

"Steven, you have to get out of bed, don't you have any appointments today?" Manny might have been talking to the walls. Ever since DCF took the other two children from their care, in what some people believed was a punitive action for the bad press caused by the trial for Angelita, Steven had been down. "This bed is a mess!" Manny rambled as he put down a tray with some breakfast, knowing that he wouldn't touch it either.

"Manny, I just can't do it today. The thought of another trial paralyzes my spine."

"We discussed all that last year," Manny was a bit stern about it. "You knew that it was going to be difficult, you knew that Angelita wasn't going to survive the trial, and you certainly knew about the spotlight and the media circus."

"Yes, but I never dreamed that DCF was going to take this kind of action with the other children," said Steven visibly shaken, "I just want to scream, to cry and to crawl under a rock all at the same time." And he added with a mixture of mockery and misery, "what a way to start the new millennium!"

"We had no idea they were going to switch directors midstream." Manny was apologetic even though he had nothing to do with it. "Look, I got some more magazines and some breakfast. You have to get out of the rut."

Manuel Zúñiga consulted several of his psychiatrist colleagues at the hospital. "Dr. Pou, what can we do?" Manuel was desperate; he was at his wit's end.

"Manny, there is nothing I can do unless Steven wants to do something for himself," Dr. Pou replied.

"He is refusing to do the Zoloft. I can't force it down his throat."

II

Not since the days of Anita Bryant in the seventies had the gay and lesbian community been so vehemently thrown into action. It all started with the state of Florida not allowing gay and lesbian couples to adopt unwanted children. The Department of Children and Family Services didn't have the space or the capacity to care for these children. They were difficult to adopt because some of them were mentally ill, some physically ill, including children that had been born to mothers carrying the HIV virus, others born addicted to drugs, crack-cocaine, and FAS babies.

A series of scandals had rocked the DCF department. Overworked caseworkers had misplaced children, some had not been visited, and some had disappeared. The governor stepped into the fight and in one press conference fired the secretary of the department, a man deemed ineffectual by the media and the state government, and announced the new secretary, a woman named Ms. Susanne Ogylby.

"DCF will change radically," announced the governor. "I am proud not only to introduce to you, but to be counted as a close friend of Ms. Susanne Ogylby who will take the reigns of the department and move it in a new direction into the future."

Her first remarks were: "What DCF needs is a good Christian woman as a director, a Christian woman who knows how to raise children. The fact that these kids are wards of the state does not exclude them from a good set of values rooted in the fear of God." Those remarks created controversy right away; the press wasn't impressed by the choice and a series of articles started appearing with titles like "Who is the new DCF secretary Ms. Susanne Ogylby?" These detailed Ms. Ogylby's conservative southern Baptist beliefs and her background as a lawyer.

The most controversial situation brought up by the media, particular individuals and some members of the opposition in Tallahassee, was Ms. Ogylby's participation in a group called the Council for the Reformation of Society and Government in the late 1980s. Ms. Ogylby and Dr. George Reekers coauthored an essay entitled *The World's New Reform of Family and Government.* The Miami Herald published the whole document, and *The Key West Citizen* picked up some of the most notorious quotes from the wire.

"We deny that the Bible allows for any other definition of the family, such as the sharing of a household by homosexual partners, or that society's laws should be modified in any way to broaden the definition of family or marriage beyond the biblically understood definition of heterosexual marriage, blood relations and adoption..."

"We deny that premarital and extramarital sexual relationships, promiscuity, adultery, homosexuality, bestiality, exhibitionism, pornography, adult-child sexual relations, prostitution, sex-act entertainment, masturbation and other sexual deviations should be sanctioned or accepted as normal or legal, even if done alone or by consenting partners . . ."

"We affirm that a man's authority as head of his wife is delegated to him by God, that this means that his legitimate authority over his wife is limited by what God's Word allows him; and that all authority is established by God and no one person and no social institution has the right to exert any authority contrary to God's laws or the bounds God has set for the man's office in the family . . ."

None of this bothered the governor, who declared his support of the contentious secretary.

Ms. Ogylby's press conferences became very popular with the media. After being asked about the foster parent situation in the department, she responded, "I think being a foster parent is one of the toughest jobs anyone can take on. To know one or two slipups can bring the weight of the system down on you is daunting."

Regarding a question about why there are so many foster kids in the state of Florida she replied, "Primarily they are the result of either families not forming through marriage in the first place or because of absent parents due to divorce. These families have disintegrated because they have fallen out of God's grace. These situations are the result of the evils of our liberal, humanistic society."

Another question came her way: "Ms. Ogylby, do you as a conservative, believe in spanking children?" Her answer came fast. "I spanked my children when they were little ones. I believe it is a good way to correct behavior." The reporter continued the line of questions. "Does that mean that you will allow foster parents to spank the wards of the state?" She shot back, "That's an unfair question, you asked my personal view on the matter. And no, spanking is unacceptable as policy of DCF. We will supply counseling to foster families that have behavioral problems on a request per case basis."

134 After examining the evidence of several trials in the state regarding gay men and lesbians trying to adopt children, including that of Manuel Zúñiga and Steven Carmichael, Ms. Ogylby told her secretary that day, "I'm incensed by the fact that these outlaws of religion and society dared to challenge the system. I will show them who they are dealing with."

The secretary called another press conference. As usual, it was packed. Her opening remarks were: "The court has spoken. Gay and lesbian couples are not deemed by the state as suitable parents of the wards of DCF. Not because they are bad people, but because certain behaviors are in contradiction with our civil and Christian laws. We appreciated the work that some of these couples have done with the children. Although the system allows gay men and lesbian couples foster children, I will introduce new procedures that will reclaim all the foster care children that have been placed with these couples and place them in families that are more in accordance with state guidelines."

The Key West Citizen interviewed the couple a few days before the two other children were removed from their care. Mr. Carmichael said the following. "Until now we have fostered three children, one HIV positive girl, Angelita, who died, a pre-adolescent boy Eric and a crack-cocaine, three-year-old boy, Tommy." Visibly upset, Mr. Carmichael continued. "You know, when we got Tommy, he was almost in a vegetative, non-responsive state. After six months, he was responding to our voices and eating solid food. Yes, there is brain damage, but he is responding. What is going to happen to him now? They are going to take Eric out of his school. He will have to start all over again someplace else; these will disrupt the only stable learning environment that he has ever know. I don't understand what the new secretary of DCF is thinking."

Dr. Manuel Zúñiga, Mr. Carmichael's partner of fourteen years added, "The amount of anger that I am feeling at this moment has no measure. We will fight this new decision in court. We have received word from the ACLU that they will help us again with lawyers and fees."

III

The case had acquired such notoriety that police had to move all the newscasters and satellite vans from Eliza St. one block away to Virginia St. Some of them were parked by Bayview Park. Only Fantasy Fest gathered that much national attention. A number of onlookers and neighbors were watching too. It was announced in local news and radio that morning.

Inside the little house, Steven and Manny prepared Eric. Tommy was already in his hand carriage. "Don't let them see you cry, Eric. I won't cry in front of the cameras." Steven ran his hand across Eric's hair. "Remember this is only temporary. We are going to court to get you back," Manny said, holding Eric to his chest. "Auntie Sarah is going to fight for the four of us." Manny kissed him on his forehead. "I am not crying either. We will show them that we are a strong family."

A caravan of cars approached the house from the direction of Horace O'Bryant Middle School. Two deputy sheriff's cruisers and a black Crown Victoria with tinted windows appeared. News crews descended on them the moment they stopped. The deputies started managing the crowd so the two caseworkers could make it up the three steps in front of the purple door. At each side of the door was a flag. Old Glory was at the right, the Rainbow flag at the left.

The Secretary of DCF descended from the Crown Victoria on the other side of the street. She was dressed in a blue power suit, her black hair done impeccably. Walking with resolution, she caught up quickly with the two caseworkers. Andrew Bryans, newsperson from channel six in Miami, fired a couple of questions at her. "Is this normal procedure for the secretary to come all the way to Key West instead of sending the regional director? Is this a punitive action because this gay couple have battled DCF in court?"

"NO COMMENT!" she fired back. When the news crews picked up on the exchange, they swarmed her and the two caseworkers, shouting questions. The deputies worked hard to get to the little porch of the house.

Inside Steven, Manny and Sarah heard the commotion but didn't really grasp the situation. Sarah waited by the door and opened it when the deputy knocked. They filed in. The Secretary was between the caseworkers when Steven saw her. Her affront was complete; he lost control.

"That condescending, intolerant bitch is not allowed in my house!" he screamed as he charged toward her. One of the deputy officers cut off his path. "I wouldn't try that my friend." Manny came right after Steven and held his shoulders. Sarah placed herself between the two groups. She squared herself in front of the Secretary and thundered at her, "As counsel for Mr. Carmichael and Mr. Zúñiga, I advise you, NO, I ORDER YOU, to leave this house immediately. Your presence is not welcomed here." Ms. Ogylby smiled. The deputy said, "Madame, they are right, I will step outside on the porch with you."

They exited and hid behind the abundant foliage on the right side of the porch. The news people started asking questions again; the Secretary ignored them. On the front lawn, Ray Rivera from the Gay and Lesbian Community Center and Connie Renault from the National Organization for Women had assembled some of their members carrying Rainbow flags and other placards. They had formed a gauntlet and the media, smelling the blood and a photo op, gave them space. As they stepped toward the Crown Victoria the chanting started.

"End the bigotry, end the hate."

"Hate is not a family value."

"All families in all colors."

Inside the car, Eric was stunned. Tommy, safe and covered in blankets, was unaware of the scene. In the house, Steven collapsed on the floor. His pain screamed so loud that the sound traveled atop the crowd. The chanting stopped; some people including some in the news crews bowed their heads. The Secretary, getting herself in the car after securing the children, heard it, stopped for a second, smiled and entered the car.

As the Crown Victoria started to move, the crowd pelted it with eggs and rotten fruit. The deputies did nothing and returned to their cars. Manny had caught Steven and was sitting on the floor, rocking him gently and letting his anger loose. "*¡Vamos a pelear carajo y esta vez vamos a ganar, coño!*" "We are going to fight and this time we are going to win." Sarah was hugging them both, weeping.

A few minutes later, Sarah Smith addressed the group of people still milling around the front yard.

"Mr. Carmichael and Mr. Zúñiga express their deepest gratitude for the show of support that their neighbors and community have expressed today. They also wish that the media and others will respect their privacy at this time. There will be no questions answered; they wish to be left alone. Thank you very much."

IV

The trial commenced in February 2000. It was a trial by arbitration, in which the sides argued in front of judge Jay Johnson. Steven Carmichael and Manuel Zúñiga were represented by Ms. Sarah Smith and Mr. Cassidy Harold, against the Department of Children and Family

Services of the State of Florida represented by its secretary Ms. Susanne Ogylby, assisted by Mr. Rudolf Sharkely.

The first thing the judge decided was the issue of visitation rights. After Ms. Smith stated the position of Mr. Carmichael and Mr. Zúñiga, Mr. Sharkely stated the position of DCF using the ruling of the first trial. The judge ruled that the plaintiffs were awarded temporarily two one-hour visits to the two children each week. The visits were strictly supervised under constant surveillance in a sequestered setting to prevent flight or harm.

"That's a punitive action, your honor." Smith addressed the judge with caution. "I object."

"So be it," responded Judge Johnson, ignoring her objection.

Ogylby and Sharkely framed the "next issue to be decided" as "whether it is in the best interest of these children to be raised in a home that wasn't under the care of a mother and a father."

Mr. Harold, Smith's assistant attorney, offered an alternative view in his opening remarks, "Until recently, gay men, lesbians and other non-traditional couples were able to, according to their financial status and ability, foster children in the state of Florida. In fact, the state encouraged this situation because it does not have the resources to care for and maintain children with special circumstances such as mental, physical or catastrophic illnesses. The only reason that we are here today is the new secretary of DCF, Ms. Susanne Ogylby, is letting her personal biases dictate policy in the department."

Arguments went back and forth about Zúñiga and Carmichael's ability to raise two children with special needs. The real names were not used because they were minors.

Mr. Sharkely brought up the law of Florida that bans gays and lesbians from adopting. "Florida is the only state with a law prohibiting all gay people, couples and individuals, from adopting. It doesn't bar gays from being foster parents. Two other states, Mississippi and Utah, bar same-sex couples from adopting." And added the law from Michigan as supporting evidence. 'If a person desires to adopt a child...that person, together with his wife or her husband, if married, should file a petition.' He then added: "many judges construe the law to mean that two people must be married to adopt jointly. Gay couples, of course, can't legally marry in the United States."

Mr. Harold refuted, "the Michigan law can be read that way if a married couple is petitioning to adopt. But it doesn't say anything about a single person adopting a foster child. In fact, some judges in Michigan have awarded adoption petitions on this concept to individuals to happen to be gay men and lesbians living with their respective partners according to our ACLU colleagues in that state and the Lambda Legal Defense Fund."

"It doesn't cut both ways counselor," retorted Sharkely. "The legislature of that state is taking matters into its own hands and will strengthen that law in the next few months."

Mr. Harold brought up another example. "Florida's governor and the legislature have received close to 63,000 letters and e-mails in the last few days from people opposed to the state's ban on adoptions by gays and lesbians."

Mr. Sharkely responded, "and probably the same amount of emails supporting the ban."

"Actually 25,000," replied Mr. Harold.

Mr. Sharkely quoted some of the supporting emails, "I feel very strongly that allowing homosexuals to adopt is a bad idea, primarily because of evidence which conclusively shows that the homosexual lifestyle is a very destructive one."

Ms. Smith argued that the law unconstitutionally singles out gay men and lesbians and limits opportunities for foster children awaiting adoption in the state of Florida. Introduced by Mr. Sharkely, was a friend-of-the-court brief filed with a federal appeals court by some of the legislators that support the ban on adoptions. He summarized it out loud: "The 25-year-old law is not unconstitutional, because self-styled child welfare experts think that such adoptions not a good idea."

Mr. Harold responded with a brief filed by several children's advocacy groups supporting the ACLU's position. Led by the Child Welfare League of America, they argued that the ban on gay adoption has no basis in child welfare and "frustrates the best interests of children because it denies children awaiting adoption the benefits of permanent, loving families."

Mr. Sharkely, as rebuttal, quoted another expert on societal issues, "social science is too flawed and unreliable to support any policy conclusions regarding homosexual adoption. We understand that there is a relation between homosexual behavior and depression, substance abuse, and even suicide, and the league's studies fall short of demonstrating that the adoption law is not rationally related to the best interest of children."

"That is the most unashamed double standard that I have ever seen. The state terrorizes, diminishes and discriminates against gay and lesbian couples that would like to adopt, and then comes out and says they are unstable, thus not deemed suitable to adopt unwanted children. Such arguments," continued Mr. Harold, "seem to fly in the face of most experts' findings on the issue of gay parenting and adoption. In fact, the

American Psychological Association states, 'not a single study has found children of gay or lesbian parents to be disadvantaged in any significant respect relative to children of heterosexual parents.' The state is saying to these people you can be foster parents, and help us but you can't adopt."

"Nothing wrong with that from where I am standing," said Mr. Sharkely

Mr. Harold replied, "Just this month, The American Academy of Pediatrics has endorsed adoptions by gays, saying same-sex couples can provide the loving, stable, and emotionally healthy family life that children need. They published their case in the journal *Pediatrics*, I would like to introduce a copy as evidence so your honor can read it."

"I will take a look at it," said the judge.

"Your honor, I object, the AAP is pro gay group," said Sharkely.

"That's your opinion Mr. Sharkely," the judge admonished. "Let's stick to the facts, please."

Steven and Manny couldn't read anything in his reactions. "Manny, can you figure the reactions of this guy? I can't read him." Steven had been more himself since the trial began. The combination of sadness and anger seemed to have shaken him out of his gloominess.

After a particular tirade issued by Ogylby, Steven muttered between his teeth, "I can't believe that woman just said that!" He gripped Manuel's hand so tight that he said out loud, "Ouch, Steven," audible enough for Judge Johnson to glance their way with a 'hush' look.

In the small courtroom the public was getting restless. Deputies had limited the attendance to a hundred people. The rest of the crowd was outside, polarized by leaders of both sides of the fence. The police presence was strong. The chief of police said on a radio morning show: "as long as the two groups were calm he didn't have a problem with them."

Another heated exchange created audible reactions from the public and the judge. "Your honor," stated Ms. Ogylby, "adolescent E has expressed to counselors that he is gay. How can a child assert this learned and abhorrent behavior is his chosen sexual orientation at such a young age? This demonstrates the negative influence the plaintiffs are having on their children and the reason for DCF to oppose such people fostering the wards of the state." There were both jeers and applause from members of the public.

"I object!" Smith almost jumped out of her seat and skin, red with anger. "Ms. Ogylby is not an expert in sexual behavior to use such vocabulary, she is not a psychiatrist either." She added, "I knew when I was five!"

The public reacted, activists on both sides of the issue jeered and booed; it was too much for Judge Johnson. He banged his gavel on the podium. "The public will refrain from expressing reactions one way or the other or I will clear the court!" He was furious as he addressed the lawyers. "Into my chambers, NOW! Ten minutes recess." He banged the gavel again and stormed out into his office.

"Ms. Ogylby, Ms. Smith is right. If you try to impersonate other professionals in my court again, I will cite you for contempt." Smith was happy she scored one. The judge looked at her. "Don't start hatching your chickens yet, Ms. Smith. You are not an expert either in the 'nature vs. learned behavior' question to my knowledge, are you?"

"No, your honor, I'm not," admitted Smith.

"Try that again in my court and I will fine you, and I will write a complaint to the ethics committee," the judge admonished both of them. "Now I will strike that exchange from the record. Let's go back and be professional, not emotional."

The closing arguments came. Both attorneys stated their sides and views passionately. Susanne Ogylby delivered her argument using the mannerisms and exclamations of her father, one of the most prominent Baptist ministers in North Carolina, now deceased. Sarah Smith opted for the style of her favorite feminist, Gloria Steinem with a dash of Susan Sontag for good measure. They were both satisfied.

"Now it is in the hands of the Lord," Ogylby said to Sharkely.

"The judge will decide!" Smith said as she turned to talk to Manuel and Steven, who were seated in the first row behind her desk.

"You put up a good fight," Manuel said. "I'm not sure which way he is going to lean," said Steven shaking her hand. "You have helped us so much," Steven continued, "we consider you part of the family now."

The judge stepped into his chambers. When he came back, an hour later, he delivered his decision. He echoed the decision made by the original judge in Angelita's adoption trial.

"It is the job of this court to express opinion and to arbitrate between two parties involved in an argument. It is not the job of this court to create new legislation. I feel sympathetic to the plight of Mr. Carmichael and Mr. Zúñiga. And I do personally believe, contrary to the opinion of the secretary of DCF, that gay, lesbian and other couples outside of the definition promulgated by such department of the state can and do raise children successfully. But this is not the forum or the place to arbitrate from my personal beliefs. It is the judgment of this court, at this point, to uphold the decision of the Department of Children and Family Services because this court can't legislate. The change of this particular policy has to come from the state through its legislative branch, with the help of its executive branch. This court also urges the State of Florida and its Department of Children and Family Services to study such policy and under the advisement of experts in the field, and dialogue with other states' agencies that perform similar services, make the changes that they deemed necessary to update and make such policy more equitable. This court proceeding is now adjourned."

V

Manny and Steven started couple's counseling. Dr. Miriam Anderson helped them get through the rough parts where the pain was still raw. It took Steven a good two months to let it ease a little. There were a few more appeals and court dates and they didn't miss any of them. Most of the rulings upheld the state's law.

Two families, as defined by DCFS, were found to take care of the children to keep them in Key West. The last item to be evaluated by Judge Johnson was to increase the visitations to three a week. Sarah Smith petitioned to the court, "Both foster families are in good terms with Mr. Carmichael and Dr. Zúñiga; in fact, I have a letter from them asking your honor to increased the visits especially with baby T. Everybody agrees, including the caseworkers, that the presence of Mr. Carmichael and Mr. Zúñiga is beneficial for the young boy."

"DCF concurs?" asked the Judge.

"Yes, your honor, but the visits will have to be strictly supervised," stated Ms. Ogylby who didn't miss any of the court dates either.

Sarah looked at Steven who nodded. "We agree, your honor."

"This court also rules that minor E should remain in Key West, so he will continue his education and to facilitate access to him by Mr. Carmichael and Mr. Zúñiga," the judge stated.

The counseling sessions were going well. Dr. Anderson asked Steven in the next session; "Ok, Steven, how many clients do you have to see this week?

"Two," he answered.

"Good, that's very good," she said. Manuel was very happy too. Steven started working again. The pain and misery was more manageable and the visits with the kids helped. Tommy's neurological situation was stable. Steven's fears for his mental state subsided. The fact that the case gained national attention helped, too; Manuel and Steven were keeping track of everything that was going on.

VI

Sheri and Sarah invited the guys for dinner at Martin's. That night the small restaurant on Fleming St. was not too crowded and conversation was easy. The wine flowed and the conversation started with Sheri talking about her bar and its business; then it turned to Dr. Anderson and their sessions.

"We are doing great!" said Manny, kissing Steven on his forehead. "Dr. Anderson has helped a lot," he added.

"We are discussing ending the sessions in the near future," Steven said with resolve. "She calls it 'ending the ménage a trois' or putting and end to her 'cruise money fund," he added with a smile. "I still have some bouts of sadness and depression, but she said that it's ok. She made me promise her that I wouldn't let them get out of hand. And Manny has promised her to talk about his anger more to me, instead of bottling it up."

"I'm so happy with this turn of events," said Sarah. "Anything new with Tommy?

"It's going very well," Steven replied. "The foster parents and the caseworker have written a letter to Ms. O, detailing our regular visits and how Tommy reacts positively to them. They want the visitations increased." He seemed very proud. "We haven't heard from her yet. She probably will try to oppose it, but I have my mantra ready 'all in the best interest of the child'."

"I can't stand that woman. I don't understand, with all the stuff the press had dug up about her performance, why the governor hasn't stepped in? It doesn't make any sense." Sheri tried to reason the situation.

"It's all politics," said Sarah, her voice couldn't hide her anger and disapointment. "The pendulum has swung to the right. I never imagined that it was going to swing that far right."

"Well," Sheri said after lifting the empty bottle to the attention of the waiter who happily nodded; "Sarah and I have been discussing for a couple of weeks now how to thwart the system and still have children. That will give that bitch a run for her money!"

"Ok, honey," Sarah interrupted, "right thing to do, wrong reason to do it. This isn't about Susanne Ogylby; this is about the kids that need us."

"How about that guy that went to the Dominican Republic?" Steven asked. "He adopted the kid over there and DCF can't do anything about it. Everybody thought the kid wasn't going to make it. But he has improved so much."

"Too costly," said Manuel. "Remember we're not rich and besides, there are plenty of kids here that need us."

"Right now, the only legal way that we have around DCF is to have one or both biological parents involved." Sarah said. "Which brings us to our proposition. I don't want to have kids; I think its frightening, with the social and political atmosphere that we're living in right now. My biggest reason is the social situation of our country. I certainly would die of a heart attack; it's too much pressure. But Ms. Thing over here wants her ova to have a ten-cent dance with some of your sailors. Its her body." Sarah was emotional and a bit philosophical about it.

Manuel was puzzled but interested. "Is this wonder Gaia coming to save the day? Are you trying to rescue us?" He was smiling and touched.

"For you guys, I would do it in a heartbeat," said Sheri with resolution. "We can work out the terms of parenthood, because I don't want to be involved. Diapers and bottles of formula aren't really what I crave." She squeezed Sarah's thigh and winked. "If you guys promise in writing that you'll take the little rugrat and raise him without me, you got a deal!" She added for emphasis, "We got the lawyer right here, and one more thing, I will be the little rascal's doting auntie, I'll teach him to drink, to swear and maybe to screw. Deal?"

Steven's eyes welled, and Manny said, "You've a deal as long as you have a turkey baster, because my religion prohibits the combination of certain parts."

"Don't say another word, dear. Although I have been known for being bi-coastal, this airplane is parked in one and only one hangar at the moment." The second bottle of wine came in with the food; the waiter, hearing only part of the last sentence of the conversation, said, "Should we call a rabbi, a confessor, a firefighter or a policeman? Or maybe I don't want to know."

"You can call them all. All of them will be needed at one point or another," Sheri said as she clicked her glass with Manny.

Sarah up drew the contract with the help of her colleagues at the ACLU. It stipulated that after the birth, Sheri Gilbert would renounce all her parental rights in favor of Dr. Manuel Zúñiga and Mr. Steven Carmichael in exchange for unlimited access to the child.

The pregnancy was almost immediate and went on without major complications. Lori hired a temporary bartender and Sarah oversaw Sheri's interests in the bar. Sarah, Sheri, Manny and Steven all attended Lamaze classes together. Manny requested to be the attendant physician at birth and it was granted. When he saw her for the first time, she was all eyes and hair that showed some red highlights. The room was aglow with radiant light and he felt his own blood running through the veins of this precious female child as his hand cut the umbilical cord. Dr. Zúñiga just stood there with the baby in his hands. He came out of it when Sheri raised her voice almost to a scream.

"Let me see that baby," she commanded and Manuel placed her in her mother's arms. After a while, the attending nurse intervened, "I need to bathe and prepare the baby." Reluctantly, they turned her over.

At the ward, Dr. Manuel Zúñiga picked up the baby, by then wrapped in a pink blanket and brought her closer to the glass so Steven and Sarah could see her. Manuel mouthed at the other side of the glass, "María de los Angeles Zúñiga-Carmichael Fourth Generation Conch, born in Key West.

The Key West Citizen published the following announcement:

ZÚÑIGA AND CARMICHAEL WELCOME HOME MARÍA DE LOS ÁNGELES.

It is with great pleasure and joy that Dr. Manuel Zúñiga and Steven Carmichael welcome their newly born daughter María de los Ángeles Zúñiga Carmichael. She weighs eight and a half pounds and is healthy. María de los Ángeles is a fourth generation conch.

On the Zúñiga side she is the granddaughter of of the late Magdalena Zúñiga, songstress of Key West fame and niece of Elías, also deceased, and great-granddaughter of Judge Juan Francisco Javier Zúñiga y Valdevieso who moved to Key West from Cuba after the death of his father, Juan Francisco in 1898.

On the Carmichael side she is the granddaughter of Andrew Carmichael who emigrated from North Berwick in Scotland, and who met Liliana Vazquez, a Puerto Rican from the Bronx. She is the great-granddaughter of Howard and Agnes Balmedie from Scotland, United Kingdom; and Pedro and María Vázquez from Vega Alta, Puerto Rico. A small celebration will be held in her honor at a later date.

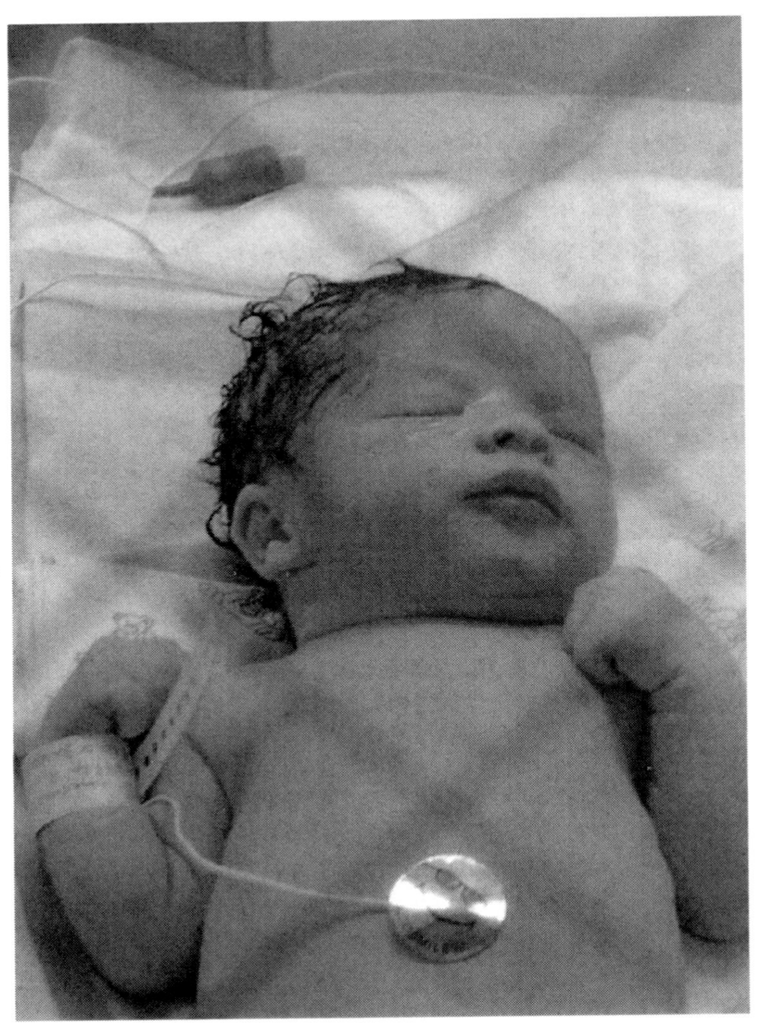

Angie a few minutes after been born.
Zúñiga Family collection.

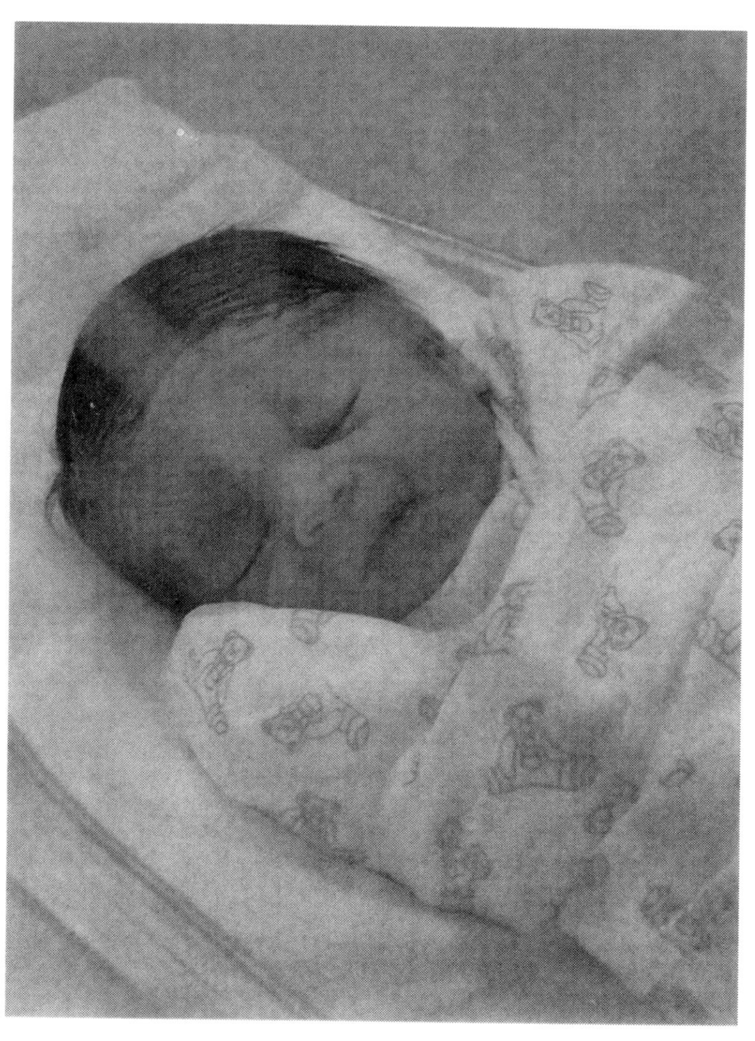

Angie's Birth Announcement Picture.
Zúñiga Family collection.

9

The *Miami Pimk Pulp* Magazine is one of South Florida's leading GLBT publications.

MARÍA DE LOS ÁNGELES COMES FOR A VISIT.

"Every morning I get up, every day I wake up, every day no matter if I'm home or in a motel or hotel or on the road, I get up and hope that every bigot and every unfair person will say, 'Damn, [s]he's up again.' " *Al Sharpton*. The action takes place around the late 2020s.

"To meet your parents?" Those two 'r's' rolled down for a few seconds. The passenger's door wasn't even closed; Emilia couldn't wait to ask questions. "And when did you tell me you wrote fiction?"

"What's up with the non sequitur questions?" I ignored Emilia's imitation of my r's. As we started toward the turnpike, I tried to give Emilia a glimpse of my family. A few hours later we were getting close to the house and I rehashed the most important facts.

"Just so you don't get confused," I told her just as the car was turning the corner from Virginia St. "I call my father Steven, Daddy, and Manny, my other father, Dad. It's funny; I don't know how it started. Daddy is at the house now because one of his clients cancelled an appointment. We couldn't have better timing."

Although I had called him in advance and alerted him of our visit, Daddy seemed startled.

"Hello, Angie, such a nice surprise." He kissed me and hugged me.

"Stop with the mushy stuff," I protested.

"I will smother you one of these days and will enjoy every little minute of it," Daddy responded, as he turned his attention to Emilia.

"Angie? That's funny. Wait till we get back to the office." Emilia was amused I had a nickname. María or María de los Ángeles was the way I was known in the office.

"You better not try that, or I'll personally kick your butt," I advised her.

"Hello, I'm Steven Carmichael, you must be Emilia."

"Emilia Hall. It's a pleasure meeting you."

"You guys aren't in trouble, are you?" Daddy asked, "Not that I'm complaining but you weren't supposed to be here until next weekend."

"Yes, Daddy, I'm running away from the law and decided to come here because no one knows my parents live in Key West. Emilia here robbed a bank and I decided to give her a ride to escape too." I nudged Emilia who grinned and nodded vigorously. "No, the cases on the docket were shuffled around due to a family emergency of one of the judges."

Daddy was amused. "You and your stories. You guys must be starving. It's almost noon. I'm having a salad and some soda. Come in and get some."

We entered the house through the side door that took us directly into the kitchen. This part of the house was still just as I always remembered. The walls were painted lime green, Daddy's favorite color. The trim was all done in white and a bay window dominated the whole space. Dad had placed shelves in the metal structure of the window and our plates and knickknacks were all displayed there. The surrounding space was used as a counter. Looking at it from the door, the left side had all the cabinetry, the stove, the dishwasher and the sink. A wall unit and the fridge dominated the other side. In the middle, sat the table with two side leaves. When closed, it is a rectangle; it opens as a round table that can seat up to eight people comfortably. When we came in, it was full of Daddy's real estate paperwork—contracts, regulations, MLS books—sourrounding a salad bowl.

II

A few years ago, I started working with the ACLU in Miami. After a long deposition for a child abuse case, Emilia Hall had invited the whole team of lawyers to her apartment for some relaxation, shoptalk, strategy and wine. This was the first time I was invited to her space outside her office. Emilia is tall and redheaded with a mischievous smile. She is a kid in a rather big body. Always, she is well dressed without overdoing it. She prefers pencil type skirts with a matching jacket. She wears a small set of baby dot earrings paired with a single strand necklace or a small chain. She never wears rings or bracelets that would distract from her hand movements.

Her apartment was decorated in classic nineteen fifties style; wood furniture from the period and a digital-rotary phone complete the retro look. Emilia came from what before the twenty-first century was called old money, although she isn't pretentious about it. She didn't feel guilty about it, made no excuses, but she wasn't in the habit of flaunting it. She joined the ACLU because she really believed in it. We're good friends because we understand each other. If I step out of bounds she offers, sometimes a gentle other times a not so subtle, reminder of place. I wouldn't hesitate to do the same thing.

Now we are in the middle of an appealing case. Still in 2027, Florida is the only state in the union not allowing people of the same gender to marry.

"So you're working on the legalization of gay marriage in Florida?" Daddy re-started the conversation.

"Not directly, but it might have some consequences in that area," said Emilia.

"The case is about a female to male, transgendered person who had gone through gender re-assignment surgery in Massachusetts, had legally married a woman and settled in Florida. He now wants to divorce her." I started rattling off the details.

"Because they were married in another state, no one knew that John Doe was originally a woman. As the divorce proceedings were taking their course, the gender conflict surfaced. The judge was blindsided and couldn't figure out what to do."

Emilia stepped in. "Now, the legal person known as John Doe could not divorce his wife because he wasn't a man in the first place, and thus wasn't legally married. The case was dismissed. The judge stated that he wasn't going to be forced to set precedence on this issue."

III

Daddy had cleared some of his stuff off the table and quickly an array of snacks and beverages replaced them. Emilia went back to the conversation we were having in the car.

"Mr. Carmichael, did you…"

"Steven, please," Daddy interrupted her.

"Did you know that Angie is writing?"

"Oh please, do you have to start that crap again?" I was annoyed. "I started writing in high school. I never thought anything about it; it was a natural progression," I said, zeroing in on my salad.

Daddy figured out what was going on. "Let me tell you a story," he started.

"Oh, not the kindergarten story again, please!" I said, embarrassed. He ignored me. It was like I wasn't in the room anymore.

"But Angie, I do want to hear the story," Emilia protested.

"I was worried about Angie when she was a baby," he told Emilia. "I thought there was something wrong with her, but I didn't tell Manny anything." His face showed how concerned he was at the time. "Angie didn't talk much at the beginning, and she wouldn't walk until well past her first birthday. Manny wasn't concerned at all. He has always been in awe of the miracle of her birth, so I didn't share my concerns with him."

"Of course, I wasn't aware of this, and I thought of my childhood as normal." I tried to interject, but it was a useless attempt to get a word in. Daddy was filling our soda glasses and putting more salad in our bowls as he kept talking.

"Her first day of kindergarten was painful for me. I understand that it is distressful for every parent, but for me it was a nightmare," Daddy continued. "I was so afraid of how the other kids were going to react to her, given my suspicions." He looked at me. "You cried a little and after finding the toys on the corner of Ms. Nevarez' room and your friend Jorge, you adjusted." Daddy smiled; he always smiled when he told this story.

"I don't remember much of that day other than meeting Jorge." I thought Emilia needed the explanation. "What attracted you to Jorge? Do you remember?" Emilia pressed on.

"I don't know. He was kind to me. He became my friend for many years. We went to school together and kept in touch with each other in college where he studied for his accounting degree and I went to law school at the insistence and inspiration of my aunt Sarah. He died of complications due to AIDS a few years ago. Yes, Daddy, I do remember the exact day but I'd rather not go there. So stop looking at me that way," I said sternly as I remembered his face and looked at my plate.

Daddy continued, "I watched as Angie labored over her assignments and my suspicions didn't go away. The first day I saw her with her pencil in hand, every time she tried to erase something, she made this big hole in the paper. I wanted to cry. I couldn't figure out why she was having so much trouble doing her schoolwork. I was afraid there was something really wrong with her cognitive abilities. I kept my fears to myself. But Angie is stubborn and determined and got through it all. And when her first grades came in, they were all A's and I cried; I cried from joy and relief."

"Daddy, how many times have you told this story?" I asked a bit bothered.

"Arghh! I know, it doesn't mean anything to you, but it does to me!" he said. "Then Manny bought her that calligraphy book. God, did you toil over that one? It did help with your penmanship but you still went through the paper when you erased." He laughed out loud.

"I was an average kid in high school," I said. "Jorge was the better student and the better poet; he won a prize in middle school and got published in the school district newsletter. I was very jealous. There was one thing I was better at though, telling stories. He couldn't catch me. I got myself out of any situation, using my gift. Actually, I think that everybody knew I was lying, but the stories got so long and elaborate that my teachers, rather than listen to them, let me go about my business. I read voraciously. And Daddy indulged me with a different book every week. It started when I was thirteen years old."

"Here, you read this," Daddy would say, "handing me a copy of *The Diary of Anne Frank* or *Ivanhoe* for example. When I was sixteen I discovered that Daddy had written some poems to Dad. I found them in his closet drawer," I said, still working on my salad. "María de los Angeles," Daddy said, he uses my full name when he is trying to scold me. "Give me those papers back and don't go through other people's things without permission."

"Too late, I've read them already," was my answer. "These are not bad," I said handing him back the papers. "That spiked my interest in writing. A few months later, when the English teacher asked for a description as an assignment, I wrote a description of our kitchen. She read it out loud in class. I was so proud; I decided that was what I wanted to do for the rest of my life. The high school newspaper got a poem or a story penned by yours truly in every edition. You just have to take my word for it, because I didn't save any of it."

"Well that's too bad," Emilia intervened. "Are you sure there isn't some of it running around?" She looked at Daddy and winked. "I'm pretty sure my parents wouldn't let any of that go if they knew about it. My mother even saved my kindergarten drawings."

"Honey, karma is such a nasty thing. I have saved most of it," Daddy said, beaming with pride. "You got mine; I got yours. I am planning to embarrass her further, if she ever becomes famous."

"I'm pretty sure there will be plenty of opportunities to embarrass her, and what happened to your writing dream?" Emilia asked.

"Law school," I answered.

"Angie went to law school," Daddy said. "Manny was surprised by the choice, but it runs in the family."

"I wanted to go to Stetson University. At the time, I didn't know much of the family history, but Dad told me that my great-grandfather was a lawyer who studied at Stetson. I knew it was destiny. I knew it was a connection I wanted to make. And stop with the looks!" I warned Daddy again. "I don't consider myself superstitious; it was something I needed to do; I don't know why."

Daddy cleared the table and refilled the soda glasses. He took over that part of the story because I wasn't sure of what really had happened. "Manny went to the northeast, to Amherst. He started law school but switched to medical school the year after," Daddy said as he sat down. "He's never said it out loud, but I believe he wanted to escape the so-called family curse. You know, booze and drugs." He turned serious. "I never met your grandmother. She died when Manny was very young. But apparently she was a force to contend with; he still bottles up most of these things."

I tried to change the subject. "Well, I applied myself to my studies; I wanted to be a lawyer, so the writing went by the wayside. I wrote a paragraph here and there, nothing of note. I didn't keep any of it. I tried to fit into a couple of writing groups and send some stuff to magazines. But I couldn't fit; my writing style and my stories ruffled some feathers. The rejection letters bothered me." I was trying to dismiss the whole thing.

"Tell Daddy where you went to school," I asked Emilia to shift the theme of the conversation.

"Stanford, my family usually went east, and I wanted to break that tradition," Emilia replied.

"And I bet you that is why you chose the ACLU?" Daddy asked.

"Right." She smiled.

"So what is it that you guys are trying to accomplish with this case?" asked Daddy. Without waiting for a response, he continued, "I still have all the paperwork from our trials and appeals. There were a couple more appeals that we could have filed, but Manny and I got more or less what we wanted. We lost all the battles but we ended up winning half the war. We foster other kids for short term. We proved to the office of Children and Family Services and the State that gay parents are good parents," Daddy stated, "Tommy's foster parents adopted him and welcomed Manny and me as part of the family. Tommy turned out to be autistic and had some brain damage, but he responded to stimuli. We worked very hard and we all believe that he led a happy life until his death from pneumonia. We had a celebration of his life at his home and another right here. It was truly a celebration. I have to say that both Manny and I are very grateful for his gift to us and we don't regret any single minute of it." He looked at the living room and smiled.

"Where is Eric?" I asked. I had told Emilia about my brothers Tommy and Eric. She also got an earful about the rest of my chosen family during the three-hour car drive from Miami to Key West.

"Eric is now the director of AIDS Help here," Daddy explained to Emilia. Like Tommy's, his foster parents adopted him and let us be involved, too. He had some problems in high school. It's not easy to be in that school and be gay but we all pitched in and helped. He struggled and graduated, then started at the community college here and completed his degree in counseling at the University of Miami," Daddy said.

"See, Emilia, I told you, I am blessed with the greatest family in the world."

I kissed Daddy and he hugged me and said, "We are blessed by you. Honey, I hear your Dad's car outside the house. Go and get him."

The side door opened and Dad entered. The family *always* entered through the side door—only Jehovah's Witness and strangers ever came knocking on the front door. His hair was salt and pepper now; he had a bushier mustache, and long crows feet framed his eyes, all those years of putting the light lamp in kids' eyes, squinting to see the other side.

Daddy looked at his watch. "It's that time already, and I haven't even started dinner. We've just been chatting away here in the dining room."

"Hello," Dad kissed Daddy on the forehead. "How was your day?" He hugged me and added, "Steven texted me and I couldn't get here faster. How are you?" He extended his hand and introduced himself to Emilia across the table. "Hello I am Manuel Zúñiga. Very nice to meet you. It's good to put a face to Angie's stories."

"Emilia Hall, it's my pleasure."

"Dad, did you call Eric and the others?" I asked, hoping for a family dinner.

"Eric has his board meeting today. He will join us as soon as he can, and don't you forget that he has other obligations too. Sarah is at the courthouse in Marathon and Sheri is covering for someone at the bar." He was talking on his way to change his clothes.

"I was hoping," I said.

"You will see everybody," Daddy replied. "Now let's get some dinner together. All of them will come and go at some point." And he added, "Emilia, I have tried unsuccessfully to teach this child to cook. It's one of the items on my bucket list that I will leave this world without fulfilling. This cross is too heavy to tolerate," he said, rubbing his eyes faking tears to Emilia's amusement.

"Daddy, don't be so harsh," I protested. "You have a different philosophy of cooking than I do. Emilia, in his mind cooking meals means more than nourishment; it means cooking with others and strengthening relationships. In my world cooking is about fixing something quick, feeding the masses or the lonely, and moving on as soon as possible and without having to do dishes. I venerate my dishwashing machine the same way that Daddy idolizes his Cuisinart. If you want to witness this, take him either to the kitchen accessory section in Sears or the Home Depot. He has been banned from both places for looking lewdly at appliances." Everybody laughed.

"Since the middle of last century the art of cooking," Daddy said, "eating together and table conversation has died slowly. When I was growing up I learned to cook from my mother who had to work outside the house and still feed my brothers and me. Now not many people cook, and they try to learn from the television or the computer. They never touch the food or smell the flavors. Now come and help me." He was already prepping the kitchen.

"Emilia, get ready, he's determined," I said giving in to a long lesson that would be finished when everybody was seated at the table. "Daddy's mother was a Puerto Rican married to a man from Boston and when his parents divorced, Daddy helped his mother with the cooking." Emilia was checking the cooking from her chair when Daddy noticed her.

"Child, come over here. How are you going to learn anything from over there?" He opened a bottle of white wine. "You know, guys," he said as he gave us each a glass, "the secret of a great meal is having the cook well oiled and I don't mean with grease."

When Emilia laughed, he said, "Gringos don't know how to cook;
 Manny is not any better. They think Caribbean cooking is *chile verde*; that's Mexican for Pete's sake! Emilia, this is a *pilón*, a wooden mortar, it was my mother's. It's been seasoned by the years of using it; smell it."

Emilia came forward apprehensively and brought her nose close to the odd looking thing. It was fragrant with the smell of garlic and *culantro* leaves, onions and *achiote* seeds. Her face lit up. "This smells wonderful," she stated, surprised.

"OK, you are going to make the *sofrito*," Daddy said.

"Oh, oh," I said, "you better make it right, otherwise he will cut off your right hand and feed it to the pigs!"

"You have pigs here? I've heard about the chickens and the scorpions!" Emilia said demonstrating her city roots.

"No, silly, it's another of Daddy's expressions," I said.

"Now pay attention to what you are doing. This is as close as I get to consecration," Daddy said, to Emilia's delight, since she was of good

Pentecostal stock. "You put in the garlic and the onions, this is the foundation of a good *sofrito*. Onions first. You can make as much to put aside or as little as you need for the meal. Fresh is better, though my mother froze it for weeks and used it as she needed. Always use long leafed *culantro* next. The Italian cilantro is like a drag queen substitution and then you finish it with regular green peppers and cumin. That is the base of any good Puerto Rican dish."

Emilia got into it. Maybe it was the wonderful smells or the first glass of wine but she was pounding away *la maceta,* the pestle, into the *pilón*. She is a hands-on person. "I like this," she said, as Daddy was pouring her another glass of wine.

"Be careful of that stuff," I said. "It's going to be a long time before dinner, so pace yourself."

"Leave the girl alone," Daddy said. "It's probably the first time she has ground anything. She is releasing some pent-up energy."

"Angie," Daddy said, "get the *caldero* ready." The best way to describe a *caldero* is a Dutch oven. They are made either of aluminum or steel. The steel ones are preferred but the aluminum is the cheaper. They come in several sizes, depending on your family size or need. Daddy has a five-pound one of steel for small dishes and a twenty-five-gallon one of aluminum for extended friends and family occasions. They can be used for many different meals but mostly they are used to cook rice, the main staple of the Puerto Rican diet.

"Are we having white or yellow rice?" I asked.

"*Arroz con pollo*," he replied.

So I fried the *achiote*, annatto seeds, in pork fat from the tin fryer he keeps near the stove. The fat drippings turned orange in less than a minute. "How many people are coming?" Even though I knew how many, I always asked, just in case.

"Make enough for six. I'm cutting up the chicken now. Don't forget to get the *achiote* off the pan, the drippings will get bitter." Daddy held his favorite knife and after six precise cuts, a whole chicken was cut-up, its back bone, ribs separated and he diced the breasts.

"That's very impressive, Steven!" Emilia said still standing nearby.

"My mother taught me," Daddy replied. "It isn't difficult at all, you have to know where bone connections are." He showed the pieces were the knife cleared its way. "Then you dice some of the white meat and the dark meat and add everything to the *caldero* and brown it just so. The chicken will get the perfect color and the fat will get the flavor."

As the meat made contact with the fat, the *caldero* hissed and crackled. The aroma of the spices swirled around the kitchen as I stirred.

"I'm telling you Emilia, Daddy can feed an army on short-term notice."

"What a wonderful smell!" Emilia exclaimed.

"And dessert?" I asked Daddy.

"There is Queen of all Pudding Pie in the fridge. I made it yesterday."

"What kind of pudding is it?" Emilia asked.

"It's guava pudding." Daddy responded, "I use real guavas from my tree. No need to use that crap they sell in the supermarket, full of sugar and preservatives."

Emilia had a quizzical look.

"Have you eaten a guava ever?" I inquired trying to read her look.

"Noo," she said, "don't they have worms?"

"Noo," I mimicked her, "not if you know how to care for them. We can have some tomorrow. As for the pudding, it's like nothing you have tasted before. It just melts in your mouth; if you know how to do it right."

The conversation turned back to our visit when Dad came into the kitchen refreshed and wearing a ragged and torn yellow t-shirt; it was splattered with different color paint spots. His faded jean shorts completed the outfit. The denim was so worn out it looked like cotton.

"Did you win the case of the guy that used to be a woman?" Dad asked Emilia.

"No, but we are appealing the decision," Emilia responded as she washed her hands and returned to the table with her wine glass.

The side door opened again and Eric entered. He was tall with dark hair to match his skin, broad shouldered and toned. He had a smile that could melt the ice caps off a mountain. He hugged me from behind as I still was minding the *caldero* where the *arroz con pollo* was simmering.

"Hey, little sis, are you still developing?"

I hit him in the head with the wooden spoon I had in my hands, turned around and kissed him.

"Ouch, I'm so sorry, you *are* a grown woman now," he said with feigned surprise, turning around to the table were Emilia was seated. "Oh my, where are my manners?" he said with a tone of affectation. "Is this my new sister-in-law?"

"I know how to pick them, don't I?" I replied and added, "No, Mister. I can't commit to a relationship right now; this is my law partner at ACLU, Emilia Hall, and NO, she is straight." For emphasis, I turned around and asked her, "You are straight, aren't you?"

"Last time I checked, the little LED light was flashing straight." Emilia was quick to pick up the banter.

Eric sat beside Dad who put his arm around him.

"How was the board meeting?" Daddy asked.

"Everything is drama, drama, drama, for these people; everything is such a difficult and tedious task. They can't agree on anything. It's like dealing with little children. But we made some progress, tabled a couple of motions, and decided to disagree until next Tuesday at five o'clock when all the lines will be drawn and redrawn in the sand; a couple of cement walls will be built, and in the end we'll hash out all our differences. God, I'm ready for a martini right now."

"You'll have to settle for white wine or beer," Daddy said.

Eric walked to the fridge and grabbed two beers, one for him and another for Dad, who nodded to him.

"How's your mother?" Daddy asked checking the *sopa de plátano*, plantain soup, which has been quietly cooking on low over another of the stove's burners. "I've been cooking this soup for her."

"Mami is fine," responded Eric and added, "Papi is in Atlanta dealing with some family business. One of his aunts is getting worse so the family is preparing. I'm sorry I can't stay tonight. I promised Mami that I would eat with her, and then I have a date. How long are you guys going to stay here?"

"Just for the weekend," I said. "We have to go back to work on Monday."

"What's going on with that case about the guy that was a woman and married another woman and now is trying to divorce her?" Eric asked.

"We lost it, but the appeals process is going on," Emilia answered and added, "Wow, is everybody in your family interested in this particular case?" I had no time to answer the question.

"That case sounds so creepy and confusing."

"Not as creepy and confusing as you on a date!" I added, getting back at him.

"Well, at least I get called back!" He jabbed me.

"Kids, you are going to scare our visitor away," Dad interjected.

"Believe me, my family is scarier when they get together," Emilia declared.

Dad's phone rang and he stepped into the living room to answer it.

"Are you sure you can't stay, Eric?" Daddy asked. "You can have a bit of the soup and I will send you with a container for Mami. She loves it too."

"Ok, I'll have some. Where are Sarah and Sheri?"

"That was Sarah," Dad said coming back to the table. "She is just past Bahía Honda. I told her you were here for the weekend, and she said that she would be here soon. Knowing the way she drives she will make it in fifteen."

"Don't exaggerate, Hon. The fact that she has more tickets and higher insurance premiums than anybody in the state of Florida doesn't make her a bad driver. She is just too intense," Daddy said. "Come on, let's get this table ready for dinner. Eric, put the leaves up and get the extra chairs. Emilia, there are table linens and napkins in that cupboard next to you, pick the color of your choice. Angie, get the dishes."

The production of setting the table started and everybody was busy and excited. With the table extended to its full length, the kitchen seemed smaller. My family likes it that everything is within reach, which makes dinners cozier, and no one gets away from the table long enough to miss anything, unless they are going to the bathroom.

The side door opened one more time and it was Sheri, red hair aflame after her last visit to her stylist, her eyes framed with gold-rimmed glasses, carrying her beloved black poodle Newton and two extra bottles of wine.

"I thought you had to cover for someone who didn't show up at the bar tonight," Daddy said. "I'm so happy you could make it."

"Well, Sarah called me from the road and told me Angie came for the weekend with a friend. So I couldn't miss it for the world. Besides she threatened me that if I couldn't find anybody to tend bar, I was going to end up on the sofa. I can't permit that, so I found someone to cover for me," she said laughing.

"I'm Sheri Gilbert, my dear," she said to Emilia.

"Emilia Hall, pleased to met you."

Newton went under the table where he lay patiently. He probably knew it was going to be a long night. A few minutes later Sarah whistled in, complaining about the driving in the Keys. There was another round of introductions and more wine was served. Another hour passed, with the family filling Emilia in on so many stories so that she got a pretty good idea of what it was like to live in Key West.

Dad's cell phone rang and he stepped into the living room to avoid the noise. When he came back he looked at Eric. "Have we forgotten something?" he asked, eyebrow arched.

"Ay, my date!" Eric almost jumped across the table and picked up his plate and silverware.

"No, your mother. Forget your date and take care of her tonight," Dad said patting him on the shoulder. "Are you OK to drive to her house? Or do you want me to drive?"

"No, I'm okay. Sis, call me on the cell tomorrow. Let's the three of us go to breakfast or something. I still haven't told Emilia everything there is to know about you," he said smiling and went around the table saying his goodbyes.

Daddy reminded him, after his hug, "Don't forget the soup for your mother. I'll call her tomorrow."

"Yes, Daddy." He hurried out.

Chaos returned to the table. Sheri was telling Emilia about the bar and the clientele. Sarah, knowing she had two captive lawyers at the table recapped the stories of all the trials she fought with my parents, and how she met Sheri and decided to move to Key West to chase after her.

"Can you believe, I've been chasing this woman for the last twenty-four years and she still plays hard to get?" Sarah said, to everyone's cheers and laughter.

"I don't play that hard to get; she's just getting slower," Sheri answered.

"Well," I said, trying to get over everyone's voice. "We have an announcement to make."

I could only hear Sheri's high pitched excitement, "WE? Are you guys getting hitched here in Key West?"

"NO!" I protested, "Emilia is straight. But you're not too far away from the target."

"Let me check!" Emilia said to Sheri, "Nope, LED isn't flashing a rainbow flag," and added, "but still the weekend is young."

"Then, what could be more important?" Sheri asked, puzzled.

"I'm going to work on the marriage equality issue." As I said it, the table fell silent for a second, then a flood of excitement came across. Sarah was telling Emilia and me about all these contacts that we should make. She offered her help. She was going to dig out her notes and give them to us. Sheri was all excited about going to testify this time around and how Newton was going to testify with her. I looked around the table and took a deep breath, located Emilia accross the table and said, "This is the reason I can't stay away too long."

"What?" asked Emilia as she shoved another bite of Queen of all Pudding Pie in her mouth.

The Key West Citizen published the following item in its social pages:

KW NATIVE TO FIGHT FOR GAY MARRIAGE

Citizen Staff

A Miami lawyer from Key West has joined the ACLU in its fight for gay marriage. María de los Ángeles Zúñiga-Carmichael is working with lawyers in the national American Civil Liberties Union who are advising ME=V, the Marriage Equality Equals Voice organization.

The ME=V advocacy group was founded to press for the legalization of gay marriage in Florida, one of the last states in the union that still bans it. The group is helping a local gay couple appeal the ban in at the state Supreme Court as well as the 11th Circuit Court of Appeals in Atlanta, Ga.

The original case that spurred the ACLU and MV=E to action was the lawsuit pop star MileM filed against longtime partner, Olympic gold medalist and fashion model Julie Ardens. Though the separation reportedly is amicable on a personal level; MileM is fighting for what she says is her half of the famous couple's millions in assets, as well as for shared custody of their three children. The couple married in New York but moved to Key West looking for a less hectic lifestyle.

Zúñiga-Carmichael graduated from Key West High School, finished her BA at Florida International University and earned her law degree at Stetson University. After passing the Florida bar, she joined forces with MV=E and the state American Civil Liberties Union affiliate in the JOHN DOE v. Florida case.

The transgender case, which is still in the courts, is

considered pivotal in the gay rights movement. After gender reassignment surgery, Doe, born a female, married a woman in Massachussetts and they settled in Florida. Now legally a man, he tried to divorce the woman. The Florida Supreme Court annulled the marriage, agreeing with lower courts that it never existed as gay marriage is illegal in this state. MV=E joined the ACLU in appealing the ruling, but the state's 3rd District Court of Appeal upheld it.

In the MilaM v. Ardens case, the federal 11th Circuit Court of Appeals in Atlanta, Ga., has agreed to hear arguments. Legal analysts have said the arguments probably won't change the courts' position of not interfering with state marriage laws, though some have argued that a case for interstate commerce could be made, given the couple's huge assets. That would allow federal law to trump any one particular state's law.

"Although this particular case triggered the formation of MV=E, our overall goal is to legalize same-sex marriages in Florida, the last state in the union that still bans it," Zúñiga-Carmichael said. "Growing up in Key West, where everyone is pretty accepting, it seems incredible to me that the rest of the state apparently refuses to join the 21st century."

The *Miami Pink Pulp*, a LGBT magazine, published the following interview.

MARÍA DE LOS ÁNGELES ZÚÑIGA-CARMICHAEL TALKS ABOUT HER LEGAL FIGHTS AND HER FAMILY

MPP Staff

María what is your reaction to the courts in the state of Florida acting on gender and/or sexuality?

They are playing morality with social issues. I'm just a citizen helping other citizens who have rights according to the constitution of the United States of America.

In 2013, the Supreme Court of the United States ruled in two important cases regarding same sex marriage. Since Florida's lawmakers haven't changed their position in these matters, what's next?

For those people who live in states like Florida where their marriages are still not recognized, these rulings are a reminder that we can't wait for justice to be handed to us. We're going to have to roll-up our sleeves and get our hands dirty. These rulings are a major step forward for the country, but for Floridians they fall far short of justice and are more than anything a call to action.

ME=V isn't the only group in Florida fighting for marriage equality. Is there a difference? What does your group offer that others don't?

Not only are there other groups and organizations but also some of them have been fighting for a long time. I don't think this is detrimental to the movement, the more the merrier. I look forward to working with other organizations if the need arises.

What do you think of the Florida state senators and legislators' refusals to even discuss marriage equality in the State?

As I said before, the only reason for our leaders' refusal to accept marriage equality is based on a warped sense of morality. Most people live in states with full marriage equality, with the state and federal protections families need. Florida LGBT people are legal strangers in their own state.

What do you advocate people in the state of Florida to do today?

I want people to talk to their family, friends and neighbors about why marriage matters and about why no loving, committed couple should be excluded from marriage. Now is the time to be vocal, be visible!

Playing the devil's advocate, I would like to flip the coin on you, do you know any LGBT person or couple who is opposed to marriage equality.

I don't know of any particular person or couple who opposes it, but I wouldn't be surprised that there might be someone out there. Like any other aspects of life, people have their own reasons to agree or disagree with an idea.

Can you give us your side of the story about your recent arrest at a Miami Council meeting?

I was part of a contingency of protestors organized by ME=V. We were distributing leaflets against marriage discrimination when a woman started screaming at the top of her lungs that I had assaulted her. The meeting came to a halt and the police move in to arrest all the protestors. She was still screaming when the police arrested me even though I had distanced myself from her. Turns out she is the wife of activist pastor John Morass from the Church of Jesus and Mary The Family Enforcers, a non denominational church whose mission is to counter protest groups working on social changes that they oppose. All meetings are broadcast. After the tapes were reviewed, the charges were dropped.

Are you planning to take legal action against them?

No, I believe they have a right to protest, as I do. Their methods might not be considered authentic but they aren't illegal. It was the police who jumped the gun, so to speak, on that one.

Can we talk about your family? Their story, as I researched it, is necessary for other people to understand who you are and where you're coming from.

We can, but be careful.

Angie you aren't the first member of your family to show such an outspoken attitude against the courts. Your pedigree is peppered with it. You're proud and unapologetic about your family heritage. Can you tell us about your parents?

My parents are Dr. Manuel Zúñiga and Mr. Steven Carmichael. They are among the first couples in the state of Florida to fight the ban on gay/lesbian adoptions. Even before I was born.

Do you feel particularly sensitive to people being boxed in by their sexuality?.

Because of the world I've been brought up in, I just don't put people in compartmentalized boxes. I don't think, oh, that's a bisexual person, that's a gay person, that's a straight person and certainly that's not the way I want people to think about me.

Now that you have picked up the torch lit by your parents, how have their struggles shaped the way you are facing your legal battles?

They are very proud of who I am, of course. I have always felt humbled by

their convictions and commitment to themselves and to their children. Even as I was growing up, they fostered children for short periods of time. In their own way, they proved that gay parents can and do raise children successfully.

I have to ask, are you gay?

I told you to be careful; it's no one's business but mine. I'm not in a relationship right now. I am very proud of who I am. I've no regrets and I don't apologize. If you don't like it, so be it.

Do you have any kids? Do you want to have any?

No I don't have children. I don't know the answer to wanting to have any. It's not in the cards right now.

Going back to your growing up in Key West, did you ever discuss your parents' sexuality?

I had a wonderful upbringing. I didn't have any adjustment problems that were different from those of any other kid growing up in Key West.

In fact I can almost claim that it was lame and boring, but that's not entirely true. My family situation was so open that it wasn't discussed. It was something we never talked about, because it was there in plain sight. I grew up in a house where gay friends and straight friends mirrored each other. They came and went, and there was no questioning, no doubting and certainly, no assumptions.

In the 90s, while they were in the middle of their first trial, your sister Angelita died. Did they ever tell you about those times?

Yes they did. Angelita is as much a part of my life as Eric and Tommy. Our lives have nourished each other. I know it's hard for other people to understand that. It is my calling not only to make them understand but to show them those relationships up close and personal.

What other lessons have you learned from your parents and their principles?

The older I get, the more I realize that life, sexuality, and the whole mess that comes with it is never a black-and-white issue. Who cares? Does my family like it? Absolutely! I know that I have complete and unconditional support from my parents and my immediate family.

The house at the Eliza St.house before Angie was born. The carport and the side door were added later.

The dining room at the Eliza St. house before Angie was born.

10

Trailer parks are home to many families in Key West. Some parks have been here before the 1970s. Irene's trailer was placed in its lot in 1973. Courtesy of the Bishop Family.

EDEN'S SHORE PARK

In the wild, "Conchs are eaten by several species of predators. Human beings and the spotted eagle ray. The starfish inserts one of its arms in the opening then, it forces its own stomach out of its body, sticks it inside the conch and digests the conch right inside its own shell. The hermit crab devours the animal and takes over the shell. The octopus can extract a conch from its shell by using its suction cup-like arms. Evidence of this can often be observed by snorkelers [and divers] who may notice piles of empty conch shells surrounding an octopus's den." In Key West, the predators of the "conchs" and the "bubbas" are themselves. The action takes place during the late 2020s.

Morning in Boyton Beach, Florida. Neelam Zakir finished his yoga routine. Not far away a teapot was protesting its contact with the stove's burner. Neelam stretched one more time before collecting his mat and heading for the bathroom, cup of tea in hand. The hot water felt good on his back and the bathroom smelled of a combo of tea, dandruff shampoo and bath gel.

The voices of the morning news came clearly now from the bedroom TV. Shaving cream, lathered, massaged the bottom of his face. He changed the blade in the razor and applied more cream carefully while the TV blasted the latest figures on the housing market. Small cut; he dabbled a glob of hair gel and the blood was contained. Brushed teeth, uppers first, right upper side, left upper side. Bottom, left, right; gargle. Hair gel, so '80s but it's the only thing that can control his hair-whorl from rebelling against gravity. Quick look in the mirror, and he noticed a couple of extra pounds. "Got to start walking in the mornings again," he thought.

A few paces and Neelam stood in front of his closet door. As he opened it, the smell of cedar filled his nose. All the clothing was organized by type: jackets, vests, long-sleeved shirts, short-sleeved shirts, each division coded by color. He chose a starched, blue, long-sleeved oxford and a purple silk tie. He walked back to the small chest of drawers beside the bathroom: underwear. Picked up a pair of gray Calvin Klein boxer shorts and khaki socks. Are we frisky today? he thought. Ironed khakis, black belt and black shoes. Cufflinks, his father's wedding band (on the middle finger) and a watch completed the look; he put his glasses on. He was ready. Meeting first thing in the morning with the law partners.

Neelam entered the conference room, with its floor-to-ceiling windows. The senior partner, Mr. Martin, and two other partners were huddled together, enjoying the sound of their own voices. Martin signaled everybody, time to start.

"Neelam, this company recruited you two years ago and we're very happy with your work so far," said Mr. Martin. The other two nodded in agreement.

"Thanks for your confidence," Neelam said.

"I've a close friend who owns Labardee Development. He is looking to develop some properties in the Florida Keys and he hired us," Martin continued. "He looked at three properties; two of them are Upper Keys waterfront and one is in the center of Key West. This one will be the easiest to develop, according to his plans. The people on it don't own it; they'll be easy to get rid of. He wants to go for the landlocked property. The problem for my friend is that he needs to change the zoning code before he buys the property. Without the zone change, he doesn't want to buy it. Son, we need a friend in Key West."

"Are you offering me this assignment?" asked Neelam confidently.

"Not only am I offering it to you, we've decided that depending on your performance, you'll be one step closer to full partnership in the firm."

Neelam beamed with self-assurance. He had worked very hard for this moment. "Thank you, sir, I'll give it 110 percent." The other two partners stood up, and everybody shook hands.

"Ok," said Martin, "back to work."

II

The iguanas saluted the sunrise at Eden's Shore RV Park in Key West, taking in the morning heat to warm themselves. Princess, Irene Bishop's black lab-chow chow mix, peered out the glass back door of the trailer. She barked at the iguanas, which in return gazed at her and stuck their tongues out. A hen with her brood of chicks crossed the street for more garden digging and feeding; the rooster flapped its wings and crowed before it followed the group.

Ever since her husband died, Irene had worked two jobs, the emergency room night shift and the electronics area at Sears three days a week. She owned her trailer, but Mr. Gregory owned the land.

Tomas "T" Gregory inherited the park from his father, and at several meetings with the tenants he had assured them that they were safe. Then the housing market went haywire, instigated by speculation. Several times a week the trailer park office received calls, mostly from the elderly residents, panicked by the latest selling rumors.

"Huh!" Irene thought. "I'll believe it when I see it."

III

Morning traffic in Miami—horns were blasting and many middle fingers were standing in attention. Even 25 floors up from Brickell Avenue you could hear the commotion of the world below. "Jesus, it's only 7 in the morning!" Angie thought. Quick run to the bathroom, one short look in the mirror. "What a freaking mess you are today."

The smell of coffee filled the small apartment, combined with the stale remnants of the microwaved pasta from two nights ago and the Chinese beef and broccoli from last night. "*¡Por Dios, Angela, limpia este reguero que tienes aquí!* For Pete's sake Angie, please clean this mess," Daddy's voice came loud and clear in her mind. She sat down at a table littered with papers, her laptop, law books, depositions and dirty dishes. Wearing a blue T-shirt and her favorite shorts, coffee cup in hand, Angie woke up the computer and started working on her case.

An hour later, she was stuck on a legal point. "Oh, my God, look at the time! It's almost 8:30. Fucking meeting at 9!" She ran to the bedroom, clothing strewn around in piles. "I haven't done the laundry, crap!" She put on her last pair of clean underwear and looked into the empty closet. A lonesome black cocktail dress peered out of the corner. She could hear it screaming; "Not me! Not today!" She grabbed it and put it on. She picked up a beige blazer from the floor, smelled it, approved it and completed the ensemble with a scarf. Work was only 15 minutes away.

IV

Eden's Shore was comprised of 200 or so trailers and a few RVs. When Irene moved in 20 years ago; it was well maintained, a haven for retired people. It started in one little corner, when the Navy needed to expand their living quarters in the 1950s and built 15 emergency units made of cinderblocks. The rest of the lot was put aside for future building. The Navy then ceded the property to the city when they downsized in the economic crisis of the '70s; Mr. Gregory's father bought it and developed it.

A few trailers were moved in 1972. Brand-new Firelights with two bedrooms and one bath, a full kitchen, faux wood paneling on the walls and a shaggy red, white and blue carpet honoring the upcoming U.S. bicentennial. By the time Irene's husband found it under seven layers of other carpets, just placed one on top of the other, it had turned an orangey color. Their trailer was on a corner lot at the far west area of the park, number 73.

They bought the dilapidated trailer for $10,000 in 1984 and in the first two years put about $20,000 into renovating it. They gutted the place, rewired it, and put in a new bathroom and kitchen. Joe died of a heart attack a year after renovations were completed.

The kitchen smelled of sweet Arabica coffee today. "Miss you Honey," Irene sighed, finished her coffee, and went to get dressed. She had a couple of vacation days, so she picked her favorite blue and green caftan from the closet. Yesterday she got a haircut. The stylist at Delano's convinced her to try something different, and she ended up with a spiky do and highlights that reminded her of David Bowie's Ziggie Stardust.

But this morning, she saw the highlights emphasized her blue eyes and she liked it. Even though she did not usually wear make-up on her days off, she decided to show off her new do. She took care in putting her face on and came back to the kitchen. Princess tilted her head inquisitively, figured out something was up, and started prancing around her.

"Oh, don't get all excited! Go fetch your leash."

Princess ran into the living room and came back with it. Irene gathered some bags and leashed her. Princess knew they were going to the dog park. On the way to the car Linda, Irene's next-door neighbor, looked out her kitchen window. "That can't be Irene," she thought. "What the heck is wrong with her?" She opened the window and yelled:

"What has gotten into you, missy?"

"Don't know, but I kind of like it." Irene replied, as she opened the car door. "The hairstylist told me if I didn't like it, to just let it wash out in a couple of shampoos. Wanna go to the dog park?"

"Nah, I already walked Tiger and I'm getting ready for work, but call me tonight," Linda said. "I'm making *ropa vieja*, shredded beef, for Jerry. Can I set some aside for you?"

"You know I'm not turning that down!" Irene said. "Thanks!"

Like everything else, the dog park was a microcosm of Key West. The people with their Afghans and Shih Tzus shared this patch of land with the mutts and the homeless who camped there. The conscientious owners cleaned up after their furry family members. The lazy ones were scolded by the others and, if repeat offenders, kicked out.

Irene had brought a folding chair, because of her knees. Princess ran around and greeted all the regulars and sniff-checked the newcomers, if allowed. Being big and fluffy had its advantages in the upwardly mobile world of the furry castes. Not to mention the fact that she had THE only purple tongue and blue lips, which made her a pretty fashion-forward pooch. Irene heard the owners of two Great Danes chewing the rawhide close by:

"This time it's for sure," the tall one said. "A friend of mine who works at the county building told me that someone representing a corporation from Boyton Beach requested plans, blueprints, surveys and historical information about the property."

"Nah," said the other. "Same old rumors."

Steve Carmichael entered the dog park from the Casa Marina side. He came with his neighbor's dog and 10 children, some from his street, some from the youth center where he volunteered. Irene had met him and his partner, Manny, a pediatrician, when they brought one of their foster kids having an asthma attack to the ER. The kid recovered and Irene kept up the acquaintance, not too difficult on a small island.

"Steve, I need to talk to you," said Irene, holding Princess close.

"Are you OK?" he said. "You sound so apprehensive."

"I'm OK but I just heard…" and she communicated the whole story to him. "I think they are right—and that's 200 working families and old people. Where are we going to go?"

"Let me talk to Manny, and I'll get back to you," he said. "I wouldn't worry about it until something is published in the paper or we have a solid lead. I haven't heard anything yet." Then Steve was whisked away by the dog and the kids.

Boynton Beach-based Labardee Development made a tentative but strong offer on the Eden's Shore property. The company's plan was to build a luxury residential complex in Key West. But bureaucracy and a lack of greasing the right hand, or a left one, for that matter, would stall it. The coconut telegraph went wild as rumors of eviction notices sprouted like latticed bougainvilleas in the middle of the summer. Linda came out as Irene's car pulled up by her trailer.

"Someone said that Michael and Karla got eviction papers today," she told Irene.

"I thought I was going to die here," Irene replied. "I really thought this was going to be my last address."

"Maybe we should rethink that," Linda said as they entered their trailers.

V

Angie Zúñiga Carmichael came for her weekend visit with her Dads. Manny started the usual discussion of the latest news, "Key West is not losing its community," Manny said. "The community is changing."

"And what that's supposed to mean?" Angie replied, mystified. "That in this tourism-rooted economy, anything goes?"

Steve said from the kitchen, "Honey, do you remember Irene, the lady who helped us in the emergency room? She's been bending my ear every time she sees me at the dog park. You know she lives at Eden's Shore behind Sears. Apparently someone is trying to buy the park."

"Steve, you know those rumors have been floating around forever," Manny said.

"Well, she believes this time it might be true. Can you find out?"

Angie was upset. "Just what we needed, another fucking developer out to displace people," she said. "When is this shit going to stop? Mobile home parks are the last affordable workforce housing. The old Cubans are dying, the Haitians are scared to death and don't rock the boat. The rest are illegal alien employees. You know that, Dad, don't you? Even teachers and public defenders are scared off by the high cost of housing and insurance."

"So what are YOU going to do about it, Angie? Steve, I'll see what I can find out. I'll make a couple of phone calls, but it will take some time."

"Can the residents stop this?" Angie asked. "Do they have any recourse?"

“I heard that a group of residents is suing their park owner up on Little Torch Key, but it’s an uphill battle,” her father replied. “The government can’t stop people from selling their property to whomever they want.”

“Well, Dad, you asked what I wanted to do about some of the crap happening in this town. I would like to help, but I need to do some research first.”

“I’m not sure that you want to do that,” he said. “You know what some people here can do to others when they get in their way.”

“So what are they going to do to me? Smear me like they do everyone else?” she asked. “Isn’t affordable housing for the workforce important to anybody? It’s an impossible idea to bring all the service industry people by bus from Homestead. Isn’t?”

Angie fell silent. Steve made a mental note of the whole discussion for later. Manny went into the kitchen to help with dinner. As they ate, the discussion revolved around Angie’s Walmart case. Eden’s Shore went to bed like the rest of paradise.

184 Next day, on her way back to Miami, Angie had three hours to think about it. She wanted to find a way to help these people. “I know it’s the market; I know it’s capitalism, but they can’t be thrown out on the streets,” she murmured to herself.

Manny made a few calls; the rumors were partially true. Labardee Development was looking for possible projects. They had requested some public documents and contacted the owners of several properties in the Keys, including Mr. Gregory, and its representatives had asked about the feasibility of changing the zoning designation for the park.

Two days later, Irene cornered Steve at the dog park again.

“Irene, Manny couldn’t confirm anything in particular, but something is going on. Here, you might like to keep this person in mind.”

Irene looked a bit skeptically at the business card: “Who’s this?”

“A good lawyer,” he replied.

A couple of days later, Irene contacted Angie. Irene repeated her concerns. The next weekend, Angie made a point of meeting Irene. The meeting lasted a couple of hours; the lawyer promised to continue her research and to keep the communications open between them.

VI

The first informal meeting of the residents was happenstance. Linda heard another rumor and waited for Irene. It was about noon.

"They're saying that the eviction notices will be in the mailboxes tomorrow!" Linda said, alarmed.

"Who are they?" countered Irene.

"Alex on lot 151."

"Come on," Irene said. "I'm going to find out for sure."

The walk from her trailer to Alex's was short. Alex was walking his two Pomeranians.

"Alex, Alex, wait a minute!" Irene said. "I have something to ask you."

"How can I help you *mi vida*?" He always used cutesy names for the ladies.

"Who told you that the eviction notices would be here tomorrow?" Irene was direct.

Alex hesitated for a moment and looked puzzled, trying to remember. "Let me think, I was talking to Mike; that's probably when it came up. It might be another rumor. Those freaking Haitians, ever since they started to move here…." He mumbled something else as he hurried the dogs along and was closing in on his trailer.

"Things are very tense right now," Irene told him. "Rumors aren't helpful to anyone." Alex had already closed his door, but she had spoken loud enough for him to hear.

Mike, one of the park's handymen, ran around in an electric golf cart. If you needed anything, you waited for the cart to come around and stopped them. Irene waited to hear the motor on the cart and ran out: "Mike, stop!" The cart made a quick U-turn and came to a halt beside her.

"Yes, Mrs. Bishop?" said Mike.

"Who told you that the eviction notices would be here tomorrow?" Irene folded her arms under her chest and looked at him like only grandma looked at her grandkids when they were in trouble. He lowered his eyes.

"Freaking Alex, he can't keep anything to himself!" Mike tried to explain. "The Haitians were all huddled in their little corner down at the other side of the park. I was going by and saw all the commotion; I thought they were fighting and went over there to help, but they weren't fighting, they were discussing the eviction. Guy heard one of the Mexican bus drivers talking about it on his cell, on the bus home. I didn't know Guy spoke Spanish, but he swears that he heard the driver say it. Mrs. Montparnasse was all over the place with it."

"Did you contact anybody in the office?" Irene asked, shifting her weight from one side to the other.

"I was going to, but around the corner came Alex with his stupid dogs —he's always screaming at those dogs. I tried to get away, you know, but once he traps you, you are stuck for at least half an hour talking nonsense. He didn't give me a chance to escape, and I told him what they were all taking about and forgot to talk to Mildred in the office."

"Mike, you know better," said Irene sternly. "We have enough problems the way things are now. One third of the park is in hysterics, the other is paranoid and the rest are dealing with the consequences. I'll talk to Mrs. Montparnasse."

Odette Montparnasse's trailer, number 200, was at the far northeast corner of the park. Anybody standing on one of Santa Clara's apartment balconies next door could look down into Odette's little garden, where she grew vegetables and herbs in a 2-by-3 foot patch of sand and potting soil mixture. Irene was hit first with the heavy oregano scent. When she knocked on the outside door of the trailer, two inside doors opened, with two different people answering the front door. This didn't surprise Irene. She had heard how some of the trailers had been converted into several family units.

Odette's body was broad and solid, but she moved with the grace of a swan, especially when using her hands. As she came down the two steps that separated her door from the front door, she gently pushed closed the second door and the face of the second person back into his domain. Her skin had a wonderful warm sheen accentuated by the chartreuse of her tunic and matching scarf that kept her dreadlocks in check. The scent of oregano from the garden was overpowered by patchouli.

"How can I help you?" she asked, offering Irene one of several chairs on the tarred pathway that led to a gate onto Northside Drive.

Around 3:30, cells were ringing all over Eden's Shore as more people joined the conversation. Richard Malinowski came after his nephew texted him. He suggested putting together a concentrated front against the selling of the park. He offered to contact a lawyer/friend to seek advice regarding this situation.

"What time is it?" asked Irene.

"Almost four," someone answered.

"Someone get Mildred on the phone before she closes the office and ask her about this."

Turned out Mildred didn't know anything about it. So the impromptu meeting continued. Food was brought in and someone suggested they all wear yellow t-shirts, with some message to make a visual impression. Discussion continued about lawyers and strategies. Mrs. Montparnasse decided to contact a lawyer that she met in Miami for guidance.

That night, that corner of the trailer park was alive with the sound of cooperation, laying out plans on how to deal with the upcoming storm, whether it was coming or not. They parted friends, each one held one end of the same flat bed sheet. The fourth corner was a weather vane.

VII

The first round against Labardee Development would be at the city Planning Commission. Usually these meetings were boring and uneventful, with petitioners, or their representatives, requesting changes, and making presentations to the board. The six-member board consults with the city lawyers, and then makes a recommendation that goes to the City Commission for final approval. When conflicts arise, the matter is sent to the City Commission directly. The agendas for any meeting about city business had to be published a minimum of a week in advance. Through this announcement, the residents of Eden's Shore figured out two things: who was looking into buying the park and that they wanted to change the zoning designation. Texting and chatting phones worked late into the night.

The morning of the Planning Commission meeting, a contingent from Eden's Shore was already seated inside the auditorium at City Hall. Some were wearing yellow T-shirts proclaiming: "No zoning changes @ Eden's Shore." A local shop had donated the shirts. Other residents milled around outside and in the parking lot. When the meeting started, every seat was filled, with lots of people standing.

The committee went through the regular agenda, approved residential variances and miscellaneous projects, and then they got to the item that everybody was waiting for: the Labardee Development. The secretary didn't finish reading the item when the chanting started: "Labardee, Labardee, please go back to Boynton Beach. Labardee, Labardee, please go back to Boynton Beach."

The chairwoman tried unsuccessfully to restore order: "We respectfully ask the public to refrain from disturbing this meeting…." but the chanting drowned her out: "No zoning changes for Eden's Shore," chanted one side of the room while the other side chanted: "Labardee, Labardee please go back to Boynton Beach."

As the meeting descended into pandemonium, two members of the commission tried to address the chairwoman.

"Madam chair," Juan Luis Garriga shouted over the crowd. "Madam chair, I must recuse myself from this vote. I live at Eden's Shore."

"Labardee, Labardee, please go back to Boynton Beach. No re-zoning for Eden's Shore."

"Madam chair," shouted Sonny "Skinny" Sawyer, "I also must recuse myself—my Aunt Norma Cartagena lives at Eden's Shore."

The meeting was adjourned in chaos.

VIII

In response to all the questions, blogs, tweets, postings on Facebook, emails and phone calls received by each Key West city commissioner, Mayor Richard Laffitte called for a workshop.

The active members of Eden's Shore homeowners association convened again to continue their preparations. After an hour of discussion and brainstorming, it was decided that three lawyers would present a unified front to the commission: Angie Zúñiga who was representing Irene Bishop; Reinaldo López who was representing Richard Malinowski; and Aaron Vontrease, who was representing Odette Montparnasse and some of the other Haitian residents. Angie was appointed to speak for the group. In Key West, politics are a grimy contact sport. The city had a mayor and five commissioners who made decisions, helped by the city manager and a cadre of lawyers. While the city government was designed this way to prevent corruption, it didn't prohibit the usual shenanigans from happening—especially when juicy contracts and development projects were up for grabs.

Everybody was present at the workshop. Even 20-year Commissioner Rafael "Ralph" Ponce showed up in an attentive mood. Usually, he avoided community workshops. He always said that they were a waste of time. The scars of old wars demonstrated Ponce's political longevity.

His gray hair had been jet black and slicked back in his first term. His skin was the color of dark mahogany and his fine features were the guarantee of his success. He knew everybody, and everyone who was anyone knew him. But now his skin was a dull-brown. His pants size had increased, indicating his taste for a good meal, good bourbon and a good cigar.

He had moved to Key West after working as a show producer in Miami and using his power of persuasion and the word of friends, got a local bank to lend him the money to buy the "Laced Teddy," a sleepy bar with a following of blue-minded people. It was hidden between Charles Street and Telegraph Lane. Because the lane was off Duval Street, he started a new program: The Naked Lunch. He had read the book, and figured out a gimmick. The new format attracted a crowd of out-of-towners, swingers, voyeurs, and the occasional scholar who got the literary reference and wandered in thinking it was a tribute to William S. Burroughs.

"Every important author had a connection with Key West, why not Burroughs?" Ponce was quoted in an article at the time.

He knew when the scholars came in, they'd sit down uncomfortably and go through with it. On occasion, one of them would dare ask a waiter: "Isn't this the William S. Burroughs' house museum?" The response was quick: "But of course it is…this is just a re-enactment!" In a few years, Ponce turned the whole block into an adult entertainment compound by adding more venues.

Ponce became a commissioner when a coalition comprised of church elders, politicians, and citizens called "Key West and the Keys for Kids" in the late '90s tried to enforce existing laws and lobbied for new regulations to clean up the town's image.

Like-minded merchants and entrepreneurs helped him get elected; he hadn't lost an election since. Against the KWK-Kids coalition's efforts, Ponce marketed the "anything goes" tourist image that allowed, for example, family restaurants alongside The Naked Lunch. "Mom and the kids can go next door while dad has a drink and enjoys his eye candy," he was known for saying.

Ponce liked the taste of small-town politics, and decided that the political arena was as satisfying as all his other pleasures. As long as the voters gave him a mandate, the flow of cruise ships, the availability of T-shirt shops, tattoo parlors, bars, and non-stop partying were secured as an integral part of Key West's economy. Allegations of corruption, money laundering, sex trafficking and other illegal activities were raised, but nothing stuck. The commissioner was very proud of his clean record and reminded anybody who dared to question it.

Ponce's world revolved around his complex of businesses and the continuation of Key West as an adult party destination. Any big celebration with the word "fest" in it made the commissioner feel tingly inside; any reason to close Duval Street from the Atlantic to the Gulf for a whole weekend made him salivate. Any project that could bring more people down to the Keys, and faster, was a great idea that shouldn't be dismissed without careful consideration.

The voters of Florida approved his favorite idea in the 1990s. It was abandoned due to cost and the housing crash, but it still got him as giddy as a parochial schoolgirl in ponytails and patent leather shoes. If you got two bourbons into Ponce, then mentioned "fast track monorail" you'd better buckle up for at least two hours of a non-stop monologue. Ponce fancied himself the less wealthy Flagler of the 21st century, and he believed the taxpayers and the government should foot the bill for the whole thing.

During the now-notorious redevelopment of the Truman waterfront returned to the city by the Navy last decade, his office door never shut. His phone became the great communicator. The legal and economic legacy of those dealings had not yet been settled.

Today, Ponce wasn't bothered by the fact that he had to get up early for the workshop, even though he had been up late talking to Neelam Zakir, a young lawyer from Miami, about a developing company's new projects in the Keys.

IX

After four years of constructions delays, an over-bloated budget, excuses from the contractors, changes in variances and an FBI investigation on corruption charges, the new City Hall on White Street wasn't finished yet. The workshop, called by Mayor Lafitte, was moved to the Old City Hall on Greene Street. The building was constructed after the Great Fire of April 1, 1886, finished in 1892, and remodeled a few times later.

The staircase that leads to the entrance was too big for the building; city coffers were depleted before its conclusion; it gave the building a sense of incompleteness, an architectural inferiority complex that ran through its bricks and mortar. The stairs at night served as the concrete bed of the homeless, panhandlers and hustlers. The occasional patron from Sloppy Joe's, a few steps away, contributed organic fluids enhancing the stairs' natural colors and required a daily spray from the Fire Station No. 3 truck.

The edifice was given an oversized bell tower, as an affront to its size. The clocks on each of its faces showed different times. The inside was as dissonant as the outside. Its dark wood-paneled main hall made it appear hunchbacked and closed in. The rows of theater-style chairs faced a dais that wanted to be a grand stage but had to settle for being the front of a classroom.

Everything in the room is too big: the heavy oak counter with its leather-backed chairs for the commissioners; the oversized signs for their names; a small area for the city staff, city manager and city lawyers all clustered together. Computer equipment, TV cameras and recording devices sum up the claustrophobic atmosphere that begs for some idiotic teenager to scream "fire" at the top of his lungs. So far, the story/history of the new building is following on the footsteps of the old one. The more the things changed in Key West, the more they stay the same.

There were rumors about concerned, well-connected citizens calling the commissioners the night before the workshop, discussing the direction of developments in the city. The room was packed to the rafters for the workshop.

Zakir was wearing a blue Armani suit, a crisp, white Oxford shirt and a light blue tie. "Nice," someone heard Ponce say out loud. The young gun was ready; he did everything that his boss asked and a bit more. Zúñiga wore her favorite black pantsuit and a print shirt.

Neither the owner of the trailer park nor anyone from Labardee Development showed up. Zakir had assured them that the meeting was just a formality and that their interests would prevail at the end. The lawyer for the commission called the workshop to order and explained who was going to speak when.

Zúñiga started in a firm tone: "Mobile home parks are an important housing resource in the state of Florida. A report in the 1990s states that around 28,000 trailer lots are located in Monroe County, and roughly 200 of them are located at Eden's Shore RV Park, which are subject to Chapter 723, known as the Florida Mobile Home Act. This law applies to any residential tenancy in which a mobile home is placed upon a rented or leased lot in a mobile home park in which 10 or more lots are offered for rent or lease. In the context of escalating development pressures and the displacement of mobile home owners from their homes, Labardee Developers have applied to the City of Key West to rezone the property on which Eden's Shore RV Park is located. The city shouldn't allow it."

Zakir countered: "The request was to rezone the property from MH-1 (mobile home park) to PUD (Planned Unit Development). Labardee Develpment is looking for appropriate properties to develop. Eden's Shore may or may not be the right property for constructing town homes and single-family homes."

Zúñiga pressed her point: "Approximately 200 households own their mobile homes and lease lots at Eden's Shore. The park has been there since the 1970s. New construction will displace the residents. Florida Statute Section 723.083 requires that when a local government considers rezoning a mobile home park out of existence, it must have a relocation alternative."

Zakir intervened: "The residents are overreacting. All we want is to change the zoning. The park has not been sold."

"The park has not been sold, but your client will buy the park if the zoning is changed," Zúñiga retorted. "Can you admit that fact? Where is your client going to put the residents? You aren't even a member of the community.… Where are they going to go? Can you answer that?"

"There are other parks…in the county." Zakir countered hesitantly.

"Twenty-five miles away from Key West!" Zúñiga noted.

After a long discussion about the free market, property rights and capitalism, Commissioner Ponce forced a "straw poll." He said he would approve the rezoning if the vote was taken today. Commissioner Juliette Busto said that she wasn't sure: "Losing around 200 affordable housing units doesn't make me comfortable at all." Commissioner Kirk Kerr sided with Busto. Commissioners Victor Borgia and Michelle Provoski sided with Ponce.

Mayor Richard Laffitte said, "For the record: I'm not wasting my time on a vote that's not binding."

Commissioner Ponce dismissed the comment, delighted with the results so far. He figured he could convince the commission that the requirements of Section 723.083 had been met.

At the public input part of the workshop, Irene objected: "You want me to drive up the Keys on US1 after my shift at the emergency room to get home? How about Mr. Malinowski, who depends on a beat-up truck to do his handyman work? How about Mrs. Montparnasse, who doesn't have the money to buy a car to get to and from her job at the supermarket?"

Commissioner Ponce was condescending: "We all have to adapt to the new circumstances of our city. Have you used our wonderful bus system?" The audience groaned. "We can't halt progress," he said. "And after the fast monorail is built, US1 will be for sightseeing only."

Ponce continued: "I concentrated on what the number of available mobile home sites were regardless of whether you can move your house there. The statute makes no requirement that it should be determined whether the mobile home owners being displaced could relocate their units to an allegedly available mobile home park in the area or not. The statute allows for abandonment; therefore, I couldn't include in my decision making process whether the trailer can be moved or not." It was a clever and confusing statement used as a diverting tactic.

Commissioner Provosky added: "I agree that other suitable facilities such as apartments are not within the financial means of some these people, but I don't think we should take affordability into account; there is housing out there, way, way above what would be adequate."

Even though these positions were vague and imprecise, Ponce and Provosky stuck to them like barnacles underneath a live-aboard boat. Ponce thought he could turn Kerr around; he was happy.

Zúñiga asked, unyielding: "What is that supposed to mean? The Commission's finding of adequate mobile home space or other suitable facilities available for relocation is an incorrect interpretation of the statute. It is our intention to continue this fight at the circuit court level as soon as this whole process is put in motion."

The mayor, looking tired and fearing a drawn-out and unpleasant lawsuit in an election year, called for a meeting between the city and its legal team to assess the consequences of granting the change of zoning designation for Eden's Shore RV Park.

"Why?" screamed Ponce.

"I want to be on solid legal ground. What's wrong with exploring the legal options?" replied the mayor.

Ponce's hair reflected a tint of the red flowering quickly over his complexion. He looked directly at the lawyer and asked: "Can this be done in a workshop?"

"This is technically not regarding the workshop per se," answered the city lawyer. "The mayor is asking for a future meeting between the city and its lawyers for legal consultation. He can do that any time he wants. It is up to the commissioners to say yea or nay. There is nothing wrong or illegal about it.

"OK, let's do it," said Ponce.

"One moment," Busto intervened. "No discussion? Not on my watch! I think it is a good idea that as a city we look into our legal options. There is nothing wrong with making an informed decision. Would you agree, Commissioner Ponce?"

Ponce's response was terse: "I have no comment at the moment." He swiveled his chair loudly and uncomfortably toward Commissioner Borgia.

"I don't need a closed meeting, I believe that I'm very well informed as of today," Borgia said. Commissioner Provosky agreed. "I'm well informed too."

"More information is good information," Commissioner Kerr asserted.

"A motion must be made and seconded," interceded the city lawyer. Mayor Laffitte looked at Commissioner Busto, who caught the low ball on the fly.

"I move that the city of Key West have a closed meeting with its legal team, client to counselor, regarding Florida Statute 723.083 and its application toward existing trailer parks inside the city limits." The mayor beamed at Ms. Busto's eloquence.

"I second it," Commissioner Kerr chimed in.

"Roll Call!" the clerk announced.

"Commissioner Borgia?" "Yes"

"Commissioner Busto?" "Yes"

"Commissioner Kerr?" "Yes"

"Commissioner Ponce?" "No"

"Commissioner Provosky?" "No"

"Mayor Laffitte?" "Yes"

"Motion passes 4-2. The City of Key West…." The clerk read the motion out loud. "Should we set the date?" she asked.

"Might as well." Ponce was visibly upset. "The sooner the better. How about next Wednesday? It is our regular meeting; we can do the meeting with the lawyers in the morning and add the 'zoning' question to the good of the order section." He was a bit more composed now.

"My," said the mayor, "if I didn't know better, I would think that Commissioner Ponce is hoodwinking the rest of us. Are you OK with this, Commissioner Ponce? You were quite unsettled a few minutes ago."

Ponce answered, "I'm holding my cards close to my vest."

X

The commissioners spent the days before the meeting fielding public comment, positive and negative. Ponce answered any and all questions with a well-rehearsed, "I have not made up my mind on anything yet. Let's see what the lawyers have to say."

Busto was clear on her stance. "These parks are important to the city. There is a quarter of our population there, so we have to be really careful with our actions."

The Wednesday morning closed meeting went fast. There was vigorous discussion about the consequences of the zoning change and the displacement of the people living at the park. As anticipated, the commission was divided between the camps of Ponce and Busto. She had found the brass ring in the argument: Eden's Shore residents could move their mobile homes to another park or move their families without moving their trailers.

Ponce stated again, "There is no requirement that the residents being displaced could relocate their units to an available mobile home parks in the area. Each of them will receive their $2,000 from the company and leave."

Busto charged ahead, "The statute is open in this regard. Because it is written in general terms, it is up to the city to enforce this clause or not."

Ponce turned to the city lawyer: "That's not right. Is it?"

"It's a plausible interpretation of the statute," the lawyer replied.

Ponce turned to Busto. "They are getting $2,000 for their ramshackle trailers, maybe more. It's not like they're leaving empty-handed!"

Busto fired, "Empty-handed? Are you that callous, Mr. Ponce? I can't believe what I'm hearing," she said, her voice rising. "What about building a new hotel on Hilton Haven Drive and giving each of the homeowners $5,000 for the houses that they've been living in and maintaining for the last 20 years? Including yours!"

"It's not the same thing. We are comparing apples to oranges. Hilton Haven has NICE houses; Eden's Shore has derelict trailers," Ponce said coldly.

"When was the last time you entered Eden's Shore, Mr. Ponce? That's my district. After the last hurricane, every single damaged trailer was replaced by a new, prefabricated structure. Or have you forgotten passing that city law a few years ago? Let me remind you, Mr. Ponce, that you agreed with me that we needed to remove and replace the damaged trailers with better-built structures. It was you who recommended the new type of structure. And it was you who suggested a way for the people who couldn't afford it to negotiate with the local banks for its completion, because, in your own words, if I remember correctly. 'It would help with the appearance of that particular trailer park to our visitors,' or have you forgotten?" Busto was beaming. Ponce was furious, red-faced again.

Commissioner Kerr intruded, "The pool of affordable housing in the Keys has been depleting since the last decade; we all know that. The true affordable house has gone the way of the dodo bird. We still aren't dealing with the main question, which is, where are these people going?"

"Not only that," Busto interceded, "We haven't voted on the rezoning yet. Commissioner Ponce's arguments are all hinging on the fact that the zoning is going to be changed. I promise you, that without a solution for the residents, I will oppose this change."

Commissioner Ponce's face reflected his discomfort.

"We are coming to the end of the closed session, and we haven't moved an inch toward a resolution. Can we recap?" Commissioner Provosky asked.

"My basic question has been answered," said Mayor Laffitte. "I agree with Commissioner Kerr. I need to know where these people are going to move. Without an answer to that, I can't back the rezoning effort. Who's interested in this change?"

"Can we get this company to make a proposal to the commission?" asked Busto.

"I would agree to that," said Kerr.

"OK, are we all on the same page?" Mayor Laffitte asked. "We are going to decide whether to enforce the relocation clause on Florida Statute 723.083 pending a presentation made to the City Commission by Labardee Development to address such a question. Do I have a motion on the floor?"

"Yes, you do," said Busto.

"I second it," stated Kerr.

The clerk called the roll and the motion passed 4-2.

"Commissioners, let's break for lunch and prepare for the next meeting," Mayor Laffitte said as staff and lawyers collected their computers and tablets. Commissioner Ponce was observed gesticulating wildly to his cell.

At the afternoon meeting, the public endured every item in the agenda; numb buttocks shifted in the movie-like rows of seats, the squeaks of un-oiled vinyl on metal parts distracting some staff members. The slow march of the mundane city business continued through discussions on items such as naming a city street and dedicating another pocket park to Wilhemina Harvey.

Then, about seven o'clock, the people in the yellow "No zoning changes @ Eden's Shore" T-shirts got what they were waiting for. Commissioners opened discussion regarding the petition to re-zone the park from MH-1 to PUD.

"We have to protect affordable housing for the people who live and work in Key West, the people who clean the hotel rooms, the waiters, the teachers," Irene Bishop said when she urged the commissioners to kill the item. "I don't have anything against any corporation, be it Labardee Development, Kmart or Sears, but I wouldn't invite them to dinner or to a commission meeting."

Richard Malinowski told commissioners, "You have an opportunity to take a stand similar to the founders of the nation in the Declaration of Independence. That document promises its people a right 'to the pursuit of happiness.' You can take a stand tonight, a stand against the greed that has gripped our island since the last century. Say no to the speculators, say no to the outside interests that lurk behind the ambitious, the covetous and the spoiled members of our society."

The speeches were passionate. The small hall resounded with voices that were trying to drown each other out. The mayor had to intervene several times, as did the city lawyer and the city manager.

Neelam Zakir said that no monetary offer had been made to the owners of Eden's Shore. The statement was received with chants of "We won't be displaced; we won't be displaced" by the residents of the RV park

and their supporters. Among them, also in a yellow T-shirt, was Angie Zúñiga Carmichael.

Commissioner Ponce reminded the crowd that a resolution passed that morning requiring Labardee Development to make a formal presentation to the commission.

"They bought you!" screamed someone in the crowd. The mayor threatened to clear the hall if order wasn't restored.

It took Commissioner Borgia's motion to table the item to quiet the room down. "Mayor Laffitte. It is almost eight o'clock and we aren't even close to a solution. I move to table this item to the next meeting for a fresh look at the facts and a well-thought-out solution."

"Do I have a second?" asked the Mayor.

Ponce leapt at the opportunity to close the meeting, to regroup and restate the strategy. "I second." Kerr, Provosky and Laffitte agreed. Busto voted against it. The item was tabled and sent to the next agenda.

The crowd expressed its unhappiness loudly: "Ponce, we'll remember in November; we'll remember in November."

Interviewed by the newspaper after the meeting, Ponce was terse. "This is a thorny issue; passions are aflame. We have to cool down and come back to it."

Two weeks later, Commissioner Busto opened the meeting with a motion to move Eden's Shore to the top of the agenda, to the delight of the crowd, which was bigger than the last meeting and full of yellow T-shirts now being sold online to help pay for the legal fight. Commissioner Kerr seconded it, and a unanimous vote followed.

Busto led the charge. "After the presentation from Labardee Development, there is no doubt in my mind that this is a land grabbing maneuver to displace the residents of Eden's Shore. It has to be stopped."

Ponce intervened, using the same old arguments and the crowd reacted the same way. He kept harping on the condition of old trailers. "Some of those trailers have been in the park since the '70s! How secure are they?" He almost had to scream over the people's voices. Mayor Laffitte called the residents to order, threatening to clear the room if order wasn't restored.

The Old City Hall meeting chamber was packed and the crowd broke into applause as the speakers voiced their concerns about the residents' displacement. "Do you remember the movie 'Jaws'? Do any of you have a doubt that nature will find a way?" asked a resident, drawing applause from the crowd. "I have no doubt that nature will find a way to amend this wrong." Mrs. Montparnasse said. "Leave life alone." The crowd applauded and cheered.

Commissioner Kerr asked to be heard. "I'll go on record as saying I hate trailers; they're absolute junk. But don't take away the tin-lined cage a guy's living in until you can replace it." The crowd applauded once again.

"Until we get some direction from the federal government, I'm not doing anything," Busto said. "I mean someone on the mainland has to have dealt with this situation before us. I can't believe we are the first city in Florida with these issues. I don't believe in re-inventing the wheel.

There must be someone out there with the answer and I intend to find either the answer or the person who can give us the answer to how to implement this statute. Until then, I'm not going to vote to displace any resident," she said. "There is no secrecy here. We're, or at least I am, trying to be as transparent as possible."

"I'm not into buying housing for the people," roared Ponce from his seat. "It will be a waste of taxpayers' money and deceitful." He didn't finish his statement.

Busto was livid. She stood up and roared: "Really, Commissioner Ponce, a waste of taxpayer's money? Did you say that it would be deceitful? Do you want to go there?" Busto asked. She had everybody's attention. "Do you want me to remind you of the issues regarding the construction of the City Hall? In public? On the record?"

Commissioner Ponce bowed his head. He knew that Busto had him; she was smiling. The public erupted; the mayor asked the police to clear the room. After a 15-minute break, the commissioners indefinitely tabled rezoning Eden's Shore. Then the commission went back to business, hearing a proposal to raise rent at the Yacht Club, which was still paying $1 a year to the city. They also heard from boat captains who complained about parking issues at the city marinas, in light of their proposed rent increases.

Busto and Kerr spotted Neelman Zakir after the meeting, talking on his iPhone.

Busto looked at Kerr, "I wonder who is on the other side of that phone line?"

"Not me, and I'm so glad," Kerr laughed.

"I'm a bit disappointed," Martin told Zakir, "but I still have faith in you. I knew it was an uphill fight."

"Thank you," said Zakir. "Commissioner Ponce assures me that we could try again soon."

"I'm pretty sure of that, but come back to Miami as soon as you can. Close up the business with our client and the commissioner," Martin said. "There is work to be done on other accounts and I could use your help."

"I'll be at the office the day after tomorrow. See you then."

Neelam put the phone in the inside pocket of his jacket. As he turned around, Commissioner Ponce grabbed his arm.

"Young man, you put up a good fight. We survived to give them hell another day." Ponce's arm snaked over Neelam's shoulders. "But tonight we relax and enjoy a good drink."

"I don't know about drinking, commissioner," said Neelam. "But we need to close a few business items. I'm going back to Miami. My boss wants me back as soon as possible. How about a quick assessment meeting?"

"Can I throw in a couple of sandwiches and a shot of tequila? asked the commissioner.

"I don't know about the tequila but I could use a bite," Neelam was hungry.

Ponce got together some of his people, reps for the client and Neelam, who held his iPhone to confer, tweet and instagram with his boss.

"It's kind of late to hold up the workers at the restaurant," Neelam pondered.

"They were cleaning the kitchen," Ponce said. "I promised to double thesous chef's nightly tip in exchange for a few sandwiches and a couple of appies. He was happy to comply not only for the money, but his boyfriend caught him a couple of days ago, sending nude selfies to someone else," Ponce explained as he laughed. "He could use a couple of extra hours not being at home."

"I don't understand how people believe they can get away with that crap without being caught," Neelam added smiling.

The meeting was a post mortem for their failed strategies and an assessment of what could or couldn't be done.

After a couple of hours of back and forth, *dimes y diretes*, no clear agreement was reached about what was the next step. The client reps and Neelam's boss concluded that a cooling period was in order. The client wanted to revisit some of his other choices for the development.

The table they were working at was littered with paper plates, crumpled paper, a few beer bottles and a couple of shot glasses. Everybody involved was tired and happy that it was over. As Neelam was packing his gadgets and notebooks, Ponce offered a ride.

"I can take you to your hotel, my car is in the back."

"No thank you, Commissioner, I can use the walk. It's only two blocks away."

"Suit yourself," Ponce added as he picked up stuff and cleaned the table with the happy sous chef who put the wad of extra earnings in his pant's pocket and changed from his coat to a t-shirt. He paused a minute and winked at Ponce as he put on his t-shirt revealing a chiseled fit torso.

"Andrew you fucking show off. That's what gets you in trouble, moffo." Ponce said as he laughed. "How's Stewart?"

"Still sulking.... He'll get over it. Who can say no to this?" He said as he patted his abs and smiled.

"Wait until metabolism catches up with you," interjected Ponce as he patted his stomach and ushered everybody out. The room smelled of the remnants of the food, drinks and cleaning solution as the hired cleaning crew, from another of his companies, finished their shift around them.

"You sure you don't want a lift?" he asked Neelam again.

"Positive."

Andrew passed them on his scooter, stopped and high-fived the commissioner; "You moffo go home and stop being a dick. Stewart is a good guy and you're going to regret it." Ponce admonished the young man.

"Yes, boss." Andrew sped away.

The conversion of trailer parks in the Keys and Key West is nothing new. This picture shows construction at Jabour's Trailer park in downtown Key West for a new hotel and underground parking garage around 2014. This project sparked litigation between the residents of the area and the developers.

After political action and protests from the public prevented the sale of Treasure Island Village park in the 1990s, its owners quietly sold it at the end of 2013, displacing the families that lived there. Developers turned the park into high-end residences in 2014.

The air was snappish and Neelam felt great. Adrenaline was rushing through his body again when he came through the lobby of the Westin. Inside his room he changed into his favorite shorts and opened up the laptop and worked on the billing for the case. Mechanically he opened his email account and checked for his secretary's emails. New depositions for the new case, a few memos from Mr. Martin, some good, others... naw. An email from his mother, complaining she hasn't heard from him. A tweet from one of his peeps inviting him to the latest trending Miami Beach spot. He labeled that one "urgent" so he wouldn't forget about it. Earmarked some of the secretary's emails and a couple of audio memos, morning had crept on him.

Shit, it's morning. He lay down on the bed cover and closed his eyes. Forty-five minutes later, he was as restless as before. Martin had agreed to the extra day, so why not make the best of it. Got ready, casual today. He didn't go far; at a Front street store got his mother a Key West hand painted wine glass and a naughty t-shirt for his dad.

Tweet from Madge, his secretary, reminding him of the morning meeting via computer feed. Neelam ran back to his room and opened

his laptop.

"Morning, Neelam," Mr. Martin said. "The good news is the client will retain our services. Now let's review your notes from yesterday." Around the table the other partners discussed and offered Neelam advice. This was the procedure for every important client. Neelam offered his opinion on the others' cases as well. Neelam felt the meeting took forever. He even yawned audibly enough to grab Mr. Martin's attention.

"Neelam, are you OK?"

"Sorry, just a bit tired." Neelam could hear the noises that mark the end of the meeting. Computers shutting down; chairs been moved. People stretching.

"Don't forget to do your follow-up phone calls people," Mr. Martin was trying to make sure everybody heard him. "I don't want emails or tweets. I can't stress enough the value of real communication. Neelam, don't shut down yet." Conversation in the background lasted for a few more minutes.

"Neelam, you're on the right track," said Mr. Martin. "You take direction well, and I like that. Now make sure that you talk to Madge, she has some questions about the billing and get ready for tomorrow. It's going to be a long day. Be careful on the road."

"Thanks, Mr. Martin. I will see you tomorrow at 7:30." Neelam closed the feed and worked with Madge and spent the rest of the morning reading up on the new case. At eleven, check out time, he contacted the front desk and added an extra night even though he was leaving that afternoon. He needed the time; he wanted to try to sleep before heading north. Around four, Madge finished the billing and had called it a day. Neelam made his follow-up phone calls to the client, Ponce and others. That lasted another forty-five minutes. He tried to sleep, no luck, he just laid there with his eyes closed. He finished his bag, took a hot shower and lay down in his bed for what he thought was a few minutes. When he looked at the clock on the nightstand, it was about 6 in the evening.

He quickly got dressed and headed for the lobby to check out. As he left the parking garage of the Westin Hotel, he looked across the stop sign on Greene and Whitehead streets toward Clinton Square and saw the Tea Pot Coffee House. A quick turn left and a dash in for an Earl Grey to go. Around the block and it was a left at Duval and Greene, then a right on Simonton and up to Eaton where he hung a left and was on his way back to Miami. A quick look on the back mirror and a wonderful pink, yellow and purple sky said goodbye. "Don't worry, I will be back," he said out loud turning his black BMW left onto North Roosevelt Boulevard, under a new round of renovations after the ones performed around 2013 failed. In his rearview mirror, Neelam saw a big pink ball of fire among the clouds.

By the time Neelam hit Big Pine Key, the caffeine in the tea started to wear off. At the Bahia Honda Bridge, he decided to push it all the way to Marathon and assess the situation after the Seven Mile Bridge. The BMW was purring, the music was right and Neelam was cruising along.

The headline of the front page of *The Key West Citizen* read:

ANOTHER FATAL CRASH ON THE SEVEN MILE BRIDGE

Citizen Staff

Investigators say the driver of a black BMW sedan fell asleep before crashing into a fuel delivery truck on the Seven Mile Bridge killing himself and the truck driver.

Neelam Zakir, 28, of Miami died along with Ibrahim Patchet, 45, of Miramar. Witnesses saw the dark northbound car veer into the southbound lane, hitting the tanker truck head on, said Florida Highway Patrol spokesman Lt. Chris Santangelo.

The truck, carrying about 8,000 gallons of gasoline, jackknifed and burst in a ball of fire visible for miles that took two hours to extinguish. Both Patchet and Zakir, still in their vehicles were pronounced dead at the scene.

Patchet, a truck driver for the last 20 years, was a father of four. Zakir was single.

The bridge was expected to reopen about 9:30 a.m. today said Sherriff's office spokeswoman Danette Baso, 14 hours after the crash near Mile Marker 41. FHP was clearing the road and state officials were to assess the safety of the bridge, Baso said. As of 11:00 p.m. press deadlines, engineers with Florida's Department of Transportation had found only minimal damage to the bridge.

Crews responds to a fatal accident on the Marathon side of the Seven Mile Bridge. Parts of U.S.1 can be shut down for hours after one of these incidents. Photo by Rob O'Neal.

Epilogue

Scratchy is hunting for food and catnip around the writer's studio.

EPILOGUE

Late 2020s

I come back to Key West every possible weekend for many reasons but no matter what is happening in my world, the house on Eliza St. is my refuge. Daddy's love of cooking comforts me, and Dad's arms protect me. Even before leaving, I'm already missing it.

Daddy takes care of his business and participates in several children's charities; Dad still works at the hospital with pediatric AIDS. They continue to foster children, but because of their busy lives, they do it for short terms. They help anybody that is in the process of adoption and keep abreast of the judicial goings-on in that arena.

Sheri and Sarah have added two more poodles, Galileo and Madame Curie, to their fur family. Sarah commutes all over the Keys and has her own practice. She has made many friends among the police force both city and statewide due to her driving record. Sheri has stopped bartending but still has an interest in the Black Onyx.

Emilia and I have forged a very strong and lasting friendship. She got married and has a lovely daughter, who is my goddaughter. Her husband, a partner in an important Miami law firm, gets amused when people think that Emilia and I are a couple. It might annoy Emilia or not, depending on her mood that particular day. We still work together at the ACLU in Miami and we are still fighting the causes that are important to us. Several appeals are pending. Judge Johnson has agreed with us several times, so the odds are improving. The judge has been nominated to the state's supreme court, and we will follow him there.

One night after writing the last paragraph of one of our briefings, with Chinese food containers and half a bottle of wine strewn over the table,

I said to her, "Emilia, I'm tired of all this legal language. I want to write something else."

She replied, "You should give serious consideration to writing that book about your family."

"Nah, it would turn into a legalese thing fairly quickly. I mean fiction, something that could or couldn't be attached to the facts of what really happened," I said, kind of excited.

"You can't get it to be any more fiction than Key West and its quirky history," Emilia replied.

"Yeah, that's what we need. Another four generations of a Conch family saga based in Key West," I pointed out cynically. "I even have the title," I said as I ripped off the first page of the yellow legal pad I was using. I took a black broad marker and wrote: *The Funerals of Key West.*

Emilia laughed. "That's way too corny."

"Yep, and Hemingway just dropped his Underwood on his big toe at the house on Whitehead Street."

"And it bounced off his toe and killed one of those six-toed cats that he never had," Emilia was rolling on the floor laughing. "Wait, wait, I got the beginning paragraph. She started narrating as she was writing on her legal pad:

> *It was a dark and stormy hurricane night in the Florida Keys. All was murky and quiet at the house on Whitehead Street. At the author's writing study in the back of the property, only a kerosene lamp alit the standing table where the writer was engrossed deeply into the craft. Cliquety, click, click, cliquety, click, click, clapow! The writer returned the carriage of the typewriter so hard with his enormous hands, that it flew of its hinges; it landed on his right big toe, bounced off again landing on the head of the unsuspecting six-toed cat, sleeping close by. Only a moan was heard, then it exhaled.*

> *"Damned machine" the writer screamed as he held his toe and looked at the cat.*
>
> *"Damned… Scratchy!" he yelled as he held the lifeless feline on his massive hands.*
>
> *He petted the cat one more time, opened the nearby window, tossed the cat out, peed and, after putting the carriage back in its place, continued writing cliquety, click, click.*

"Emilia, I can't believe you just came up with that!"

"Why not, I don't believe in sacred cows!" Emilia said, bringing the wine glass to her lips. "Now let's get back to work."

The window of the Hemingway House detached writing studio as seen from Olivia St.

The Hemingway House became a tourist attraction in Key West in the 1960s. Other houses owned by renowned authors in Key West have remained in private hands. Photos courtesy of the Monroe County Library.

Postscript

Photos courtesy of Rob O'Neal and Mike Hentz

POSTSCRIPT: OF LITERARY AGENTS, MOVIES, MICROBUSES AND DRAG QUEENS

> "The more things change, the more they stay the same..." Key West has changed a lot, but it also has stayed the same. People come and people go, some try to change things, some fight to keep it the same. It is the process of the ebb and flow of its man-made tourist beaches on top of coral rock.

"Angie, did you give me the copies of the depositions for the Walmart case?" Emilia's voice came from her organized office.

"I gaze them or yer dest this mirming," came the voice from the other office. She could hear the ruffle of papers being moved around.

"Angie, take your pen out of your mouth. I can't understand a word you're saying. What about the depositions?"

"Here." Angie came in with several thick file folders. They have a system of color-coding the files according their content; green files were reserved for witness' depositions. Angie was wearing a pair of jeans, a silk flowery blouse, and a baseball cap with her hair in a ponytail coming out of the back. The pen had moved from her mouth to the back of the hat. A pair of low-heeled pumps completed the outfit.

"No, you said that you placed them on my desk this morning." Emilia, impeccably dressed in an Alexander McQueen suit, smiled as she examined Angie's ensemble. "You haven't gotten to your laundry yet, huh? Though I have to say that you have an uncanny ability to look absolutely adorable in shabby chic!"

"I love you too, but I don't have a husband/washer/dryer combo in my apartment."

"There is this thing called the dry cleaners, dear. Everybody has access to them in our modern world," Emilia said as she was leaving for court. "I'll see you later today. Don't forget dinner tonight."

"Whatever," said Angie.

II

"This courtroom is stuffy today," thought Emilia as she sat at her table. "Another humid day in the Sunshine state." The room was the usual courtroom setting, two seating areas for the public divided by the path leading to the judge's bench at center stage flanked by the flags of the state and the nation. The seal of the state was behind the judge's seat atop the photograph of the president.

"Morning." Edwin Carter was already seated. Tall, slender and in his early fifties, Edwin had a long career with the American Civil Liberties Union and was happy to be second chair. Well dressed but casual, his demeanor was as relaxed as his easy smile. He was a good friend of both Emilia and Angie and looked after them like family.

"Morning," said Emilia. She gave Edwin a hug and then shook Evalina Williams' hand. Evalina was an intern studying law at Florida International University.

"Are we ready?" asked Emilia.

"Charge ahead, boss," answered Carter.

The opposing counsel table was a sea of blue custom-made suits and red power ties. "So nineteen eighties," thought Emilia. The first chair was Jack Lee; he made his career defending corporations, the Republican Party and some of the most notorious personalities of the media and entertainment industries. Tailored from head to toe, nothing was out of place. Also in his early fifties, he resembled his namesake, Robert E. Lee, with his height, silver hair and perfect complexion.

The first round on the Walmart case was two hours long. Emilia and her team argued several points: everything from low wages, employee break times, and the possibilities of advancement for women in the company. Opposing counsel bogged down the court for two more hours with all sorts of information on labor laws, comparing them with the actual company practices. They also placed in front of the judge binders and binders of paperwork on women who had climbed the company's corporate ladder.

"How many of these women have become top executives?" Emilia asked. "Let's take for example, the case of Mrs. Smith—not her real name—who has been a regional manager in Miami for the past fifteen years. She hasn't advanced to the next step. How long does it takes a male employee to go from regional manager to regional vice-president?"

The judge looked at the blue suits, who were conferring feverishly.

"Any number of years. There isn't a set curve," answered Lee with resolution.

Angie pushed a button on her hand-held control and a chart appeared on the courtroom's screen. "Our research illustrates that it takes a male employee an average of four to five years to access the next step. Mrs. Smith has ten years of experience over the latest male co-worker who had advanced to the next. What's the hold-up?"

The next table resumed the intense conferring.

"OK, it's one thirty; I've had enough numbers for the morning," said Judge Kay. "Let's break for lunch. Mr. Lee will answer the question when we come back at three o'clock."

Evalina went back for an afternoon class at the university; Edwin and Emilia sat down at the Cafeteria Única, around the corner from the courthouse. It was decorated with posters of Cuba and Puerto Rico, framed with abandon and without a cohesive style. The tables and chairs looked like an odd collection from a secondhand store, but all had the same checkered red-and-white plastic tablecloths, with a bottle in the middle that contained some ixora flowers in varying stages of decay. Around the flowers were different arrangements of commercial salt and peppers, bottles of homemade hot sauce, and napkin holders. The floor was clean, but the thick smell of old frying oil that hadn't been changed hung in the air. Everything was deep fried and carefully scooped in the ubiquitous square red paper baskets.

Emilia and Edwin ordered sodas and Cuban mix sandwiches.

They chit-chatted for a while, waiting for the food to arrive. After a few minutes the waitress Amelia came with the food. Known to all the lawyers in Miami, Amelia was a dark-haired beauty past her thirties, clothes a bit snug, but not enough yet. Her bright red lipstick and next-door beauty parlor manicure with rhinestone nails that couldn't hold anything right were as sensual as her legs, which supported not only her body, but also her legend as one of the most incredible dancers in the area. She called everybody *Mami* and *Papi*.

"*Aquí están sus sandwiches*, here are your sandwiches *y Mami, al tuyo le puse menos mayonesa que al de él porque nosotras tenemos que velar la línea.* I put less mayo in yours because we have to watch that stuff. *Pero al de él le puse más porque lo tengo que engordar un poquito* I doubled his, because I have to flesh him out more *pa'que cuando me saque a bailar, pueda con to'esto que Dios me dio y que no me quita nadie*—so when he goes dancing with me he can be man enough to deal with all of this womanhood that the good Lord gave me which no one can take away." Her nails caressed Edwin's face as lightly as the flutter of butterfly's wings. The whole place laughed, as usual. Then, as in a command performance, she pivoted and danced back to the kitchen.

"You remember when you dropped some files yesterday in my office?" asked Edwin.

"Sure, did I miss something? I can ask Angie to bring it to us." Emilia bit a chunk out of her sandwich.

"No, you didn't miss anything. I got extra files."

"Huh?" Emilia stopped mid-bite and looked at Edwin, puzzled. She gulped some soda. "Which files?"

Edwin slid a purple folder in front of her, "I didn't know you wrote fiction," he said, wearing an impish grin.

"What?" She opened the file. "I don't write. This is Angie's 'purple file,' her book. It's more like a stress release thing."

"Really? You're kidding me; she wrote this?" he said, "I thought it was you. Well, I'm in more trouble than I thought. I figured it would be hard to get you to let me help you with it. But now I have to contend with Miss Stubbornness herself."

"What are you talking about?" Emilia was both amused and annoyed.

"Well, I really liked what I read so far. So I took a little liberty and emailed one of the stories to a literary agent friend from Chicago. She's really interested."

"No, you didn't," Emilia replied. "She's going to flip out. She's such a flake. She probably was overwhelmed the day she gave me the files and didn't realized that she included the 'purple file' as she likes to call it. Purple is her favorite color. I don't think it's meant for publication," Emilia said, putting aside her sandwich. "We have to go back."

"Well, you think I should just give her back the file and forget the matter?" Edwin finished his soda, and put down some money on the table before they walked out. "Of course I'll apologize, but she gave you the file."

"I don't think you have to worry too much about it. It wasn't intentional. The way her office is organized, it's a miracle that she can find anything at all. Every time I look at her desk, the hair on the back of my neck stands up. She's a brilliant lawyer but a messy person." Emilia's pace was picking up, even though they were already close to the courthouse.

"Slow down! We still have fifteen minutes, and we're less than a block away from the courthouse."

"Sorry," Emilia said, pausing, "I had this conversation with her about it a few months back. Anybody who writes wants to be read, in my opinion. We discussed it for hours. My argument was the *Diary of Anne Frank*. She died and she had no say in the matter of publication, but because her father made the decision, we now have a document with an important insight into the mind of a young woman in the middle of the most traumatic event of the Twentieth Century." They turned the corner toward the building's front door.

"Was she opposed to your argument?"

Emilia paused for a moment, remembering the conversation. "I think I gave her something to think about. She admitted that she's not writing a diary, otherwise I wouldn't have seen it." They went through the first set of doors and presented their badges. The duty guard checked them against her list. "I believe she started writing a few months before that conversation."

They got to the second group of guards, where their briefcases were checked and they went through the new metal detectors. "We're having dinner tonight at the house. You're welcome to join us. Give me the file; it will be the excuse to pick up that conversation again. I do agree with you, she can write and she has good timing." She stopped and added, "And it should be shared." She put the purple folder in her briefcase as they exited the elevator.

"Can't be there tonight. I've made plans. But how about my apology?" Edwin almost whispered.

"Nothing to apologize for—text her. We all know now that it was a mistake. I'm curious, what was the reaction from your friend?"

"She's very interested. I haven't seen her this excited about a possible book in a while." Edwin, always the gentleman, opened the door for Emilia.

Emilia's heels echoed her entrance to the courtroom. The opposition counsel's table was swimming again with blue-suit activity.

Jack Lee turned around and stood up. All he needed was a saber at his side to complete the look of the most famous painting of the old general. All Southern charm and gentility, he bowed his head in salutation.

"Counselor, the sound of your lovely shoes makes my heart skip a beat. I hope you had a wonderful lunch," he smiled, adding, "Mr. Carter, it's good to see you too."

"I hope you had a good lunch, too, Mr. Lee, always such a charmer," Edwin replied. The guard in the front cleared his throat. The afternoon round was about to begin.

III

Angie arrived at Emilia's house late. Emilia was running late too. Robert was almost finished preparing dinner and had little Olivia in her high chair. She was already fed. Angie hadn't changed; she came directly from the office. A shadow appeared in the kitchen door window.

"Door is open, Angie."

"How did you know it was me?" she asked as she came in.

"Emilia always uses the front door," said Robert.

"Here's your wine. Emilia just texted me; she'll be here in a few minutes," Robert said as he pointed to the glass. "Olivia, say bye-bye to auntie Angie. You're going night-night," he said as he held the baby out to Angie. She played with Olivia for a few minutes before handing her back.

"I'll be back in a few, you know where everything is." He walked toward the bedrooms.

"This smells delicious. What is it?" Robert's answer from the bedroom was unintelligible. The front door opened, heels announcing Emilia.

"Honey, is Angie here yet?" she called.

"Yes, dear," answered Angie. "Hand over my purple file. Edwin texted me. You might've thought he hacked into the CIA; he was so apologetic."

"He thought it was mine." Emilia laughed. "You should have seen his face when I told him it was yours." She walked past Angie and into her bedroom. As the conversation continued she changed into more comfortable clothing.

“What, I don’t look like I could write?” Angie was annoyed.

“Of course you do. In fact you look like Willa Cather,” Emilia said as she came back into the kitchen barefoot, in a cozy jogging suit, purple file in hand. Angie had poured wine for her.

“Yes, but of course, Ms. Toklas,” Angie said. They both laughed.

“You’re both so high school,” said Robert as he came into the kitchen. “At least use references that people will know, not stuff that has to be Googled to make sense. Anyway, Olivia is down for the night. Turn the microphone up. I installed the new cameras in her bedroom today. Check out the monitor.” He pointed proudly to the computer monitor atop the cabinets. It gave full view of Olivia’s bedroom as part of the latest in home fashion monitoring devices. “What’s that?” he asked pointing at the file.

“Honey, you’re looking at the first oeuvre by Ms. Emily Dickinson…oh, excuse me, Ms. Angie Zúñiga Carmichael.”

“Well, I was going to keep it to myself,” Angie said, “but SOMEONE went into my office and STOLE my work. And BTW Emily Dickinson was a poet not a novelist, just so you know.”

“I know. So we’re a novelist now, how interesting…AND BTW to you too…if the cat is out of the bag, it’s your own doing. Your office is a mess, and you mistook your file for some office work. You ought to be more careful in the future.” Emilia punched Angie gently in the shoulder.

“OK, OK, it was my fault.”

Talk of publishing, writer’s rights and literature punctuated dinner. Robert had been unaware of Angie’s aspirations and, like Emilia, encouraged her to pursue it. “What you need is a good lawyer,” he said, and they all laughed.

“You should think about movie rights,” said Emilia.

"What? I don't think it's that good," Angie said.

Robert rolled his eyes. "OK guys, you can chew all the fat you want, though it's getting late. We all need to work tomorrow. I'll go and check on Olivia and bid the fair maidens adieu and good night. If you guys polish off that second bottle, Angie is sleeping on the sofa."

IV

Patrick "Pat" O'Celacanth was in his office, looking through some old photos. He liked to remember how much work he put in on his ladder to the business world. Patrick, William "Taz" Morgan and Dick Dullea founded Historic Quests in the 1980s. They pulled together what little money they had got together to start. Originally they wanted to sell history to the tourists who came to the Island, but it proved too costly and had too many legal requirements. Dick left the company to pursue other ventures; Pat and Taz shifted their focus just enough to tip-toe around the legal stuff. As long as they didn't claim historical certainty, they could say whatever they wanted. History has always been a pliable medium. Historic Quests became Hypnotic Quests, and now was one of the most profitable entertainment businesses on the island.

They started out with walking tours, but it cost too much to hydrate the tourists, especially in the hot months, and some of them didn't want to walk at all. The tours were shortened and bicycles substituted. Still it was too physically demanding for many of the visitors.

So they came up with the idea of open-air buses. The City Commission at the time allowed them only microbuses, given Key West's narrow streets. They kept modifying the open-air idea until they arrived at the current model. It looked like a worm, cut lengthwise, sporting a summer hat with windows that can be easily lowered down when it rains. The vehicles were painted bright red with yellow decals depicting the company's logo. Today both motorists and pedestrians consider them the rats of the city streets.

"Taz, I just got off the phone with commissioner Ponce." Pat usually shouted across the office; he had been losing his hearing.

"Yeah, what the old fart has to say?" Taz came closer to the desk.

"You remember that lawyer kid who derailed the development of Eden's Shore behind Sears?"

"Sure, she's the daughter of that pediatrician that married that other guy, isn't she?" Taz scratched his head.

"Yep, one and the same," said Pat. "Well, apparently she wrote a book that's creating some buzz in the business."

"Legal book?" Taz was curious.

"No, it's based on the history of her family, but fictionalized." Pat paused for a minute but Taz was mum. "My kind of book. Ponce says there's talk about a movie. He thinks, and I agree with him, there's money for all if we play it right." Taz was still quiet but attentive. "The first thing is to get a copy of the book."

One flip of the iPad and Pat was set up for the night. He read it, and he liked it--a lot. After a few days of pondering, he came up with a plan. "Remember," he said to Taz after hearing his objections to the plan. "All we have to do is tip-toe around it; it's fiction, for God's sake."

V

Hands were shaken, other hands were greased, and Commissioner Ponce did his best job politicking and maneuvering. A new route among the many companies that peddle historical entertainment was born. It started at the depot on South and Simonton streets. Pat wanted beautiful women dressed in 1940's garb, with impeccable coifs and hats to lead the tours. An employment company interviewed many applicants, and when it got down to the leading contestants after two weeks, a small pool of possible candidates came up. Pat thought carefully about it and went for the drag queens.

Different from some of the other candidates, Porsha del Puerto showed up every single time punctually, dressed on point, and sober. A statuesque figure dressed in a bright red Chanel knockoff suit, platinum blond hair reminiscent of Jayne Mansfield, she delivered the script with a flawless Southern twang.

The first stop was a dilapidated apartment building in Bahama Village chosen to be Magdalena Zúñiga's home. The tourists ate it all up and took pictures of everything, including startled residents who happened to look out the jalousies of their own windows, and the chickens roaming around. Click, click, click, said the iPhones.

Next were the judicial buildings on Whitehead Street. Tourists were told that it was here where Judge Zúñiga worked and Elías Ramírez was found guilty and sentenced to death.

The tour passed the Hemingway House on the way to Truman Avenue. The visitors were driven down to Duval Street where the microbus turned left. The old Viva Zapata restaurant used to be in the 900 block. The building was being renovated, but meanwhile posed as the Medianoche Club. On this stop, Porsha was joined by a trio of singers who regaled the tourists with 1940's songs, in English and Spanish. A delight in sequin gowns and elbow gloves, one of them "died" gloriously at the end of the last song. Click, click, click. A tourist tweeted her friends about the horror of witnessing a woman dying and no one doing anything about it. The friends called the police, who explained it was an act. It wouldn't be the last time that happened.

Along Duval Street, toward the Gulf, tourists were shown places to drink and eat, advertisement plugs paid for by the businesses owners. Porsha answered all sorts of questions. Right on Eaton Street, right again on Eisenhower Drive, which was the edge of town in the twenties and thirties. A beautiful white house with a turret stood alone on a corner lot. Now a Key West real estate mogul owned it. Eighty-five years ago, a young judge who emigrated from Cuba, his wife and three daughters bought it. At each of the stops, Porsha del Puerto delivered a monologue with gusto. There wasn't a dry eye in the microbus after she recited the particulars of the judge's death.

The vehicle drove back to Truman, which became North Roosevelt Boulevard and turned left. Porsha told her audience some facts about the city-owned Garrison Bight, pointing out the floating restaurant whose owner had paid for this privilege. The tour leaving old town, turned right on First Street, heading to Atlantic Boulevard turning into the circular drive entrance for the 1800 Atlantic Condos. That was the cue for the next group of actors to set up shop in the opposite corner. While the microbus rounded the driveway, Porsha told everyone the story of "Siña María" and an actress dressed as a homeless woman threw T-shirts and small bottles of water to the tourists.

One morning the actors were delayed by another three-year construction project in another part of town. Unbeknown to Porsha and the tourists, a real homeless woman was resting at the corner. The bright red vehicle with flaming yellow logos and decals, the overdressed über-blond guide, and the flurry of iPhone cameras and mega slick video recorders overwhelmed the schizophrenic woman, who thought the devil himself was addressing her as fire and brimstone rained down. She threw whatever leftover food, dirty laundry, and anything else in her cart at the tourists. Click, click, click. Cameras followed as she ran screaming and cussing down Bertha Street toward Smathers Beach. One of the tourists uploaded the video on YouTube and it garnered over three million hits.

The tour went back up First Street, took a right on Flagler Avenue past The Salvation Army building and the Thrift Store were Siña María had bought her first pair of used sneakers. Then came Key West High School. The buildings were new, but Porsha told the audience that the site had been there for more than fifty years. Several movies had been filmed in the modern jail-like hurricane proof building. As she discussed some of these films, the microbus turned into Hamaca Park.

Porsha points out at the place were Elías Ramírez had his last conversation with David Findley. Several tourists later claimed that they photographed a spectral figure resembling Mr. Findley. Some of those shots were posted on the company's web site, where online visitors were welcomed to make up their own minds. The website also features tweets, other postings, letters and scanned-in handwritten notes from the followers and believers of Elías and David sightings and deeds among the living. Flowers, rainbow flags, candles and other offerings appeared in that area of the park every December 22nd, the anniversary of Elías' death.

After more pictures and a leg stretching at the park, the tourists piled back into the microbus, where Porsha was joined again by some of the re-enactors including the "dead" singer who caused the almost weekly consternation back at the Duval Street stop. Refreshments were served and unmelodious singing and merriment punctuated the trip back to the depot at South and Simonton.

A cash bar greeted their return and a computer station was supplied where the tourists uploaded their pictures and wrote the latest testimonials. The gift shop was stocked with copies of the book, *The Funerals of Key West*, framed pictures of the tour participants and T-shirts. The bigger sellers were "I've seen the head at Hamaca Park," and "David touched my cheeks before the shock." The designers did not miss the sexual references and innuendo that had become part of the Key West tourist mystique of the last two centuries. The tour happened only once a week and reservations were required before boarding. It was so popular that it was booked months in advance.

VI

Emilia peeked into Angie's office, where her friend was buried under the Walmart Case.

"Angie, would you please clean up in this office. It reminds me of that hoarders show on TV." Emilia was standing at the doorstep.

"I kno ware everythand is," Angie said, pen in her mouth.

"Obviously not where your phone is. Would you mind answering it? Your agent is calling you. She has good news about the book."

The next day, buried on the left bottom of page 7A of *The Key West Citizen*, alongside the obits appeared the following:

KWFC NEGOTIATES FOR FILM ABOUT LOCAL FAMILY

Citizen Staff

> *Negotiations have concluded between the Key West Film Commission, literary agents and the independent film company InUrbane to begin the filming of the Zúñiga family's story depicted in the book The Funerals of Key West. None of parties involved disclosed details of the final agreement. City Commissioner Ralph Ponce's involvement has puzzled some, who wonder if the politician has a financial stake in the movie. Ponce did not reply to The Citizen's repeated requests for comments.*

CHARACTERS, EDITORS AND OTHERS (INCLUDING THE AUTHOR) HAVE REACTED TO THIS BOOK. SOME OF THEIR MUSINGS ARE TRANSLATED INTO ENGLISH FOR THE BENEFIT OF THE READER.

LA INSPIRACIÓN HARTA DE APOYAR ESTA OBRA ATORMENTA AL ESCRITOR A TRAVÉS DE UN SONETO.

¿Tú tratas de imitar escritura?
Tú que tienes poca mente y está ausente,
Que a tus méritos está resistente,
¿Es que no tienes ninguna cordura?

Maniático de atar, es locura.
¿Es tu falta de ser lo mas prudente?
Tu harta necedad ora es contundente,
Debes dejarte de tanta frescura.

Y vive en la eterna seguridad:
De que nadie es profeta en su tierra,
ya no sigas en esta certidumbre.

Es obvio que el seso no te da lumbre.
Tu musa se convirtió en fiera,
¡te gastó una buena broma de verdad!

INSPIRATION, TIRED OF SUSTAINING THIS WRITING PROJECT, TEASES THE AUTHOR VIA A SPANISH SONNET.

Fool, are you trying now to imitate writing?
You of little sense, which is mostly absent,
your mind is dead, and your merits not present.
You must be insane! She stated not chiding.

Are you that crazy, to try your hand at flying?
Do you think prudent, to show lack of talent?
Your follies demonstrate you're deficient;
you should leave behind your constant gliding.

You should remember the old wise proverb:
which says: "No one is a prophet in his own land."
And I have no more gifts for you to proffer.

It's obvious, there's no light to this process.
And a beast instead of a muse you command;
who had a laugh at your "so called" success!

EL AUTOR CONTESTA A SU MUSA EN UNA DÉCIMA.

Quiero hablar a mi musa,
que así tan mal me ha tratado.
Que me llama autor malogrado,
y de mi escribir, abusa.
Y se afana sin excusa,
de mi burlarse y agraviarme.
Ella pretende dejarme
sin libro, prenda y dinero,
¡que es su requerido anhelo,
de mi novela librarse!

THE AUTHOR RESPONDS TO HIS INSPIRATION'S CHARGES, WRITING A SPANISH DÉCIMA.

I want to speak to my muse
who has treated me so badly.
No author, she calls me coldly,
my writing she boldly abuse.
And she tries without excuse,
makes of me, the butt of her joke,
no clothes, without money, just broke.
It is her required longing,
(my mind and soul eroding)
my book and novel to choke!

SHERI LOHR WROTE THIS POEM FOR MAGDALENA AFTER READING *"IT'S BEEN TOO LONG."*

MAGDALENA

¡Canta angelito! Canta, ¡Por Dios!
Sing for the ones who love you;
Sing for all your ghosts.
Sing for the guy at the end of the bar
and the girl at the end of her rope.
Sing *bienvenidos* sweet dark night
and *adiós* to yesterday's hope.

Sweet *sinsonte* sing for us. Sing your breaking heart.
Sing for the dreams that shatter
and lovers who must part.
Fallen angel, raise your voice
to reach for heaven's door.
Send your song to holy heights
your wounded soul will see no more.

Named for the sainted sinner, gifted by God's grace,
how did your promise turn to smoke
and vanish without a trace?
But lift your crushed and tattered wings
for one triumphal flight
and let your notes emerge from ash
to blaze eternally in light.

SHERI LOHR ESCRIBIÓ UN POEMA A MAGDALENA DESPUÉS DE LEER, *"¡CÓMO HAN PASADO LOS AÑOS!"*

MAGDALENA

Sing little angel! Sing for Heaven's Sake!
Canta a los que te quieren
Canta a todos tus fantasmas
Y cántale al tipo sentado en el bar,
canta a la niña desesperada.
Canta *Welcome* a la noche oscura
y *good-bye* a la esperanza de ayer.

Dulce *mockingbird* cántanos, de tu pobre corazón.
Canta por los sueños rotos.
Y de amantes que han de partir.
Ángel caído, eleva voz
a las puertas del cielo,
llega a las sagradas alturas,
que tu alma herida no volverá a ver.

Honra a La Pecadora, llena eres de Gracia,
¿cómo tu promesa tornó en humo
y se desveneció?
Levanta tus alas rotas y maltrechas
para un vuelo triunfal,
tus notas emergen de cenizas,
cual llamas eternas en la luz.

LASSIE WROTE A LETTER TO NEWTON AFTER READING THE STORY OF ANGIE'S VISIT TO KEY WEST

Dear Newton:

I heard about you and couldn't wait to put my paw to paper. Newton, you need a few pointers from someone who has been there.

They say fame is futile; they lie through their teeth. Not only am I famous, but also I have sired a whole line of descendants who are still working. I wish the same for you. Start reproducing now, the sooner the better.

They say beauty is vain; they lie through their fangs. I have a hair color for humans named after me. Your black curls should be patented; please talk to your human about this.

They say that animal acting careers are short. They lie through their molars. There are movies, TV series, board games and dolls patterned after my image. I have had a 70-year career under my collar. Look around you, Jack Russell Terriers (Eddie in Frasier, and Uggie who has made three movies and counting), and those pesky Chihuahuas from Hollywood are all making money. Don't underestimate the power of marketing. If your human doesn't follow up on this, bite her on the ankles until she understands.

Don't waste your talents for a treat!
Sincerely,
Lassie

NEWTON REPLIES TO LASSIE:

Dear Lassie, Paw High Four to you!

I pondered your thoughts carefully and discussed some ideas with my mom. It didn't take much time to convince her, since your arguments were so well constructed. We decided to get an agent or agency to manage my budding career. After weighing our options, she signed me at BiSCuiKt (Bailey, Shapiro, Cochran & Kardashian) Animal Modeling and Acting Agency. They offer a diverse portfolio with acting, modeling, training and singing lessons.

Hollywood here I come!

Newton

PS. I envy your prowess as a stud, but since I was adopted at the local refuge, my ability to...hum...how can I put it in delicate terms...to create several generations of artists has been severely severed.

N

ANOTHER WRITER WROTE A POEM AFTER READING THE STORY OF ANGIE'S VISIT TO KEY WEST

THE JUDGE, ANGIE AND ME.

In Fiction:
Doña María Isabel shouted from the niche besides yours.
Arturo Rivera scribbled until the day of his departure.
Carmen and Siña María are waiting for your return.
Magdalena is singing, venting her rage at such wrong.

In Life:
Lois C. touched me today, as she rests nearby you.
Julia never met you, but yearns for your advice.
Linda is looking for you, in the traces of her face.
Lolo is writing with my pen to make it right.

In Life:
You're resting alongside the tales and the murmurs of your death.
Are you walking alongside North Beach Drive?
Or maybe you're looking out of the turret's window,
for CeCe and John Jr. are outside playing in the sand.

In Fiction:
Angie and me? You ask, looking at me from the edge of the page.
We are interlacing descriptions, distilling smoke prisons
to house conscripted words, which might or not be yours,
inscribing bits in floating paper pieces of your story in ours.

OTRO ESCRITOR ESCRIBIÓ UN POEMA DESPUÉS DE LEER LA HISTORIA DE LA VISITA DE ANGIE A KEY WEST

EL JUEZ, ANGIE Y YO.

En la ficción,
Doña María Isabel gritó desde el nicho, al lado del suyo.
Arturo Rivera escribió hasta el día de su partida.
Carmen y Siña María están esperando su regreso.
Magdalena está cantando, desahogando su rabia por tal mal.

En la realidad,
Lois C. me ha tocado hoy, mientras ella descansa a su lado.
Julia nunca lo conoció, pero desea escuchar sus consejos.
Linda está buscándolo, en las huellas de su cara.
Lolo está escribiendo con mi pluma para corregir la historia.

En la realidad,
Descansa junto a los cuentos, y los rumores de su muerte.
¿Está caminando por North Beach Drive?
O tal vez mirando desde la ventana de la torre,
porque CeCe y John Jr. están jugando afuera en la arena.

En la ficción,
¿Angie y yo? Pregunta mirándome desde el borde de la página.
Estamos entrelazado descripciones, destilando cárceles de humo
para albergar palabras alistadas, que pueden o no ser las suyas.
Inscribiendo en pedacitos flotantes de papel su historia en la nuestra.

TEXTING CONVERSATIONS BETWEEN THE AUTHOR AND AN EDITOR ABOUT ANGIE'S VISIT STORY.

When necessary for clarity, the excerpts from the text are in regular type and inside quotes marks. The questions/comments from the editor are in italics. For those of us who were born before texting ... btw= by the way, wth=what the heck, bc or b/c=because.

Editor: (pp 151) IF [Angie & Emilia] *were friends for a long time, she'd already know everything about the family history.*

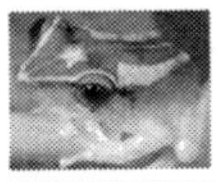

Author: Not necessarily. Do you tell EVERYTHING to your BFF?

Editor: *what is the point of him being startled?*

Author: Dictionary says: "to surprise or frighten (someone) suddenly and usually not seriously."

Editor: (pp 162) *Angie? It's not a funny nickname*

Author: HUH? WTH? I think you're going to have a lot of hate tweetts from people named Angie when this is published.

Editor: *why did they come early, btw?*

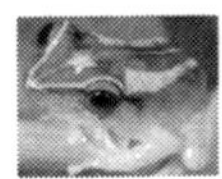

Author: Good point, will add explanation.

Editor: You have to call the fathers Daddy Steven and Dad Manny.

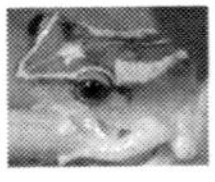

Author: No, she sounds childish. An adult artist used the same terms [Dad/Daddy] in a recent TV interview. It wasn't confusing at all.

Editor: (pp 152) *Regarding the description of the kitchen.* "Just now it's piled high with Daddy Steven's real estate paperwork — contracts, rulebooks and MLS lists — surrounding a big salad bowl at center." *That's an odd segue*

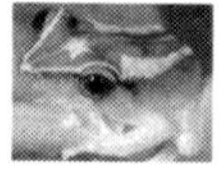

Author: HUH?

Editor: (pp 153) *What are the 2 laws? No gay marriage & what's the other one? Confusing paragraph.*

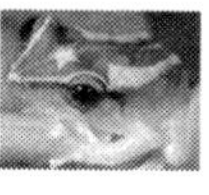

Author: Opposition to Gay Marriage and Proving Your Gender when applying for a marriage license. Yes, the "lawmakers" in Florida did think about these things. I don't think is confusing at all. It's infuriating and intrusive but not confusing. But will rewrite

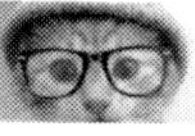

Editor: *So that was the ruling? That the marriage was/is invalid? Maybe want to say how long marriage was.*

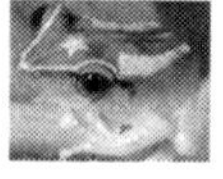

Author: Yes. Thinking about it, ten years? Maybe. Is it that important?

Editor: (pp 154) *The conversation about the "wife" of the transgendered person, makes the discussion difficult to follow. If they are defending "john doe," why would they talk about the wife?*

Author: Angie had a lapse of judgment. I'm deleting that part of the conversation. Good catch! OK, its changed.

Editor: (pp 154) *Delete the word "again." Emilia didn't know how long Angie has been writing.*

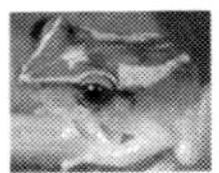

Author: Deleted

Editor: (pp 154) Daddy figured out what was going on. *But we haven't, so this sentence is annoying.*

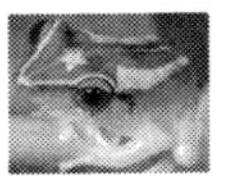

Author: How's this annoying? The fact that he tells Emilia the story, lets the reader know "what was going on."

Editor: *When I say so, ;) Change it.*

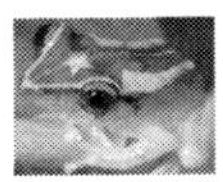

Author: Hum…I'll think about it.

Editor: (pp 155) "I was so afraid of how the other kids were going to react to her." *At 5, she would have been walking & talking. Maybe elaborate on probs.*

Author: It's a parent's fear. Fear is irrational, it doesn't need explanation.

Editor: *What is the point of the kindergarten story? How does it relate to her writing again?*

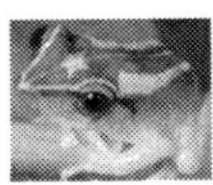

Author: In Steven's mind, it's evidence of Angie's determination and development as a lawyer, as a person and as a writer.

Editor: (pp 155) "We stayed friends until he [Jorge] died." *Does Emilia already know about Jorge? She should if they're such good friends.*

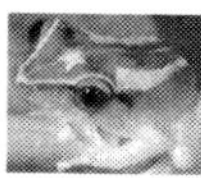

Author: You keep missing the point about it...

Editor: (pp 155) "He died of complications due to AIDS sometime back—a few years ago or so. Yes, Daddy, I do remember the exact day, but I don't want to talk about it. Stop looking at me like that." *How is he looking at her? Why would he think she wouldn't remember the exact day?*

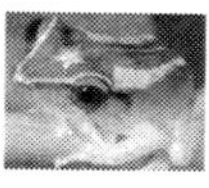

Author: Q1, as only a doting father could look at his daughter. Q2, because it's important to her.

Editor: (pp 156) RE: erasing holes in the paper. *So what? All kids make mistakes.*

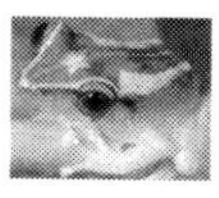

Author: It's important to him. #parenthood.

Editor: (pp 155) "Arghh! I know, it doesn't mean anything to you, but it does to me!" he said. *Odd sentence. Again, why?*

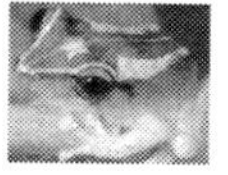

Author: I think sentence explains itself.

Editor: (pp 156) ...he [Jorge] won a prize in middle school and got published in the school district (NEWSLETTER?).

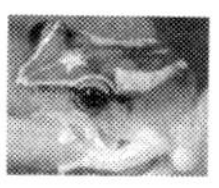

Author: Good point, fixed.

Editor: (pp 156) “Daddy gave me a different book every week. It started when I was thirteen years old.” *That seems old. Why that age specifically?*

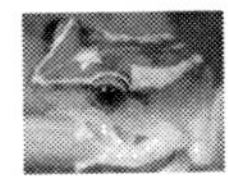

Author: Because that’s the age that I started reading seriously.

Editor: (pp 156) *Add a quick poem they wrote, then below a quick poem angie wrote reflecting it, but about the kitchen + love. Love in the kitchen.*

Author: Good suggestion about the parent’s poem. Re “kitchen+love” that sounds like the movie 9 ½ weeks … not apt for this chapter.

Editor: *Yuk, you’re sick, sick. #sickpuppy*

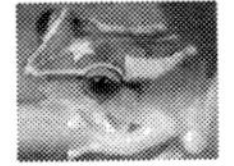

Author: :)

Editor: (pp 156) Re Angie’s assignment: *is the porch significant in some way? I would change that to the kitchen.*

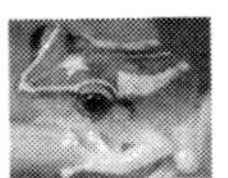

Author: My, are we obsessed with the kitchen? ;) Good point will think about it. #loveinthekitchen.

Editor: (pp 157) *Stetson reference seems irrelevant, unless other chapters relate.*

Author: yep

Editor: (pp 157) “I never met your grandmother,” *Huh? I’m assuming other chapters are referenced here.*

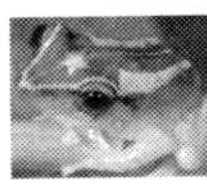

Author: Yep, you got it.

Editor: (pp 157) "but I didn't fit in, and I ruffled some feathers" *how did she ruffle feathers? I'd add "with my liberal views" or algo.*

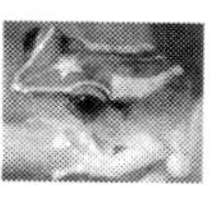

Author: Me gusta cuando escribes en español ... Oops I'm channeling Pablo Neruda...Good point about Angie's writing, fixing it. I don't think I should make it about "liberal" views, just about writing.

Editor: (pp 158) *Who the F is Tommy? You're talking about the 2 dads being foster parents, but now you're suddenly talking about other foster parents?*

Author: No, Manny and Steven had two foster kids, older than Angie. Tommy (who died) and Eric. Check family tree. Oops forgot to send you that. Sending it as we speak.

Editor: *Go it, its OK.*

Editor: (pp 158) *"Dad came through the side door. Everybody came through the side door, only Jehovah's Witnesses and strangers ever came on the front door."*

Author: Love that sentence, I'm stealing it!

Editor: *You're welcome. I want a footnote and royalties.*

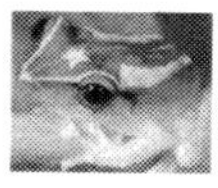

Author: yes on the footnote, strikeout on the royalties.

Editor (pp 158): *Is manny an ophthalmologist, an optometrist, I can't remember. Didn't he go to law school at Amherst?*

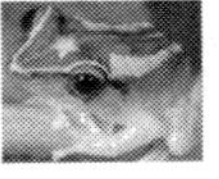

Author: Already fixed, but a good reminder. Will look at it again. He started law school but decided to go into medicine.

Editor: (same page) *The dads must have heard about Emilia b4 this, right?*

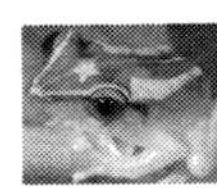

Author: Good point, fixed.

Editor: (same page) and Sarah is at the courthouse in Marathon. *May as well say plantation key, that's where the monroe county courthouse actually is.*

Author: I'm not sure. Tavernier is farther than Marathon. Even Sarah can't drive that fast.

Editor: (pp 159) RE ERIC: "He had some problems in high school. It's not easy to be in that high school and be gay; but we all pitched in and helped. He struggled and graduated, then started at the community college here and completed his degree in counseling at the University of Miami." *Why is he gay? Meaning why are we supposed to already know this? That's how it's written. As if he's gay bc his parents were gay? I don't get it.*

Author: Why Not? He was born that way. Go LADY GAGA! :). I guess you have never seen *The Torch Song Trilogy* movie from 1988.

Editor: No, I haven't seen it, should I?

Author: You should.

Editor: (pp 160) "Emilia, get ready, he's determined," I said." *Determined to tell his story? To tell his philosophy of cooking? Determined to cook?*

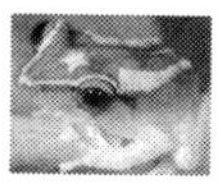

Author: Read it in context. The answer is in the sentence. Or … maybe Steven is determined to kill Angie and Emilia and boil their skins to make lampshades of it. Darn, that book is already written.

Editor: *Funny, crai crai funny.*

Editor (pp 160): "No, silly, it's one of Daddy's expressions," I said. *Maybe put saying also in spanish here? I'm assuming it's a PR saying.*

Author: OK, not a PR saying but might be interesting in Spanish. Looking into it.

Editor (pp 160): "Now pay attention," … "This is as close as I get to consecration." Emilia, raised a Catholic, was amused. *I threw in the catholic part*

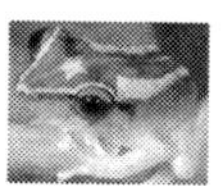

Author: Sorry, Emilia is Pentecostal, but she understood and she was amused.

Editor: *change the drag queen sentence–not clear*

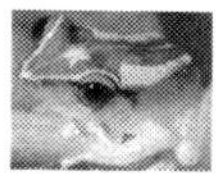

Author: I'll kill for that sentence.

Editor: *Really*?

Author: Yes

Editor (pp 161): *may as well say how many gallons the small calder is; it begs the question.*

Author: OK Fixed

Editor: (pp 163) "Hey, little sis, are you still developing?" he said. *That question sounds weirdly sexual, at best inappropriate.*

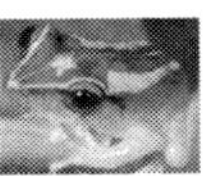

Author: Hum…I grew up with two brothers; you've no idea the things siblings can say to each other.

Editor: (same page) "Oh my, where are my manners?" he said with a tone of affectation. *Do you mean a funny voice or did you mean to put affection?*

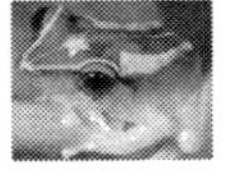

Author: No, he is using an "affected tone of voice."

Editor: "I know how to pick them, don't I?" I replied. *Is she joking that she always gets pretty women? Usually ppl say that if they pick bad ones.*

Author: No, I have heard it the other way.

Editor: (pp 163) "No, Mr. Eric — I can't commit to a relationship right now!" *Who's saying this?*

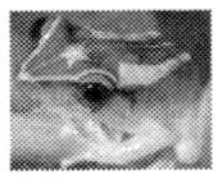

Author: Angie is saying it

Editor: "Last time I checked, the little LED light was flashing straight," she laughed. *Strange expression.*

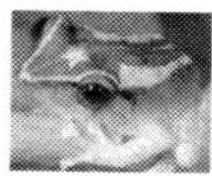

Author: Actually I think it's pretty funny.

Editor: (pp 164) "Well, at least I get calls back!" he said, jabbing me. *Awkward sentence.*

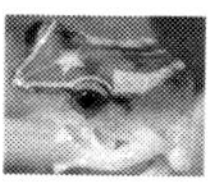

Author: Why?

Editor: *Usually when people make these types of jokes, they are referring to a specific incident to which you may want to refer.*

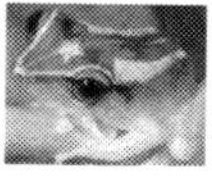

Author: Not necessarily.

Editor: *OK, whatever.*

Editor: (pp 165) "Besides, she threatened me that if I couldn't find anybody to tend bar, I was going to end up on the sofa ..." *the sofa thing doesn't make sense. Are they a lesbian couple? And did she find someone to cover? Need to put that in if so—otherwise it's confusing.*

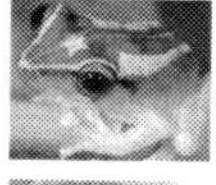

Author: Sofa=Couch. Yes they're a couple. Yes she found someone bc she showed up at the house. It's implied.

Editor: (pp 165) ...Sarah whistled in, complaining about the driving in the Keys. *The drivers or the traffic?*

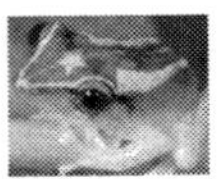

Author: Does it make any difference?

Editor: (pp 167) *You don't have to say* "using her joke a second time" *reader will remember. I still think it's an odd, not-funny phrase, tho.*

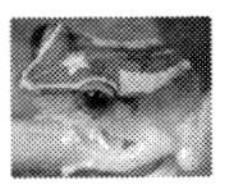

Author: OK fixed. I do think is hilarious.

Editor: (pp 167) *"I'm going to work on the marriage equality issue." In Key West? Or just in general?*

Author: Very good point. We'll make it local.

Editor: *That makes sense if it were local work, in KW, tho Angie would know those contacts.*

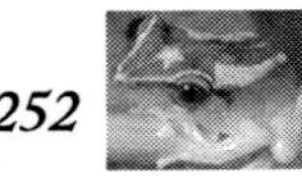

Author: Not necessarily she's been working in Miami until this point.

Editor: "Sheri was all excited about going to testify this time around." *Why would Sheri testify? In what case? And why would she be a witness? Unless Angie is reviving her dads' case somehow.*

Author: No, they have been eating and drinking is just banter around the table. But I'm changing the ending, its too melodramatic.

Editor: *good I wasn't happy about it. I also think the interview is too long. Can you change it?*

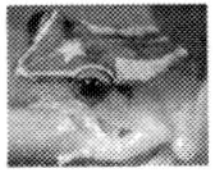

Author: I'll think about it. But I wouldn't change it, if it's going to change the outlook on Angie's character.

AN EMAIL FROM A FRIEND WHO CONSULTED ANOTHER FRIEND ABOUT LEGAL ISSUES PRESENTED IN EDEN'S SHORE PARK.

Hi Edgardo:

Richard read the ms and suggests:

The process of asking for and obtaining a zoning change is much more technical, bureaucratic and complex than set forth in the story. However, he thinks that changing the story to reflect the actual process would be a mistake. It would destroy the flow of the narrative and introduce too much extraneous material, pulling focus away from what the story is about. He suggests that you keep it as it is, and if you are worried that it will be criticized as inaccurate, add a note at the beginning stating that you have condensed and simplified the permitting process in order to focus on the human impact of the social forces at work.

A TWEET FROM ONE OF THE EDITORS REGARDING EDEN'S SHORE PARK.

The first two paragraphs from this chapter make my head spin. Can you tone it down a bit? #headspin

ANOTHER EMAIL FROM AN EDITOR REGARDING EDEN'S SHORE PARK.

We're almost halfway through! I'll send more later. This really is very engaging, Edgardo. I saw a commercial for an upcoming reality show about a trailer park called *Myrtle Manor* and I thought of my friends at Eden's Shore. I forgot they weren't real!

A WELL-KNOWN KEY WEST FEMALE IMPERSONATOR AND POET WROTE A LAUDATORY POEM TO PORSHA DEL PUERTO AFTER READING POSTCRIPT.

LaKesha Drag Queen Princess of Duval StreetTo Porsha Del Puerto Working Drag Queen of Hypnotic Quest Tours

I, Lakesha, am the product of an allusion
draped in gold;
you, Porsha, are the Divine result
of eyeliner and Chanel.
Your Steed is a red and gold microbus,
a glass chariot.
Mine is a Captain Outrageous silver bicycle
with blue polka dots.

Your platinum hair
carries your fabulousness around Key West.
My purple 'fro,
adorned with sapphires and pearls,
is the envy of the heteros and the blue bloods.

Your curves are the repository,
of your shy modesty.
My curves can't be damned,
for the rumbles
caused by my incredibly beautiful hips.

Our differences end
where the ocean meets the gulf,
where the hot stream meets the cold currents.
Where Fast Buck Freddies met Coach (and died),
and the cruise ships met the defunct ducks.
Where the tourists meet the locals,
to keep the service industry going,
and the service workers afloat.

UN RECONOCIDO TRAVESTI DE CAYO HUESO ESCRIBIÓ UNA ODA A PORSHA DEL PUERTO DESPUÉS DE LERR POSTCRIPT.

LaKesha la Reina Travesti de la calle Duval a Porsha Del Puerto trabajadora Reina Travesti de Hypnotic Quest Tours

Yo, Lakesha, soy el producto de una alusión
envuelta en oro;
Tú, Porsha, eres el resultado Divino
del delineador de ojos y los lustros de Chanel.
Tu transporte es un microbús dorado y rojo,
una carroza de cristal.
La mía es una bicicleta platinada
pintada por el capitán *Outrageous*
con lunares azules.

Tu cabello oxigenado
lleva tu *fabulousness* por todo Cayo Hueso.
Mi afro púrpura,
adornado con zafiros y perlas,
es la envidia de los heteros y los de sangre azul.

Tus curvas son el repositorio,
de tu retraída modestia.
Mis curvas son el gravamen,
impuesto a los estruendos
causados por mis bellas y tremebundas caderas.

Nuestras diferencias terminan
donde el Golfo caliente encuentra al Atlántico frío.
Donde Fast Buck Freddies se encuentró con Coach,
(y murió por ello)
y donde los cruceros mataron a los vehículos anfibios.
Donde los turistas se reúnen con los lugareños,
para mantener al turismo en marcha,
y a los trabajadores del turismo a flote.

AFTER AN INTENSE DISCUSSION ABOUT THE USE OF SPANISH IN THE BOOK, ONE OF THE EDITORS SENT THE AUTHOR A NOTE.

I get it, I get it, I get it. ¡Yo entiendo!

The next time we saw each other, she was carrying a copy of Stephen King's book *On Writing*, hit me over the head with it and opened it to page 13:

> *"One rule of the road not directly stated elsewhere in this book: "The editor is always right." The corollary is that no writer will take all of his or her editor's advise: for all have sinned and fallen short of editorial perfection. Put it another way, to write is human to edit is divine."*

(King, Stephen. *On Writing: a Memoir of the Craft*. NY: Scribner. 2000. p.13)

256 **Author's reaction:** Sí, sí, yo entiendo, tú eres un ser divino, tú siempre tienes la razón, siempre, siempre, ay, ¡deja de pegarme con el libro! (Yes, Yes, I understand, you are a divine being. You are always right, always, always. Ouch, stop hitting me with the book!)

ACKNOWLEDGEMENTS

I have the privilege to have great friends who have taken the time, at different points and phases, to read and guide the unruly hand that shaped some of these words. Lynne Smith, Anne Gallagher, CS Gilbert, Anne Shaver, Sheri Lohr, Stacy Rodríguez, Laurie Hoppe, Eric McCarthy and Lisa Mahoney, I am both thankful for and unworthy of their efforts. In the end, all typographical errors are solely my responsibility.

Irving Weinman, through the Key West Writers' Workshop, gave me the opportunity to participate in three workshops where I met so many great aspiring (and now published) writers and three great mentors: Edmund White, Robert Stone and Lee Smith. I tried to learn (and I am still learning) as much as I could from these teachers and artists. Thank you, Irving.

The Key West Writers Guild and the Key West Poetry Guild, encourage, teach the craft and support both would-be and established artists. I cannot stress enough the place of groups like these anywhere that writing is discussed and cherished.

My friends at the *Key West Citizen*; it has changed, it has stayed the same. Some members have moved on, some members have been recognized for their work. I left, I came back and we are still laughing and working.

To Lolo

Lolo was all made up and dressed,
as she was every day at seven in the morning.
Foundation spread evenly,
eyebrows painted in the perfect arch;
the right amount of rouge on the cheeks,
lips flaming pink.

Today though,
she was busy correcting,
one of her little miscreant's writings…
Seated straight up because
"age is not an excuse to lose your good posture."
"You know the nuns drill the posture
on your brain …
with pain."

The sleeves on her blouse
… fluttering above the paper;
… the printed hearts
pouring their red dye all over the paper.
They were taking over the table,
… the writing, … the air.
Their perfume took over.

Her diamond ring
dripped perfect little prisms of color
that turned into little rubies
as she edited others' writing.

Occasionally,
she paused,
gathered her thoughts,
and judged the overall effect,
always proud of her penmanship.
She paused again,
scrutinized the paper,
almost like talking to it.
Caught herself almost thinking out loud.
Looked around,
to make sure nobody was aware,
smiled impishly,
and laughed.

She put her pencil down
and rested her eyes … for a minute.

The Zúñiga Family plot in at the Key West Cemetery. The author respectfully request of his readers not to disturb the family mausoleum. Zúñiga family collection.

THE STORIES

PREFACE: A CAUTIONARY TALE ABOUT KEY WEST X

JUAN ZÚÑIGA Y VALDEVIESO 1

JUDGE JOHN ZÚÑIGA 25

CÓMO HAN PASADO LOS AÑOS 47

SIÑA MARÍA 69

EL OLOR DE LAS AZUCENAS 87

IN HELL'S CIRCLE 101

THE SPOT ON THE WING OF THE ANGEL 111

MARÍA DE LOS ÁNGELES ZÚÑIGA CARMICHAEL 131

MARÍA DE LOS ÁNGELES COMES FOR A VISIT. 151

EDEN'S SHORE PARK 177

EPILOGUE 211

POSTSCRIPT: 217

June 18, 2014.

Anne McKee Artist Fund Award Ceremony
at the Gardens Hotel in Key West.

Thank You, Ms. Anne McKee.